To 1

MW00905796

The LAST
BEST
WEST
NEVER LOOK BACK

I've always
loved the
amazing heart)C A
you have for
Kids!

**SHANNON
BRADLEY
GREEN**

Shannon

 FriesenPress

Suite 300 - 990 Fort St
Victoria, BC, V8V 3K2
Canada

www.friesenpress.com

ISBN
978-1-5255-6400-0 (Hardcover)
978-1-5255-6401-7 (Paperback)
978-1-5255-6402-4 (eBook)

1. FICTION, SMALL TOWN & RURAL

Distributed to the trade by The Ingram Book Company

ACKNOWLEDGEMENT

This book has been a long, but continual process of love. Firstly, I would like to thank Nora Schmidt who published Lady Adela's story in a local newsletter in the '90's and introduced me to this remarkable pioneer woman. Secondly, I would like to thank the inimitable Jana Wilson, librarian extraordinaire, who offered me a table at the Bert Sheppard Stockmen's Foundation Library and Archives to write every Friday afternoon. Jana knew the collection inside out and pointed me toward many resources that founded the factual background of the story. She was always my biggest cheerleader and I can't thank her enough for her input, including editing, into making this book possible. Thanks also to the foresight of Bert Sheppard and the Stockmen's Foundation who lovingly created this fabulous resource. The many community histories found there that told the family stories were a treasure trove of information. Thanks go as well to Judith Barge, PhD., whose doctoral dissertation, "From Ranch to Reality: The Landscape History and Heritage of Former Settlement Schemes in the Bow Valley, West of Calgary, Alberta", was an amazing guide to the life of the Cochranes. Dr. Barge, your scholarship has preserved this fascinating story in academia, and I hope you enjoy my fictionalizing of it. Thanks to you from the bottom of my heart as well to my family members. To my husband Dr. Bryan Green, for being an avid listener as I read the book aloud to you, and for your editing suggestions which improved the story. You fell in love with my book, just like you fell in love with me. Thanks to my sister-in-law Leanne Green for your amazing editing of the original draft – twice. You rock!! To my son, Tieran Green, thank you for the amazing photo for the cover of this book, that is the view from both Mitford and the Bradley Half Diamond V homestead. You put my thoughts into vision, literally and figuratively. Your sky spirit fills me with wonder. And to my son Kai, the fire guy, Green, you lift me up. To my great grandfather, Billie Bradley, whose early death meant I never knew him, thank you for your pioneer spirit. Also, to truly amazing friends Loren Spector and Trish Quinn for doing an initial read and edit, thank you. Lastly, to that wonderful female entrepreneur, Lady Adela Cochrane, whose dreams never became a reality, but whose love for the land matches my own, thank you for your creation. I think you would be happy to know that a wonderful school bears your town's name, and that the dream of Mitford does indeed live on….

DISCLAIMER

THE EVENTS IN THIS BOOK are based loosely on the life of the characters. The roles played by all the characters in this narrative are entirely fictional. My imagined Lady Adela does, however, abide by the generally known facts of the lives of the real Lady Adela and T.B.H Cochrane. While many of the characters were real people, many were not, and a lot of imagination had to insert itself into the many different tellings of the stories.

DEDICATION

TO THE PIONEERS OF THE Last Best West – your dreams for a better life have given me a life of wonder.

HENRY DAVID THOREAU:

"Never look back unless you are planning to go that way"

TABLE OF CONTENTS

CHAPTER 1

THE SHOOT

SEPTEMBER, 1882

The dark shape plummeted downward with deadly precision, neck bent and head at an odd angle. Lady Adela Rous brought her rifle down to her hip and intently watched the pheasant fall. Her beautiful pointer had flushed the pheasant from the field, and now she turned to her obedient retriever, who sat calmly by her side, awaiting the command.

"Back," commanded Adela, while at the same time stretching her arm out in the direction the bird had fallen. The retriever burst forward with incredible energy, streaking outward toward the fallen prey. Adela's natural auburn curls reflected back the sun glinting off them. A throaty laugh erupted from her lips as her dog, hind quarters sliding, came to a stop, while he delicately picked up the pheasant and immediately turned to find Adela. With hardly a glance he was back at full speed, racing toward her.

As she awaited the racing dog, Adela looked about her with pleasure. To her left was her brother George, with his

SHANNON BRADLEY GREEN

own setter and retriever, with a handsome young man holding a rifle, chatting jovially beside him. Further back, out of the wind and under a canopy, sat her dear papa and mama with their guests.

Lady Adela, in the prime of her youth and of very marriageable age, was a woman of rank and privilege in the British peer system. She lived at Henham Hall, a Georgian manor house in the county of Suffolk. Her grandpapa, John Rous, 1st Earl of Stradbroke, had built Henham in 1790, and passed it along to her papa, John Rous, 2nd Earl of Stradbroke. Papa has raised his first family here, but after his wife had passed on, he remarried to Adela's mama, Lady Augusta, who was much his junior and she had given him six lovely children.

Adela was the apple of Lord Rous' eye. She was a keen sportswoman and loved the out-of-doors, preferring them immensely to the stilted and structured indoor environments of her day. She was happiest on a horse at a fox hunt, or in the field shooting pheasant. She was at her most aggravated at a tea or ladies' gathering, where all the women gathered to gossip. But today, in 1882, she was glowing with pleasure at the young man who accompanied her brother George.

"T.B., that was a splendid shot!" laughed Lady Adela Rous.

"Look George, he's got a lovely pheasant," she continued happily to her brother. Lord George, Viscount Dunwich, had just been commissioned in the First Norfolk Artillery volunteers. He and Adela had spent their childhood shooting, fox hunting and riding together. They were incredibly competitive, and Lord John had delighted in watching them trying to outdo each other.

"Well done, T.B.", George said, adding a third pheasant to

his brace. He would have seven or eight easily before the day was done.

JOHN ROUS WAS ALWAYS THE happiest when he, too, was out of doors. The shooting match, in very agreeable weather, was the highlight of the day. The Earl, nobleman and soldier, sportsman and peer, husband and father, had reached the remarkable age of eighty-eight. He was well known and highly respected by a large fashionable circle and numerous private friends. True, he now sat with the women, a blanket covering his knees and another 'round his shoulders, but, nevertheless, he was thoroughly enjoying being in the field with his gracious friends and family.

But hearing the sound of Adela's laughter had completely set his teeth on edge. He knew a man's mettle up front, and he was not impressed with the latest of Augusta's attempts to find a husband for Dellie, T.B.H. Cochrane.

"How many have you bagged, Dellie?" her father asked.

"Six altogether, Papa," she giggled.

"And I've only three," complained George. The family rivalry had not stopped with his ascension to the military.

"That's one to your three for Cochrane," Lord Rous answered gruffly. He was not impressed much by anything this young man did. Adela, on the other hand, thrilled him with her skill as a horsewoman and marksman.

"Now Papa, don't be so silly."

Lord Rous was annoyed by the shushing. He was still the head of the family and demanded the respect due to him.

Knowing a storm might erupt from her father, Adela deftly steered T.B.H. out of the way and over towards her mother.

Lady Augusta Rous was a generous and kindly hostess. She and the Earl were entertaining the Sir Thomas John Cochrane family from Quarr Abbey House on the Isle of Wight. Sir Thomas had been an Admiral of the Fleet but had passed away some years ago, and Lady Augusta was entertaining his widow and children.

The Cochranes belonged to the most fashionable circle in all of British Society, that of Queen Victoria and Prince Albert. John's son, Thomas B.H. Cochrane, and daughter, Anne Annette Minna, had grown up with Princess Beatrice, Queen Victoria's daughter. Augusta had met Rosetta Cochrane at another social gathering, and realized she had a young son of marriageable age. The Cochranes actually traveled in Queen Victoria's circle, so she had decided on the spot it might be prudent to entertain the family at Henham Hall in the near future.

"How is everyone enjoying the shoot?" she enquired of her guests.

"Looks like there is much hunting occurring," Rosetta Cochrane replied wryly, glancing over at T.B.H. and Lady A.

With her auburn hair and strong stature, Adela looked hale and healthy. She had a winsome laugh and kind personality and reveled in taking on any challenge nature could throw at her. T.B.H. seemed quite smitten with her, and Adela with him in return. It was just exactly as Augusta had hoped. Short of marrying into the royal family, she could think of nothing better than Adela marrying into the Queen's circle. It was the epitome of social success, and Augusta Rous was a woman who would stop at little to get what she wanted for her daughters.

Augusta looked pleased as punch with her social efforts.

She had so far achieved the marriage of only one of her six children with Lord John: Lady Augusta Fanny, her namesake child, to Cecil Fane. His mother was the daughter of the 8th Earl of Westmorland, and Augusta was happy with that. The rest of her children were as yet unmarried and finding appropriate mates for them was her main occupation now.

Her elder children from her marriage to Colonel Fred Bonham were married and had lives of their own. As they had been raised in Eden Hall, Cumbria, they lived a very long way away from the home of her second family with the Earl of Stradbroke at Henham Hall, in Suffolk. She rarely saw them.

"Well, it looks like our children are quite taken with each other," exclaimed Rosetta Cochrane, who was not titled. Her deceased husband had not inherited the title from his father, the 8th Earl of Dundonald, as he was not first born. Marrying an Earl's daughter would bring social and financial advantage to her family, which was pleasing to Rosetta.

"It looks as if they are," returned Lady Augusta, thrilled.

Both mothers were happy that their social connecting had brought about this lovely romance possibility at Henham Hall.

Rosetta Cochrane had been very, very satisfied when the invitation to a hunt had come from the Countess of Stradbroke. She had carefully managed the childhood of her children, Anne and T.B.H., as he was known (for there were so many Thomas Cochranes), making absolutely certain that the children had been available to engage with Queen Victoria's youngest, Princess Beatrice. T.B.H. was happy playing with the girls when he was little, but Mama Rosetta watched each and every move with the eyes of a hawk, and when she became worried he might be getting too comfortable playing with the girls, she had removed him from their play. Every step of his childhood and adolescence has been orchestrated by Rosetta. There had never been a question of what he would do with his life: as the son of an Admiral, it was completely expected that he would follow his father into the Royal Navy. Ever the dutiful son, T.B.H. had agreed.

The Royal Navy was indeed a proving ground, and T.B.H. had not taken naturally to the sea at all. He eventually gained his sea legs and learned to deal with the sea sickness, but he felt ill at ease with the life on board ship. He had no natural camaraderie with the sailors. After a few years, on a leave and back home on the Isle of Wight, he told Rosetta that he would not be returning.

Rosetta was devasted, and ever so thankful that Admiral Cochrane had passed away and was not alive to see the disgrace of his son not becoming a navy man. Never one to be stopped for long, the indomitable Rosetta Cochrane set about finding a young lady of wealth and title for T.B.H. She knew her family status with Queen Victoria would be of great value to all the peers of England, and she set about to find the best match possible for T.B.H.

John Rous was still as sharp as a hawk when it came to determining the measure of a man. Lady Rosetta Cochrane had told him the night before at dinner that young Thomas had quit the navy, something that would never sit well with John Rous. Retired Captain Rous had served in Wellington's campaign in Belgium and was wounded at Quatre Bras and so did not take part in the glorious defeat of Napoleon two days later at Waterloo. He had served as Lord Lieutenant and Vice Admiral of Suffolk for many years of his life. He had pursued an active life as a peer and politician and believed first and foremost in duty. Young Cochrane had only served for a few years, retiring at age twenty-seven. This fact alone did not sit well with Lord John, and the thought of this young ne'er-do-well marrying his darling Adela brought him to a fury.

All the dinner-talk last night had centered around young Cochrane's desire to join in the latest rage all over Europe, seeking fortune in the Dominions. John Rous was far too old and far too established in his beliefs to put any faith in such utter nonsense. He was annoyed that his family was quite amenable to these foolish ideas of finding fortune in the new world. It meant little to him that all the fashionable young men of London seemed crazed about adventure in one of the Empire's dominions. Australia, India, or Canada were all the young men talked about when they met in the fashionable London clubs, where they drank, gambled and quite often partook of the services of young ladies of dubious quality.

"John dear, do you see how Adela is getting on with T.B.H?" Augusta asked with shining eyes from her place at the grand dining table at Henham Hall.

Lord John barked back, "I do, and I don't like it."

"Oh, my dear, why not?" soothed Lady Augusta.

John complained loudly "This fortune finding in the Dominions is utter nonsense, and hardly the life I want for Adela."

Lady Augusta laughed nervously and remarked, "My goodness John, it's all our George talks about too. All the young men are looking for adventure."

John glanced over at Adela, who was flushed at the talk of the young men, and he couldn't help but smile. Adventure, sport and fun were all things Adela craved herself.

Of course, sporting women were well accepted in the Rous' circle. Adela was easily as good as the men when it came to the hunt. Her natural seat on a horse and uncanny connection with the dogs meant she could as easily be found in the barns discussing the horses as she could anywhere else on the Henham Hall estate.

But now, here she was giggling like a coquette! T.B.H. was preening like a peacock, basking in the glow of Adela's attention. However, it was not just Adela's attention that he was seeking. He seemed to require the attention of all present, and was not, in Lord John's mind, the kind of man one respected.

Countess Stradbroke was very concerned with connections. She often sat in library at Henham Hall, while the staff bustled about running her home, and her husband and children were busy with their own affairs, and gazed out onto the gardens to reminisce about how she arrived here at Henham.

…" Fred, you'll squeeze them to death."

She remembered her handsome first husband, Colonel Frederick Henry Bonham, playing with the little tykes while on a furlough. There was precious little time at home with his busy army career, and the little ones often forgot who he was for the first few days when he came back into their lives. Lady Augusta remembered the thrill of his visits home, always wondering if she might become pregnant after the visit.

Then the unthinkable. Not a military death, but a medical emergency that turned into death from a brain hemorrhage at the age of forty-six, leaving behind a young son and daughter, who were four and five respectively. Frederick had served his country well and married later in life to Augusta, who became the love of his life and he hers.

She was devastated.

The shock had been terrible. Augusta was only twenty-seven years old when this ill-fated event occurred. She had returned with her children to Eden Hall, her ancestral home in Cumbria, where her father, Reverend Sir Christopher Musgrave, a military chaplain, lived. Her own mother had encouraged her to attend the season in London that year, telling her that she was still a very marriageable woman. She really hadn't felt much like attending, but she followed her mama's advice and attended the debutante balls. Much to her surprise, a distinguished looking older gentleman seemed to be quite taken with her. Lord Rous, the Earl of Stradbroke, no less, was a widower looking for a new wife.

What followed was rather a whirlwind romance, with Lord Rous visiting Eden Hall and proposing a marriage to her papa. It was rather disconcerting that Lord Rous was actually older than her own father, but her parents felt entering into marriage with such a distinguished man was really quite the right thing for Augusta to do. She was now considered a mature widow, and was able to bear children, which was what Lord Rous was looking for. She felt she had been most fortunate to meet John Rous after the death of her first husband, but still missed the romance and love of her first marriage.

She was a little shocked when Lord Rous suggested that her children stay at Eden Hall. This was not a surprising thing for a second husband to demand, so Augusta felt she would have no choice, when on May 26, 1857, thirteen months after the death of her first husband, she became the Countess of Stradbroke. Lord John was sixty-three when they married.

John was not opposed to her visiting the children, so with this in mind, she left her young children in the care of her parents, and following their wishes, moved with her new husband to Henham Hall in Suffolk.

Within the next eleven years she gave birth to six children, the third being George Edward John Mowbray Rous, who would become the 3rd Earl of Stradbroke. Augusta had fulfilled her obligations very well, and Lord John was a very satisfied man with his new wife and family. His only regret was that he was getting on now to very old age, and that he would not likely live long enough to see his children marry. After all, he was old enough to be their great grandfather.

THE HUNTING SOCIAL CALL WAS a preferred event amongst the nobility and the Cochranes' visit had been filled with hunting, riding, shooting and fine dinners. T.B.H. and Adela had managed to find themselves together for every event, much to the pleasure of Rosetta Cochrane and Lady Augusta. However, Lord John had not been swayed in anyway with regards to his opinion about T.B.H. Cochrane. Both mamas were a little disconcerted about this.

At the conclusion of the gathering, on a fine autumn morning, with the sun peering down joyfully on the families, the Cochranes were packed and leaving Henham Hall.

"Thank you so much for your generous hospitality, Lord John," offered Rosetta, as the carriages pulled up outside.

"We were delighted to have your family visit, Rosetta," Lady Augusta quickly interjected, for fear that her husband might make some inappropriate comment about T.B.H. After all, Lord John often now spoke with a candor that was definitely not acceptable in proper society.

"Lovely to make your acquaintance," Lord John mumbled as he leaned heavily upon his walking stick, the only thing that kept him upright these days.

Minna Cochrane, T.B.H.'s sister, was saying goodbye to Adela. They, too, had enjoyed each other's company, although Minna was certainly not the outdoorswoman that Adela was. The talk this weekend had also centered around Minna, who was to be made Lady-in-Waiting to Princess Beatrice herself.

Adela and T.B.H. moved aside and gazed at each other raptly.

"Goodbye, T.B.H." Adela sighed.

"May we see each other again, very soon," responded T.B.H. with a long, adoring look.

Adela's little sisters, Hilda and Gwendoline, giggled at each other at how foolish their sister looked. At fifteen and thirteen, they too would soon be engaged in the business of husband finding, but for now they found it hilarious to watch their sister looking so foolish as she gazed adoringly at the disappearing T.B.H.

LATER THAT DAY AT LUNCH, Mama Rous was very animated at the table, reliving the visit from the Cochranes. Papa Rous looked very, very tired and was as agitated as Mama was excited.

"Augusta!" he growled. "I have always trusted your judgment, but I am annoyed by your interest in that young man as a suitor for Adela."

"John, dear, why ever would you say that?" she asked carefully.

"I have seen his type and he is not to be trusted!" Lord

Rous yelled and banged his fist upon the table.

"Now, John, I believe you are being quite harsh," soothed Lady Augusta. She stole a glance to look at Adela, who was starting to look like a brewing thundercloud.

Adela was the only Rous who would talk back to Lord John, and Lady Augusta could only imagine the row that was going to break out.

"Papa, I feel you are being entirely unfair," Adela started. "T.B.H. is going to the Dominion of Canada soon to make a fortune in ranching."

"Ha, fortune in ranching," seethed Lord John. "What does he know about ranching?"

Lady Augusta intervened. "John, dear, your heart. Please don't upset yourself so."

"Just keep that idiot away from Adela," raged Lord John, and with that, he threw down his napkin and pushed himself slowly to his feet.

From his standing position he bellowed out, "I recall clearly that the Earl of St. Vincent wrote a letter to the London Post about the Cochrane brothers, way back in 1806. My father spoke of it often as he was not impressed by the Dundonald Clan."

Vincent wrote, "The Cochranes are not to be trusted out of sight. They are all mad, romantic, money-getting and not truth-telling, and there is not a single exception in any part of the family."

"Is this the type of family you want for our Dellie?" he demanded.

The footman was there immediately to get him his walking stick and to help him to his bedroom, which had been relocated to the main floor as Lord John was no longer able to climb the long staircase to the second floor.

Adela sat glowering after her father left but said nothing. She was furious to think some letter in the London Post from the dawn of time could actually be taken seriously by her father.

Lady Augusta fussed about her husband, helping him to his room while all the while thinking much the same thoughts as Adela. Was John not thinking about the Cochrane's connections to Queen Victoria? That was the here and the now, not something written decades before by another fusty old peer.

Adela was not going to be put off easily from the discussion. With her father out of earshot, she turned upon her mother with great intention, when she returned.

"Mama, I am so glad you are on my side," she seethed. "Papa is being entirely unfair about T.B.H."

"Oh, my dear, I agree," continued Lady Augusta, "but you know what he is like when he has made up his mind."

If there was ever to be disharmony in the family, it was likely to be between Lord John and Lady Adela.

"Well, wait until T.B.H. makes his fortune in ranching in Canada," Adela huffed, "then he'll see how wrong he was."

Lady Augusta could only see the hurdles and she knew there would much work ahead of her if she was going to make this match between Adela and T.B.H. work.

September 9th, 1882. Be still my beating heart. What a splendid time I have had. What brilliant effects of sun and cloud and celebrated golden shades in the trees. How fine the air, crisp and cool upon my brow, and how rare the laughter of family and friends.

Does the world seem brighter each morn, the birdsong sweeter than ever before heard? Is the world simply more glorious now than ever? The sweetness of your smile; the way your eyes crinkle at the corners when you beam at me, the rich, resounding sound of your chuckle. Surely the world has never seen such, or am I as yet in love? Thomas Belhaven Henry Cochrane… the sound of that name now speaks sweetly to me!

CHAPTER 2

THE NEW ELDORADO

1883

"This is Your Opportunity – Why Not Embrace It?" read the poster in the milliner's window. The poster showed wheat lands and blue skies in Western Canada and advertised one hundred-and-sixty-acre parcels to anyone who had the adventurous spirit and a small amount of cash, to claim them. Eighteen-year-old Lady Adela Charlotte Rous lingered over the poster, thinking of her new love, T.B.H. Cochrane, and hoping for another letter as soon as the post could deliver it. Thomas was over in the Dominion of Canada with his cousin, Billie Cochrane, and their business partner, Hugh Graham. He had purchased a grazing lease sight unseen and had headed to Canada to inspect his new purchase and begin plans for the ranche he would build.

"Eldorado…the golden empire" mused Adela to herself. It was so incredibly romantic, just like her life had been ever since Thomas had spent time at her family home, and they had fallen in love.

"Canada…." she murmured, not quite as quietly as she meant to, catching the ear of her sister Gwendoline, who had just plopped an outsized hat on her head. Hilda and Gwendoline pantomimed silly lovesick faces at each other, just barely behind Adela's back, and she turned and swatted at them with her parasol.

"Shoo, you are nothing but a silly pest" she said, as they broke up into gales of laughter.

While she browsed through the hats, Adela recalled the talk she had heard when she was listening in on the men at Mama's last social. T.B.H. had been dancing with her Mama, and Adela had been listening in on the men while she waited for him to return to her. Her father's friends had been discussing T.B.H. and his father, Admiral Thomas Cochrane. They remembered how he had served as a junior officer during the French Revolutionary wars and had captured the French ship Favourite off the coast of Dutch Guiana. He had been in the Americas and took part in the Burning of Washington and the attack on Baltimore during the war of 1812. Admiral Thomas Cochrane was well thought of by them for his outstanding Royal Navy career. Those stories brought her back to remembering the fantastic tales told to her by her dear Uncle Henry, who was famous for his exploits in the Royal Navy. In 1834, he was appointed to the command of the HMS Pique, a 36-gun frigate, which ran ashore on the coast of Labrador and was greatly damaged. Uncle Henry, however, brought her across the Atlantic Ocean with a sprung foremast and without keel, forefoot or rudder, and though the ship was taking on two feet of water an hour. The story was known throughout England, and Adela felt a little stab of sadness, knowing she would never hear him tell his tales again. Uncle Henry had been even older than her dear papa and had passed away when she was only twelve. How she had loved listening to his tales as a child.

"Adela, are you ever going to choose a hat?" called Hilda. This brought Adela out of her reverie and back to her present predicament: the hat.

"I'd rather be getting a pith helmet to ride on an Indian elephant," Adela whispered to herself, as her eyes were pulled toward the Eldorado poster.

"Oh, this bothersome gathering," she complained to herself, but smiled at her sisters and pulled the nearest hat onto to her head.

"What do you think?" she called out.

"Absolutely dreadful!" replied her youngest sister, Gwendoline, who began fussing around finding just the right hat for the night.

"I wonder how many idiots I will have to dance with tomorrow night?" Adela asked herself as she purchased her hat, which reminded her of an admiral's hat, but with lots of ostrich feathers, making it definitely a lady's chapeau.

May 17th, 1884. There are days when I find the constant shopping so completely tiresome. There are far too many of these days and far too few spent on the hunt or simply riding alone, free as can be, on a wonderful mount. I must attend, yet again, another ball with my parents and sisters. Lucky George, too busy and spared again.

I have had a letter from T.B.H. It seems that, after inspection, the grazing lease was totally unsuitable for cattle grazing, as it was set in the mountains. He was

*very disappointed, but soon soothed by the magnificence
of the open prairies and soaring skies.*

*He and Cousin Billie will camp and ride for some weeks,
then will return to England. I long every moment for his
return so that I might see his dear face once more.*

Ho hum, another boring night, she thought to herself.
Just then, her sister, Lady Gwendoline, came sauntering by,
resplendent in a huge hat with enough flowers on the top to
fill half the garden.

"Mama has invited Mrs. Cochrane, again," gossiped Lady
Gwen. "At least T.B.H. isn't here to upset Papa," she continued
to tease.

"Shoo, you are still nothing but a spiteful pest," reproved
Adela, who then completely ignored her, as one can a
younger sister.

Adela drifted over to the oversized silver pitcher to sip a
glass of water that was poured for her by the footman. Like any
young Victorian lady of the nobility, Adela was not required
to serve herself, dress herself or to take care of any of her
personal needs in any way. To her relief, she spied her mama's
friend, The Honourable Emily Marion Tatton Egerton, Mrs.
Percy Mitford, who was also taking a break from dancing.
They moved out of the ballroom and into the salon so that
they could have a better conversation away from the orchestra.

"There, that is ever so much better," sighed Emily.

"Indeed," replied Adela. "It is lovely to see you again."

Emily smiled fondly at the daughter of her friend,
Lady Augusta.

"Your dear mama tells me that you have become enamored

.of a young man, Adela."

"Ah, yes, Aunt Em," she giggled. "I have indeed. His name is Thomas Belhaven Henry Cochrane, of the Scottish Dundonald Clan."

Emily's countenance darkened a little, as she replied, "Ah, yes, I do know of the Dundonald Clan, and the Cochrane family. They say they have the kiss of the devil on their cheeks."

"Oh, Aunt Em, not T.B.H.," Adela responded quickly. "He is warm and kind and very romantic. He would not raise a hand to anyone."

Mrs. Percy Mitford smiled at Adela, and at young love, blind as the poor beggars 'round St. Paul's. Instead of scolding her like her Papa would, Emily moved on to other concerns.

"What is your young man doing now?" she inquired.

"My, my, Aunt Em, that is the best part. He is currently in the Dominion of Canada. He and his cousin Billie, I mean William Edward, are inspecting the large ranching lease they purchased in the North-West Territories. Sadly, it turned out to be unsuitable as much of it was in the mountains, and he and Billie are now scouting about, having great sport, while they come to know the area.

He plans to make his own fortune in the New World," continued Lady Adela.

"And what about you, Lady Adela, what do you think of this adventure?" Emily continued to query.

"It would be my dearest wish to accompany him someday." She sighed dreamily. Emily smiled at her youthful imagination. However, in the coming years, she would remember this night and Adela's words, as she helped Adela to raise funds for some of her great endeavors. Adela would remember this night too.

She loved her mama's friend, Emily, because she did not try to stomp on her dreams. Not once did she reprimand her for her thoughts and wishes; instead, she listened thoughtfully.

Emily was married to the Honourable Mr. Percy Mitford. He was currently very interested in a new organization that he had started with some her Papa's acquaintances. They often met at the Carleton Club to discuss politics and the issues of the day. They had named their organization The Primrose League, in honor of Lord Beaconsfield, whose favorite flower was the primrose.

Emily glanced into the library of Henham Hall, where all the senior gentlemen, including Lord John, were gathered, discussing the new club.

She heard Percy say, "The Primrose League is an organization for spreading Conservative principles amongst the British democracy. We feel we need an effective voice for free enterprise in the government. We shall represent the interests of our members and bring the experience of the leaders to bear on the conduct of public affairs for the common good."

Percy rose to his feet and exclaimed, "I propose a toast, to The Primrose League, may we uphold and support God, Queen, and Country, and the Conservative cause!"

At this point, all the gentlemen were on their feet, raising their cognac snifters and slapping each other on the back. Emily smiled fondly at her husband. They unfortunately had no children, yet had remained very much in love throughout their marriage. She was proud of the new organization and happy for Percy to find such a great interest. He spent most of his days busy in his law practice, and most of his evenings at the Carleton Club with the new organization, but they did enjoy Sunday services together, and always kept Sunday luncheon for each other.

She continued down the hallway, back toward the social gala, which was filled with the young people. She spied Lady Adela trying to escape from an interested suitor and smiled kindly. She was very fond of Lady Adela. She glanced around the room and found Augusta chatting with some other mothers of eligible young ladies. As she made her way toward Augusta, the Countess caught her eye and excused herself from the conversation.

"My dear Emily, are you having a good time this evening?" asked Lady Augusta.

"I always enjoy your social gatherings, my dear," replied Emily. "Your cook makes simply the best food in all of Britain."

"She does, and we enjoy it immensely," laughed Lady Augusta.

"I was speaking to Lady Adela a few minutes ago," continued Emily, "and she was telling me all about T.B.H. Cochrane."

"Ah, yes! I am so very pleased that they met, and apparently fell in love, at my last shoot," said Lady Augusta.

"I see the hand of a very determined woman in that meeting!" Emily persisted.

"Indeed," laughed Lady Augusta. "Some of my finest work. However, there is a problem. Lord John took an instant disliking to the young man and his ideas about Canada."

"There is no surprise in that, Lady Augusta. I have just been listening to The Primrose League's declarations in your library, and Lord John is very supportive. Our husbands are Conservatives through and through, and though The Primrose League value free enterprise, I think that finding it in the wilds of Canada is not what Lord John sees as a good occupation for a husband for Adela."

"That is so very true, my dear. I fear Lord John will not relent in his dislike of the young fellow, nor will he let Adela marry the man, which would be such a pity."

"Why are you so favourable about this union?" queried Emily.

"Well, my dear, the Cochranes travel in Queen Victoria's circle on the Isle of Wight where she goes for respite from London. Their home, Quarr Abbey, is close by Osborne House."

"Oh, yes, quite right," replied Emily. "That would be a very great catch for Lady Adela."

"And luckily, she is still quite young, but at eighteen it is definitely time for her to find a husband," continued Lady Augusta. "I am definitely in favour of the match. However, the wedding may have to be postponed until either Lord John passes or he becomes unable to remember what his wishes are," she complained to her dear friend. The two old friends smiled at the reality of life where women had to work only from behind the scenes to bring about their wishes.

> *May 21, 1884. The evening has finally ended, yet I am as awake as if it were the first of morn. I think about you continually my darling, and wish you were not so far, far away in a foreign land, having great adventure without me! Surely the world moves more slowly these days as I pine for you, so alone. That I cannot even write to you saddens me so, yet I can catch my thoughts in my diary, and will do so until I can see the sweetness of your face once more.*

CHAPTER 3

THE LITTLE BOW RIVER CATTLE RANCHE, A TIMBER BERTH AND A SAW MILL

1883 – MAY 1885

Thomas Cochrane had to admit that he was stunned with the reality of the new world. It was so unlike his home in England. He arrived back in the late summer of 1883 and returned to his family home on the Isle of Wight to find that things had indeed been changing while he was gone. His dear sister Minna was spending a great deal of time with HRH Princess Beatrice when the royal family was visiting their vacation home on the Isle of Wight. Of course, this made his mama very happy. She was also very happy that he was in love with Lady Adela Rous, son of the Earl of Stradbroke. Mama was also very interested in his exploits in the Dominion of Canada, as after all, the Cochranes had quite a history in Canada.

"Well, son, tell me about this Last Best West" Rosetta Cochrane asked excitedly. She was enthralled to be hearing his stories at his first breakfast, home at Quarr Abbey House.

"Indeed Mama, it is a perplexing, but fascinating land," responded T.B.H.

"Your father found it to be the same when he was Governor of New Found Land." Rosetta Cochrane laughed. "'The people are rough, spiteful and cannot be trusted,'" Admiral Cochrane used to say.

"That was long before you knew him though, Mama, correct?" inquired T.B.H.

"Goodness yes, my dear," laughed Lady Rosetta. "He was still married to Matilda then, his first family, you know."

"Did Father tell you about his time there?" T.B.H. asked, eager to hear once again what life had been like in the Dominion for his father, when his father had been an active military man.

His mother laughed again.

"Oh yes, I heard his stories many, many times. They went like this," Rosetta continued, mimicking the voice of Admiral Cochrane.

"'When New Found Land became an official Crown colony in '25, I was appointed as its first Governor. At the time, military officers were appointed to direct colonies that did not yet have representative government. I directed the construction of Government House, located between Fort William and Fort Townshend. I split the colony into three judicial districts over each of which I placed a chief justice and two judges and brought back the poor relief system. This way those who were desperate could build roads.'"

"I should think the people would have been pleased with that," suggested T.B.H.

Mama laughed again. He would have said, "'You would

think that, wouldn't you! But they were rough, undisciplined and unruly. They drank up every penny earned.'"

She continued, "'I strongly opposed the introduction of representative government to the colony. How could such lowly people govern themselves? They needed a governor with discipline and experience to govern them, just as the navy needs officers. I created a new constitution which was granted in 1832 and was appointed as the first civil Governor.'"

"Then his story always changed," Mama went on. 'But times were not easy. I became involved in various conflicts while I was Governor, especially with reformers in the new legislature and with that damnable Roman Catholic bishop, Michael Fleming. Much of the Catholic population were descendants from the years when the French had been predominant.'"

"'So,'" she continued, "'the colonial office recalled me in 1834. Claimed I had become too unpopular. Those damn ingrates actually threw filth at us on our way down to the wharf.'"

"Yes, but wasn't Papa appointed a companion of the Order of Bath by Queen Victoria for his service there?" remembered T.B.H.

"Yes, of course, on April 18, 1839. Such a marvelous woman, our Queen," chuckled Rosetta Cochrane.

"It is wonderful to have her patronage," agreed T.B.H. "And Minna and HRH Princess Beatrice certainly do get on well."

"We hope she will be appointed as Lady-in-Waiting, soon," agreed Mama. "But enough of life in jolly old England. What of the New World?" Mama asked, with eyes glowing.

"It is absolutely breathtaking in its beauty," T.B.H. began. "The Rocky Mountains are indescribable, tall, majestic and

SHANNON BRADLEY GREEN

snow covered until late June," he went on.

"Your father would be so proud that you and Cousin William are carrying on the Cochrane family tradition." Mama's eyes began to mist over as she remembered her grief at losing Admiral Thomas.

"It will be marvelous running a big ranching operation!" T.B.H. continued enthusiastically. "There is something about all that open, unclaimed space that makes a man think anything is possible!" T.B.H. went on.

"But there was a problem with the purchase, dear?" Mama broached the tricky subject of how things had not worked out well for the two cousins.

T.B.H. replied quite heartily,

"Too true, Mama. However, where one idea turns out badly, in The Last Best West, there are plenty more to try."

"What does that mean?" asked Mama.

"Well, Billie and I have a great new proposition to look at near the Little Bow River. It will include around 51 000 acres of ranch land," T.B.H. replied. "Now all we have to do is to pull together more financing.

"This is Hugh's great skill," chuckled T.B.H. Hugh Graham was the son of Sir F. Graham and one of the partners in the new business.

Rosetta Cochrane smiled fondly at her son. Like so many women of her time, she was the second wife to a man who had lived well and lived long enough to have two families. With Admiral Cochrane now gone, and Minna so busy with HRH Princess Beatrice, Rosetta turned all her attention and adoration to young Thomas. She knew all the young men were in a fervor over land acquisition in Canada, and she wanted to be sure young Thomas was able to talk about his exploits at any social events he attended when back in Britain.

Adela was thrilled to the bottom of her soles that T.B.H. had returned home in the fall of 1883. He was full of his plans for The Little Bow River Cattle Company. He and his partners planned to stock it with a thousand head of cattle and about seventy horses and ponies.

As T.B.H. always returned from Canada to his home on the Isle of Wight, and Adela lived at Henham Hall in Suffolk, they often rendezvoused in London. Mama had convinced Papa to buy a town house for the family in London many years ago, and Adela often convinced Emily Mitford to accompany her as a chaperone when she went to meet T.B.H. He had many friends in London, so it was always convenient for them to meet at the London townhouse. Young Cochrane spent time with all the fashionable young men of London and was caught up in the near hysteria of the times about life in the Dominions.

This way, too, Adela's father, who had become now mostly unaware of his surroundings, would not be troubled by her continued relationship with T.B.H. She traveled to meet him as often as her Mama would allow, and they often met for dinner so she could catch up with all his plans. T.B.H. was busy procuring and financing the Little Bow River Cattle Company and needed to be in London for these proceedings. Her chaperone, Emily Mitford, had no problem with the two of them meeting at a stylish restaurant. It was expected that young people act with decorum in public, and she offered Adela this time to meet with T.B.H. and enjoy his company by herself.

"How are things going, my love?" Adela cooed as she swept

into the restaurant and plopped into a chair beside T.B.H.

"Things are going well with the transfer. It looks like everything will be settled by May," replied T.B.H. "I am anxious to get to Mosquito Creek."

"Mosquito Creek, that doesn't sound very hospitable," Adela laughed.

"Indeed!" T.B.H. laughed back. "However, this time I am assured that the land is suitable for ranching," he concluded.

Adela gazed adoringly at her young beau. She was as excited as the young men of London with the ideas about the New World. And T.B.H. made his exploits there sound so thrilling that she hung on his every word.

"Adela, I simply cannot wait to show you this land," T.B.H. said. "Could you ever imagine living on a ranche in the Dominion of Canada?" he asked tentatively.

"My goodness T.B.H., that sounds almost like a proposal," Adela laughed gleefully.

"My sweetest girl, that is my deepest hope. I know your Papa will never agree to it though. I am more than certain that he would turn me down if I were to ask for your hand in marriage," T.B.H. replied glumly.

"My dear Papa will not live forever T.B.H., and I can wait for you to become more settled and successful at The Little Bow River Cattle Company. When Papa no longer cares, we could be married…." she suggested.

T.B.H.'s face broke into a broad grin.

"My dear Adela. You are the perfect woman for the New World. We will have such lovely adventures and happiness there," Thomas promised.

"So, it will be our secret. We will be secretly betrothed until such time as it becomes possible for a marriage. Then we will marry right away and move to the beautiful Last Best West," Adela sighed.

"My dearest, this is the happiest moment of my life." T.B.H. glowed with love for the wholesome girl sitting across from him.

"And the happiest moment of my life too," Adela agreed to the dashing adventurer with the sheepish grin. Glancing quickly about her, Adela reached across the table and delicately kissed T.B.H.

With joined hands and hearts, the young lovers talked endlessly about what the future would hold for them.

IT HAD BEEN A LONG year, but Thomas had finally procured the lease from the Canadian government in his own name with help of former partners Hugh Graham, Ted and Frank Jenkins and Cousin Billie. The partners had decided the deal was too tenuous for them but had encouraged T.B.H. and Billie to go ahead on their own.

"This is thrilling, so thrilling," enthused Adela, her eyes shining bright with the excitement of this enterprise in this Last Best West.

"When we are married, I will be able to invest in this ranche as well," she sighed longingly.

"Well, I am convinced your papa is going to live forever," complained Thomas. "which is keeping us apart."

Papa was the most agreeable when her brother George was home on leave. George, under the courtesy title of Viscount Dunwich, was now a major in the Norfolk Artillery Volunteers. The enthusiasm for the Volunteer movement following an invasion scare in 1859 saw the creation of many Rifle, Artillery and Engineer Volunteer units composed of part-time soldiers eager to supplement the Regular British Army in time of need.

George had just completed his Bachelor of Arts at Trinity College in Cambridge, but was back to study for a Master's degree. However, going to university and volunteering with the Norfolk Artillery kept him very busy. He had no time for romance or marrying as he was a very studious fellow and was also preparing himself to take over the duties as the next Lord Stradbroke, as his father was no longer able to keep up with any of the responsibilities. Luckily for the family, there were often duties that called George home, which was a great comfort to all. Papa was calmer, Mama was happier, and Adela was just happy to spend time with her older brother. The two had been so close as children, before George had gone off to Harrow School in London.

"It will be so bittersweet, T.B.H., when Papa dies. My dear Papa will be gone, but, then I will finally be free to marry the love of my life!" she exclaimed.

T.B.H, on the other hand, was ever scouting around for new opportunities, and living up to his family's reputation as "money getting." One thing he had learned about the North-West Territories was that it was a frightfully cold place in the winter, and as there were few buildings or lodgings for him, he found it much more pleasant to return home to the Isle of Wight with its creature comforts for the winter months. By April, the snow was on its way out and warmer weather was ahead, so he usually planned to return to the West in the spring. This also meant that he could spend the winter months with Adela, which he enjoyed immensely.

He had discovered that in 1883, a certain James Christie had applied for a license to cut timber in the Dog Pound area. This license had been granted in February 1884, subject to the filing of a survey with the Department of the Interior. Upon his return in the spring of 1884, T.B.H met with James Christie and his partners, seeing a golden opportunity to set up a sawmill. He arranged to meet with Christie in Calgary, which had begun to grow from the Fort and a few tents and shacks, to a small village. The accommodations were still very spartan, but there were places to stay and places to do business.

"James, old man, I believe this lumber venture could become a capital opportunity. Settlers will continue to pour in, needing houses, and pine logs will need to be turned into lumber. There are no sawmills as of yet in this Dog Pound area. Such an odd name, Dog Pound, don't you think?" T.B.H. jested.

"Everything is named after some great Cree event in this country," James laughed. "Apparently, some poor fool wolf got mixed in with the buffalo being herded over the jump and was found dead at the bottom with all the buffalo."

"Damned odd, indeed, but unimportant in terms of sawmills!" T.B.H. agreed.

"I believe the sawmill will be an excellent addition to this lumber venture!" James Christie agreed, "and my partners are in full agreement."

The spring of 1884 brought T.B.H. Cochrane to the future site of the sawmill. At this time, he met the Count de Journal, a fellow speculator like himself, from Paris. Journal believed that the area needed some decent lodgings as none were available as of yet. T.B.H was able to convince the Count to finance a hotel while he provided the land. The Count was travelling with Joseph Limoges from Quebec, who being in poor health, was looking to relocate West. They convinced Joseph that he should operate the hotel. This made Thomas pleased as now he would have lodgings to stay in when he visited the site of his new logging operation and sawmill. Until he married Adela, he would have no money to build the fine home that he wanted. He had found the perfect location for his new town at the confluence of the Bow River and a lovely little creek that emptied into it. For T.B.H. Cochrane, the looks of a place were very important. To build a town, he knew a water source was essential, but beyond that, he had no idea what was required. It didn't really concern him.

To the adventurers and settlers coming to the area, this place was simply known as the Calgary Lumber Company site. Thomas was anxious to get started, but it all took so much patience and money.

While back in England, Thomas continued on with the legal work when he returned from his yearly trip to Canada. On April 25, 1885, James Christie assigned his rights to the timber berth to T.B.H Cochrane, Hugh Graham (Cochrane's money man), and two of the original timber partners, Francis White (a rancher) and Archibald McVittie, (a Dominion land surveyor).

When T.B.H traveled to the lumber company site in the spring of '85, he was hoping to finally get it operational. He also had in mind that the site needed a company store, and he had been busy raising funds for that business during his winter in England. I.G. Baker bull trains and the Canadian Pacific Railway were reliable transportation for bringing the building materials to the site. But T.B.H wasn't sure what he would do when the materials arrived as he hadn't found a carpenter.

Providence smiled upon him as William Sargent, a carpenter and millwright from England, arrived that spring as well, seeking a new life in the Last Best West. Thomas spent all summer supervising work with Sargent, who had traveled out with his wife to the West. Sargent began to build the store for T.B.H. Finding a qualified person to run the store would be difficult, but this was a job for next season. Count de Journal had been busy with the hotel construction and Joseph Limoge was ready to become the first innkeeper at Saw Mill, as the site had come to be known.

In May 1885, Thomas completed the exchange with the Canadian Government of his initial timber lease with the new lease, and his other venture, The Little Bow River Cattle Company, which came into being near Mosquito Creek. Thomas was the legal manager of the ranche, but it was Cousin Billie Cochrane, his business and travel partner, who had left a sweetheart at home as well, who traveled with him to supervise the ranche management.

May 10, 1885. That this day would never come has been my fear now for over a year, yet today T.B.H. tells me that it is all finally legal and that he will be leaving with Billie on the next steamship to New York, then to make his way out West to The Little Bow River Cattle Company. Finally, his dream is a reality! It, like so many dreams in my life, is bittersweet. I shall miss my darling so as he sets out across the ocean to build our new life, yet he builds it without me. Sadness and melancholy rip at my heart, yet I know one day I shall venture there with him and great happiness shall fill my every waking hour.

CHAPTER 4

A PASSING AND A WEDDING

1885-1886

The summer of 1885 passed agonizingly slowly for Adela. However, things were about to change. Papa had definitely taken a turn for the worse. Mama had contacted every doctor to be found from miles around and all said the same thing. The Earl of Stradbroke was dying.

George had taken up full time residence at home, which was a great relief to the Rous' women, but all realized that there was nothing to do but wait. What did help Adela pass this difficult time was that T.B.H. had returned home for the winter months and had not returned to Canada. The Rous family did not want to stray far from home.

T.B.H. was often a guest at Henham Hall. Papa Rous had long ceased to be engaged in the world, and therefore his presence was no longer an annoyance to him.

After a slow, painful, autumn, John Edward Cornwallis Rous, 2nd Earl of Stradbroke, departed the earth on January 27, 1886. He was ninety-one years of age. After his death, Mama flew into action, planning an elaborate funeral wake for the Earl. His funeral was held at St. Paul's Cathedral in London, so that all of London society could be invited. The funeral was a huge undertaking, and Adela and her sisters had been frightfully busy helping their mama with all details.

As was expected, all of London society indeed turned out for the funeral service and the after-service gathering. Adela and George sat together after they had completed the receiving line with their mother and sisters. It was so exhausting. It was easiest to be with George, as it was with him, and her papa, that she had spent the happiest years in her home. All her memories of fox hunts and pheasant shoots and horses and dogs ran together in her head like a crazy kaleidoscope. She remembered riding alongside her papa and George on so many occasions, which brought tears flowing down her cheeks. The awful realization that she would never see her papa again made her heart want to burst.

One dreary morning a few days after the Earl's death, T.B.H., never one to wait for long, asked Adela to join him for a walk. He had continued to stay on at Henham Hall, ostensibly to help the family with the arrangements. On the pretext of wanting to check out the horses, they headed toward the stables. T.B.H. seemed more than a little anxious that morning.

On the way, he turned to Adela and proposed,

"Adela, would you do me the honour of becoming my wife?"

Now Adela had been giving this very idea some serious thought since her papa's death. She and T.B.H. had been waiting so many years for the opportunity to marry. She knew, beyond the shadow of a doubt, that she was madly in love with the impetuous Cochrane. She knew he would give her the kind of life she could scarcely have dreamt about, and that made her very, very happy. And she had been waiting for his actual proposal since that evening in London so long ago when they had pledged their hearts to each other.

"T.B.H., I would be delighted," she agreed excitedly.

"But I will only marry you if you promise me adventure. I simply cannot spend the rest of my life buying dresses and preparing for balls and visiting other ladies for luncheon. I want to be a ranche wife in the Dominion of Canada, and never step onto another dance floor, in a gown, again."

"Oh, Adela, wait until you see Canada and our ranche!" T.B.H. enthused. "I can barely wait until I can take you there."

"I can barely wait to go there, my darling. But wait we must, and we must be very correct in announcing this engagement. As well, we must give the appropriate time now that the funeral is concluded to make our announcement. My dear Mama has been so exhausted with Papa's funeral, that we will need time for her to recover so that she can start all over again with our wedding plans."

Adela giggled with excitement.

"For once I am enthusiastic about a huge dinner and ball. Truly, I would forego the entire thing, but that is impossible for the daughter of the Earl of Stradbroke. So, if I must endure it, then I shall, knowing it is the key to our being together and my escape from London society."

"Right you are my darling, right you are. Let us wait until March for the social announcement. We can make it public, and then I will leave for Canada for the summer for the last time by myself. You, your mama and sisters can plan the wedding upon my return."

Adela agreed that this was a wonderful plan, and happily offered her mouth to T.B.H. for a kiss to seal the wonderful moment.

"And on the matter of the ring, Adela, I am afraid there is a little problem. Every penny I have ever owned is invested in the ranche and Saw Mill in Canada. Indeed, my dear mama must send me a remittance to live on so that I can travel back and forth. I do not have the finances to buy you a ring," he said sadly.

"Oh, T.B.H., you needn't worry. We will have left enough time between our true engagement and the announcement that George will have taken care of my inheritance. We can go up to London and choose our wedding rings when you return from Canada next autumn," Adela finished.

"Splendid idea!" Thomas replied with great relish.

So, the Rous family went into official mourning. Mama would be in mourning for two years; the girls and George would be expected to officially mourn for one year. Knowing this, Adela knew her wedding could not take place until after January of 1887. That meant February 1887, in her mind.

She had had to wait so long and was so impatient to get to Canada. Now that her papa was gone she was a least one year closer to her dreams. It was such a bittersweet time in her life. In order to have her own true love, she must lose her father whom she had loved so dearly.

On a lovely March day, a few weeks before T.B.H. was due to set out for Canada, Adela convinced Mama to invite him up for a Henham Hall visit. After the funeral Thomas had returned to Quarr Abbey and his business affairs, which were causing him no end of worry. By the spring of 1886 his businesses were unraveling, and he was running into financial difficulty. It had cost him thirty thousand Canadian dollars to build the mill and tramway, and both were inoperative due to the difficulty with a timber license being issued. Thomas was perpetually amazed at how much difficulty there was with getting anything accomplished in Canada.

Mama had begun taking her breakfast in the dining room with George, as they had many details to go over together in terms of the passing on of the estate. The girls had always been required to dine in the dining room for breakfast, so Adela and Thomas decided that they would announce their engagement there.

"Good Morning, T.B.H.," said George, 3rd Earl of Stradbroke. "You look like the cat that got the cream this morning."

"Well, I do believe that is exactly how I feel." Thomas laughed.

"How so, old boy?"

"As you know," Thomas began, "soon it will be time for me to head back out to Canada, to my ranche, sawmill and tramway. Each year I must leave poor Adela behind here, much to her dismay. You have no idea how many times she has begged me to take her with me, married or not. But we have been patient, and have waited for this day, when we may announce to you that Lady Adela Rous has agreed to do me the honour of becoming my wife."

Mama's hands flew to her mouth, then with a great pushing back of her chair, she rushed over to Adela's side of the table to throw her arms around her.

"Oh Adela, my dear, how this lifts my heavy heart!" Mama cried.

"We want to be proper, Mama, so will wait the full year required. We will marry in February of 1887," Adela replied.

"Jolly good idea to wait, Adela, and not entirely like you!" George teased. He continued, "Congratulations, T.B.H."

Lady Gwendoline and Lady Hilda started talking excitedly about the wedding with Lady Adela, who for once was not upset with them and their incessant talk about balls, parties and social gatherings.

SUMMER DID NOT BRING AN end to T.B.H.'s business difficulties. He required the intervention of the Deputy Minister of Interior in Ottawa to help get the paperwork in order, and this also came with a stiff back rent requirement which Thomas had to pay "under protest."

Things had not come together for him at all, and even with back rent paid, he was still not able to begin cutting lumber due to a discrepancy in the submitted survey plan. Thomas was required to engage in many actions of which he had very little knowledge, and subsequently mistakes were made that needed to be corrected. It all added up to more cost and no movement forward on his plans.

Things were going so poorly for Thomas that there was no way he could leave Canada and return home for the summer. He spent his time mostly at The Little Bow Cattle Company ranche with Cousin Billie, leaving only when his business affairs required him to travel to Calgary. There was also difficulty with the original land grant, so the Calgary Lumber Company, the name he had chosen for his business, purchased the contentious quarter section of land from the Hudson's Bay Company.

It was on this particular section that Adela's great dream was to come true.

Both Thomas and Billie were frustrated with the difficulty of getting everything in order, for it had been decided that Billie would return to be married to his love, the gracious Evelyn, his fiancé, at the same time as Thomas and Adela were to be married. Finally, the cousins felt they could leave Canada by December of 1886.

In the meanwhile, Adela was very lonely, as she had not seen Thomas since the spring. She and her mama and sisters had been very busy planning the wedding. Adela had thought that her dear brother George would give her away as her papa could not, but George had decided that he was going to take Papa's side on the matter of Thomas Belhaven Henry Cochrane, and that Adela would not be given away by the Earl of Stradbroke.

Mama, who was quite annoyed by George's allegiance to the dead Earl, decided that she herself should then give Adela away.

"I can't believe George is doing this!" Adela wailed when she found out. She and George had always been so close that she couldn't imagine him being so unkind. He was her favorite, and she his; yet he had chosen to side with what the London society men might think of him over his own sister. Adela felt fury, alternating with hurt, knowing that society seemed to always win out over family.

"Oh, Papa and George are not thinking of the social prestige Thomas has brought this family with his family's acquaintance with the Queen!" Mama protested. "This kind of social relationship is not to be wasted."

Mama had spared no expense for this wedding. Lord God above be praised to the Heavens, Queen Victoria and Princess Beatrice would attend! Mama truly felt like her greatest ambitions had been achieved with this social coup. Truth be told, it was of far more importance to her than the type of man that Adela was marrying. Augusta Rous' raison d'etre was to gain social position in society, and she had just managed to achieve the greatest success of all, the Queen's attendance at her daughter's wedding. After all, as a young woman she had married much older men for their social position, and life had turned out very well for her.

ADELA'S WEDDING DAY DAWNED WITH a constant downpour. Adela didn't really care as she would have foregone the whole thing if she could. Dark skies greeted the wedding party. Many brides would have been in tears, but Adela wasn't fazed. This wedding was merely a means to an end to achieve the kind of opportunity she wanted in her life.

The Reverend George Work, vicar of St. Paul's Cathedral, married them on February 19, 1887.

Adela and Lady Augusta walked down the long aisle of St. Paul's.

"I hope you have a long and happy life with T.B.H.," Mama whispered to her before handing her over to the beaming young Cochrane.

Her mama had fussed over every detail, and Adela had just agreed with whatever Mama had wanted. As she had learned long ago from her papa, it was far easier to just go along with what Mama wanted. Lady Rous had outdone herself, filling the rooms of the hotel where the wedding luncheon was held with large vases of flowers and hanging ribbon and garlands of flowers everywhere.

Mama had arranged that the young couple would stay at the hotel for a week's honeymoon. Then, they were to continue up to Scotland to be the guests of the Clan Dundonald relatives for a few weeks. Finally, they would return to Quarr Abbey until it was time to leave for Canada.

Champagne flowed, and a beautiful luncheon was served. Adela thought it would never come to an end as she accepted the best wishes of all her family and the guests. She got a big chuckle out of the Cochrane clan who had traveled down from Scotland. They drank champagne, but quickly switched to whiskey and proceeded to get very drunk, even though it was only mid-day. Their tables echoed with ribald jokes, loud laughter and excessive enjoyment of the event.

The elated new bride was finally able to be with Thomas, after waiting for so many years. Soon they would leave for the Last Best West, in the great Dominion of Canada, and for The Little Bow Cattle Company ranche on Mosquito Creek. She could not have been happier.

February 20, 1887. That this day should never come has been my constant agitation for over a year! Tiring as these social events are, Mama is thrilled beyond reason at how my wedding has turned out. George remained gracious, but after all, it really was the first event for him as the 3rd Earl of Stradbroke, so he needed to be on his best behavior. Minna and Princess Beatrice were very complimentary, so apparently, I didn't choose any unbecoming phrases when replying to Queen Victoria's best wishes. It is so like me to say the wrong thing and make a mistake when replying to the Queen, which would never be forgiven. Still, she seems slightly upset by something though…

CHAPTER 5

IN SEARCH OF ADVENTURE—
THE DOMINION OF CANADA

1887

She was sitting in the saloon, sipping sherry and feeling incredible. Lady Adela Cochrane looked about her on the Parisian, of the Allan Line. She reflected back on the journey that had brought her to this place. The year was 1887 when they sailed out of Southampton, bound for New York, then onwards to Canada. Adela knew they would have a long journey once they got there, but for now her mind was looking back at the journey which had brought her here.

"Cheers, my darling," she smiled to T.B.H. as she raised her glass to her husband.

Those posters from Canadian Pacific Railways, which had caught her eye on the streets of London, had been the beginning of her wildest imaginings. Who would have ever believed she would find herself here?

Adela knew she should be crying from loss to be leaving her home and family, but truly, all she felt was the relief of getting away from the suffocating society life she had always so abhorred. She was still vexed with George for his position about her marriage to Thomas. She thought about her family's motto, "I Live in Hope" that she had seen so many times above the main entry to her home, Henham Hall. She felt very close to her ancestors at this moment, as she felt that somehow, they must have understood that life was often difficult, but that you must live in hope if you were going to take from life what it had to offer. She was very hopeful that a new life was going to open up for her and T.B.H., one she was far more suited for than the stilted, smothering life of a Victorian upper-class lady.

T.B.H. purchased passage aboard the Parisian that left every two weeks from South Hampton. Saloon passage was procured, and Lady Adela's great adventure started to fall into place. They had decided to travel with three staff for their first trip, T.B.H.s' idea, as he knew the hardships ahead of them. She remembered the excitement of her childhood, listening to Uncle Henry, and all his adventures. Now she wanted to start having her own.

THE CANADIAN GOVERNMENT WAS ENCOURAGING the sale of odd-numbered sections of land in the West to any business that demonstrated its goodwill and capabilities, and a sincere interest in promoting settlement. When T.B.H. had first shared this with her, Adela had thought about it, and a plan had started to hatch in her mind. She would build an incredible new town in this new land. The more she thought about it, the more excited she became about this wonderful opportunity. At night, she would lie awake trying to imagine a world where there were no people settled in towns. She just could not imagine it. Not only were there no people in towns, but also there were no farmers either. Her rural life in Suffolk consisted of tidy farms, and, of course, Henham Hall. But this new land of Canada had only open lands and roaming savages. It was incredibly romantic to her to think of moving away and building her very own village.

Now, you may think that Lady Adela was very conceited to think about building her own village, but you must remember, she had grown up at Henham Hall, the daughter of an Earl, and therefore was quite used to being part of the most important family in a very large area. In her mind, she was simply creating a new Rous family dynasty in a foreign land.

It was hard to imagine this land, and yet, when Mama had renovated Henham Hall, the architect, Edward Barry, had included one wall that featured a remarkable frieze depicting a savage fighting a bear. Of course, the frenzy about the colonial lands of Britain was all the rage, and even the architects wanted to be sure to include these ideas in the décor of the day. This was the only visual, other than the CPR posters she had seen, that gave her any idea of what her new home country might look like. Mr. Barry had suggested the frieze, as Victorian Englishmen's imaginations were completely taken with the New World. He had convinced Mama that any great home needed to include an acknowledgement to the interests of the times; and the interest was certainly in the new world of North America.

THERE HAD BEEN SUCH A flurry of activity in the months preceding their departure that Thomas and Adela had had little time to do anything but prepare for their emigration. Adela turned her imagination to re-creating an estate like that of Henham Hall in the new land. She daydreamed about what she would call the new estate but could think of nothing more fitting than New Henham. However, she remembered reading letters from Thomas and Cousin Billie describing the ranche, and Adela started to understand that a ranche in Canada might really be nothing at all like the life lived by country squires in jolly old England.

Saying goodbye to Mama, George and her sisters was harder than Adela thought it would be. Everyone decided to come up to London to see them off on the train to South Hampton. George had finished up the details of Papa's will, making Lady Adela now a woman of her own means. She had been purchasing wonderful new clothes for Thomas, which he assured her would suit him well in Canada. Steamer trunks were packed for the spring/summer trip to The Little Bow River Cattle Company ranche, their destination. Cousin Billie Cochrane and his newly married wife Evelyn accompanied them, and they would all would be staying together at the ranche.

Waving goodbye to the family in South Hampton caused Adela a few moments of sadness, but this was quickly replaced with the sense of freedom and adventure she had waited so long for. There stood her mama, Lady Augusta, the Countess of Stradbroke, resplendent in her beautiful scarlet coat and fashionable hat, waving her handkerchief at the ship. Lady Gwendoline and Lady Hilda waved their handkerchiefs too, and George doffed his tall beaver hat to them in a salute. Adela knew she would return with such amazing tales to tell them, and she secretly felt very much like Uncle Henry, which filled her with joy.

The voyage was long. Adela was often seasick as the North Atlantic was rough. The ship was comfortable, but nothing could stop that terrible feeling when the ship began to roll in the heavy seas. Adela had been ecstatic when they boarded in South Hampton, but now, days into the voyage, she was wondering about how difficult this adventure might turn out to be. She was too sick to even think about eating. To get some fresh air, she attempted to stroll on the decks as often as possible, when the rain let up and allowed her to do so. This was truly where she felt the best.

As her dear friend, Susan St Maur, was later to write in her chronicles of her trip to the Far West, "To see the world one must be callous to personal comfort; travelling does all men good; they find their level, come in contact with the enterprise of others, and see life from many different points of view." Adela was to learn stores of wisdom herself from her life in the New World.

T.B.H. spent the better part of most days in the Gentlemen's Lounge playing cards, along with Cousin Billie. He had been in the Royal Navy, so the roughness of the ship bothered him not at all. Evelyn Cochrane and Adela kept each other company, as they were to do for many years into the future. The servants kept a close eye on their ladies, but there was little they could do to ease the discomfort of the perils of the voyage.

On one of her strolls around the deck, Adela came across a small girl standing beside her mother. These were passengers from steerage, who were allowed out on the deck for short periods of time during the day. The little one seemed like an imp and was tearing around the deck enjoying her freedom. Adela could tell the mother was mortified with her child's behavior.

"Ida Cooper come this instant," the woman intoned in her full Scottish brogue. The little one stopped running and went obediently to her mother's side. Adela liked this little scamp and tweaked her nose as she went by. On Adela's next loop she saw that the woman and child were still out on the deck, but the mother was once again chastising the child. It appeared that the little girl had peed her pants, and the mother was very distressed.

"You've ruined your wee boots, lass," the mother complained loudly.

Adela realized the child probably only wore the boots to come out on the deck, and that there would be no extras to replace the ruined pair. She quickly dipped into her small purse that she kept attached to her waistband and drew out a few bills. She pressed these into the mother's hand. The woman immediately began to protest, but Adela would hear nothing of it and turned and left the astonished woman and the small rascal on the deck. She could see herself in the small imp of a girl and chuckled heartily at how she may have behaved in exactly the same way when she was a child.

DAYS PASSED. ADELA STARTED TO feel excited again about the adventure ahead. The passenger ship was only the first leg of their journey; there was a train to Canada, a steamboat and another long train ride ahead of them before they would be able to come to the ranche, where there would be many mysteries ahead.

Finally, the Parisian sailed into the port in New York.

"Evelyn, look. What a fine example of the new world for us to see."

Adela had read in the London Times how the Statue of

Liberty, 'Liberty Enlightening the World,' had been sent as a gift of friendship from the people of France to the people of the United States in 1886. She was awe-inspiring in her beauty.

EXHAUSTED, BUT VERY EXCITED, THOMAS and Adela, Billie and Evelyn drove through the New York streets, the first Adela was to see in the New World. Lodging had been arranged at the Brunswick Hotel, and Adela was relieved to look upon a hotel in the tradition of the grand hotels she frequented in London. New York surely was not like the Last Best West.

The two couples settled in for a few weeks, while Thomas and Billie went about arranging their business dealings and organizing their trip to Canada. Of course, Thomas and Billie had been making this trip now for four years, and they were old hands at what needed to be done.

The first leg of the journey was booked to Montreal on the New York Central Railway. The second leg would take them from Montreal to Toronto to Owen Sound, where steamboat passage was booked across the Great Lakes; the next leg of their passage west. The steamers took them to Port Arthur, where they would pick up the Canadian Pacific Railway to Winnipeg. The last leg of the journey took them from Winnipeg to Calgary. The journey alone was the wildest adventure Adela could ever have imagined.

The men took care of the details.

Evelyn and Adela enjoyed New York. They knew they would not need fine dresses for their new life, but instead shopped for sturdy hunting outfits and leather boots in their outings. Evelyn was quite concerned that they dress in the style of North America, so they added a few more steamer trunks to the large number already packed. Evelyn had even insisted on bringing her wedding china.

"I say, Adela, now you look like a frontierswoman," Evelyn exclaimed as she looked on at Adela in her woolen skirt and jacket and tall leather hunting boots.

"We look the same, which we could never do in England," laughed Adela, who was so relieved to be shopping for clothes that would have a purpose other than to be commented on by other women.

They dined in fine restaurants and attended the theatre, knowing that these types of activities would soon be a part of their past.

Adela and Evelyn thought New York was a fascinating city, part new world and part old. They enjoyed sharing their daily exploits with their new husbands at day's end. Life and all its problems back at Henham Hall seemed a world away, which they were, and Adela was glad of it.

THE TRAIN THROUGH THE COUNTRYSIDE of New York State afforded the two young ladies their first views of rural New York. They noticed farms, villages and towns, with strange names like Saratoga Springs and Schenectady. The towns looked different yet had a certain similarity to the world they had just left.

Montreal delighted them as well. A French city, its beautiful Old Port rose gracefully from the St. Lawrence River. It was, however, an old-fashioned place with a French looking and French speaking population. The houses of Montreal had a foreign look about them, with shuttered windows and tin roofs.

The Cochrane cousins were taken from the station to the hotel in caleches, which were modeled after those found in France during the reign of Louis XIV. These were small carriages, carrying only two and a driver, and the Cochrane contingent required a great many caleches to transport themselves, the staff and their luggage to the hotel. The men always enjoyed Montreal and were happy to stay for a week. The new wives visited the Falls of Montmorency and the well-fortified Citadel. The landscape was breath-taking with the great St. Lawrence winding its way out to the Atlantic. The countryside was dotted with villages and each of these was dominated by a large Roman Catholic church spire. After a day's tramping around the countryside, the ladies were happy to retire to the Hotel Windsor; however, their husbands found good fun in the card parlours after they had safely tucked their wives in for the night.

From Montreal to Toronto was another fine train ride, and this time the Cochrane wives found an English city. Adela marveled at how different American New York was from French Montreal and from British Toronto. These were such established cities that Adela could not fathom how different they were than the wilderness she was expecting.

The Cochranes disembarked from the train in Toronto. In 1887, it was another bustling small city with a comfortable hotel, the Queen's Hotel, to stay in. Toronto was the seat of a university, and also had a cathedral, many fine churches and other large public buildings. Its great claim to fame was that Queen Victoria's son, The Prince of Wales, had visited and stayed there. Much to her surprise, Adela found herself being waited upon by Negro servants who were very deferential; yet she was shocked by their lack of the genteel manners which she expected from her English staff. Queen Victoria would certainly never have accepted this, Adela shuddered to herself. This brought back the odd feeling she had experienced when she spoke to Queen Victoria at her wedding. It baffled her how English cultures could be so different.

The tidy country of small villages and towns disappeared on the train trip to Owen Sound. This land was forest. Hours passed without them seeing a living human.

"I think we are finally seeing a bit of our new life!" Adela exclaimed to Evelyn as she looked out the window. She was so delighted to have Evelyn with her because Thomas and Billie never took long to find a card game wherever they were.

Evelyn was surprised to find the first-class railway car was really on par with a third-class car back home. She looked on in wonderment as all sorts and conditions of men tumbled into the car. They were indeed obliged to travel with the roughest of people.

"It is quite unbelievable!" agreed Evelyn, as Adela commented to her upon the situation that they found themselves in.

"Our mamas would be truly offended to think we are traveling with these people," Evelyn commented.

However, they continued to be amazed by the hour-after-hour scene of virgin forest that passed by their windows. The enormity of the country they were traveling in was phenomenal.

May 2, 1887. So much has happened since we left
England only three weeks ago. I have tasted the life of
America, and French and English Canada and explored

beautiful cities. Canada Is wonderful, and yet I still yearn for the adventure of my new home. Tomorrow we shall reach Owen Sound and board the great steamboats that shall take us across the Great Lakes, inland seas. Every day brings new and amazing sights and my heart soars each morning as I open my eyes, knowing that when I close them again at night I will have experienced many new things that I had never known before. Is any new bride as fortunate as me? I have a wonderful new husband and a wonderful new friend in Evelyn Cochrane. I await each new day with wonder.

CHAPTER 6

SHINERS IN FITZROY HARBOUR

1870'S

Fights were the entertainment of the day in Fitzroy Harbour, Ontario, during the time of the timber trade. Irish immigrants, fleeing poverty, starvation and tyranny in Ireland, took a chance by riding empty lumber ships returning to England, and boarded these in either Liverpool or Cork and traveled to Canada. The Rideau Canal construction provided work for the poor Irish and this had been the only possible option for the immigrant Bradley family from County Kilkenney, in Ireland. They came to build the Rideau Canal and lived through the rough and often terrible times associated with its building and the growth of Bytown, located where the canal met the Ottawa River. Previously, the labour force had consisted of French-Canadian farmers and woodsmen from neighbouring districts, until the heavy Irish immigration of the 1820's brought new workers to the Ottawa Valley who were willing to work for lower wages. Bytown sprung up from the camps of the workers and later became a major lumber and sawmill center for Canada.

When the Ottawa River first began to be used for float-
ing timber to markets, squared timber was the preference.
This required the logs to be skillfully shaped with broadaxes,
giving the whole log a squared appearance. It was wasteful but
squared pine was preferred by the British for resawing.

Changes in the timber trade influenced the population
distribution of the Ottawa Valley. When the Rideau Canal
was finished in 1832, many more drifted to Bytown looking
for work. Some were employed cutting oak in western Quebec
and were dubbed "cheneurs" (oak-cutters), by the French,
which became "Shiners" in English slang. Because the Shiners
accepted lower wages than the French Canadians, conflicts
arose between the two groups.

By 1866, Fitzroy Harbour was a post village with a population of two hundred. It was located in Fitzroy Township on
the Ottawa river, at the head of the Duchesne Lake navigation,
on a small bay, dotted with islands. On the south side of the
river, directly opposite the village, was the government timber
slide, a water-filled chute built to carry rafts of timber around
the Chats Falls. Here was the home of the Kilkenney Bradley
family, who had moved into the mostly Irish Fitzroy Harbour
to work at the sawmill and timber slide. The Fitzroy Harbour
Irish were tough timber men and cantankerous women,
Orangemen and Catholics alike, who had escaped Ireland,
lived through building the Rideau Canal, and had now built
simple communities in the area in which they raised their
families. But this industry which had brought them livelihood
was waning, as the British market for lumber changed. There
was less work and more uncertainty.

Into this Irish Canadian community was born William

Percival Bradley in the 1860's. He was a typical Canadian, grandchild of immigrants to Ontario who had left behind destitution and found a new life that was much better than the old. All the Bradley men were lumber men, and all had worked in various aspects of the trade and had made a much-improved life for themselves since they had left Ireland.

Life was simple and had very few distractions. The dangerous physical work of the rivermen, along with the predominance of male settlers in the Ottawa River Valley, fostered a culture of masculinity. Fights could be seen as entertainment on a day off, with even prominent men indulging in duels.

The most notorious symbol of this culture was the French-Canadian folk hero Joseph Montferrand, a rafting foreman for the Bowman and Gilmore Company on the Ottawa River. Known as "Joe Mufferaw" to the region's English speakers, Montferrand inspired legends and songs about his legendary strength, size and exploits. Montferrand had been involved in the "Shiner's Wars" that took place in Bytown from 1837-45 between Irish and French-Canadian lumbermen. He was indeed a legend in his own time.

Young Billie Bradley grew up in the lumber culture of Fitzroy Harbour. By his early teens he was working full time as a Valley riverman. Rough and boisterous, rugged and rollicking, he lived in a time where men lived and died by their trade. The men who were his mentors were direct and daring, but simple in their actions. Good natured generosity was also a part of the lore, and these men were quick to pass the hat for a family in need. They were swift to anger and fierce in a fight, but always handled their brawls with their fists. Guns, knives and other weapons were rarely used to settle a difference.

Billie was a large boy with ragged, curly blond hair, and sparkling blue eyes.

Life on the Ottawa as a riverman made him strong at a young age. Even in his teens he was already known up and down the river for his great strength, which was highly valued by the other rivermen. The stories about him told of how he could lift a horse right off the ground with his own two hands. Of course, the men of the day taught him to fight as a boy and fighting became one of was his best skills. He became a master of the Irish Stand Down, a technique that removed maneuvering 'round the ring. He rarely, if ever, lost.

He wished he could have had a chance with Joe Mufferaw because he was sure he could have beaten him, but Joe had retired from the fighting world and could not be coaxed out to fight anymore.

Henry Bradley was Billie's younger brother by fourteen months. Henry was much smaller and leaner, with flowing red locks, and had a mischievous glint in his blue eyes. He was a fast sprinter and was deft on his feet and he too was well known by the rivermen, for his ability to hop lightly from log to log. He was extremely daring and fast and would jump in when others held back to stop the logs from jamming. Henry was incredibly charming, had the Irish gift o' the gab and was a fine dancer. His river skills made him so light on his feet that all the girls wanted to dance with the talented Henry Bradley.

He was very good with money, and early on decided to be Billie's manager when the bets came out for a fight. He only wished he could have set up a fight with Joe Mufferaw. If Billie could have fought him and won, the winnings would have been plentiful. No one would have believed that Billie could win, and the odds would have been so good that Henry was certain he could have cashed in for the two brothers.

Fitzroy Harbour had three churches to keep the rivermen in tow. Billie and Henry and the rest of the Bradley family were parishioners of St Michael's Catholic Church, where Father Patrick, or Father Paddy as most called him, kept an eye on the souls of the rivermen of Fitzroy. All endeavored to get back home for Sunday morning mass. Ma Lizzie Bradley insisted on it. Father Paddy had been known to be a pretty good fighter himself, before he took up the calling and became the pastor of souls at St Mike's.

While Sunday morning was all about Mass, once a month on Saturday evenings the church basement became the dance hall. Residents of Fitzroy Harbour turned out in whatever finery they could afford for the monthly dances. The admission was modest but added to the church coffers.

As younger teens, the Bradley boys tended to connect with their neighbors of the same age at the dance, but already the young boys and girls of the town were eyeing each other up and down, and giggling and guffawing were in abundance as the boys worked up their courage to ask the girls to dance. Henry was such a fine dancer that every girl wanted to have a chance to dance with him.

"Well, a feller can't even find a minute for a nip out the back of the church," Henry complained.

"Shouldn't be such a fine dancing man, Henry boy," Billie laughed.

"Right you are, but I do love the dancing," he laughed back.

"Colleen O'Donnell has certainly got her eye on ya, boy," observed Billie.

The boys quickly scooted out behind the church for a swig of the homemade whiskey their neighbor, Arthur Dolan, cooked up in his still. Due to Billie's success at the fights, they always had a little pocket money. Their wages went to Ma to help feed the large Bradley family. She would have beaten them both for gambling, which she considered a sin. Yet all the men of Fitzroy Harbour gathered round for an Irish Stand Off when one broke out.

CHAPTER 7

GOING WEST

1887

T.B.H. Cochrane stomped about in a bad temper, riled about the amount of money that he was losing at the card tables. Adela had truthfully never thought much about money in her life.

"Adela, money is a husband's concern and not a wife's," he lectured, and she knew from his tone that it would not be an area for further discussion. Instead, she hurried to the company of Evelyn. Without her mother to question about married life any longer, Adela sometimes felt very young and naïve and at times helpless, as she navigated the early weeks of her marriage. Evelyn was as young and naïve as herself and didn't have many answers, and Adela missed her mama and especially her mama's dear friend, Emily Mitford.

Docking in Port Arthur brought about a stir in Adela's heart. It was far less civilized a place than she had found so far on her journey. Thomas had been informed by his fellow travelers that three years earlier, the Montreal-based Canadian

Pacific Railway syndicate, in collaboration with the Hudson's Bay Company, clearly preferred the low-lying lands along the lower Kaministiquia River to the exposed shores of Port Arthur, which had required an expensive breakwater, if shipping and port facilities were to be protected from the waves. The CPR had subsequently consolidated all its operations there. They had erected rail yards, coal-handling facilities, grain elevators and a machine shop, all of which Adela was able to see when the ship had docked.

There was a sense of newness that was hard to miss, and this excited Adela. She began to feel that her adventure was really growing. There were not, however, any of the grand hotels she had stayed at along the way, and she said to herself, "Well, Adela, the real adventure is about to begin right now. Say good-bye to all you knew."

Lodgings were procured in a simple wooden hotel, that had rooms above a public house and a shared toilet in the hall. The servants were horrified at the prospect of their ladies using such facilities. Little did they know, that in a short time even these modest surroundings would seem luxurious.

NEXT STOP, WINNIPEG. ADELA LOVED the sound of the name of this city. It was completely unlike anything she had ever heard of before. The CPR train was quite modern and comfortable for people of means like the Cochranes. Thomas had discovered on his previous trips that the most comfortable way to travel was in the "State Room" which accommodated two persons. There being only one of these on each car, the Cochrane cousins had wagered, with the winner taking the luxury State Room, and the loser having to make do with the sleeping car. The sleeping cars had high-backed seats which faced each other, and at night these seats were arranged as beds, with an upper berth being let down from above. The State Room was difficult to procure; it was often booked in advance. Thomas had learned this as well and was therefore very organized when booking their train fares so that he might find the State Room available.

All the baggage was loaded, arranged by the Negro porters who expected a little present at the conclusion of the journey. Adela was rather fascinated by this system as it was so very different from back home. Thomas was much less than pleased by it, and grudgingly made a most meagre little present at journey's end.

T.B.H. and Billie supervised the loading of the baggage, while Adela and Evelyn found their seats on the First-Class Coach. Their servants had third class passage and were becoming acquainted with other commoners who were traveling west as well. Truly, the difference in the accommodation was not so great between the first-class and the third; yet again another new situation for the Cochrane ladies to deal with. The train itself consisted of two baggage cars, a mail car, one second-class coach, two immigrant sleepers, two first-class coaches, two sleeping cars and a diner. Another traveler informed them that several dining cars were used throughout the journey. It appeared that the diners were removed from the train during the night, and another fully loaded one was picked up in the morning. The food was very good because the conductors had the power to buy fresh fish, poultry and whatever else they could find along the way. Three excellent meals were provided each day. Adela was thrilled when she saw two Indians bring some wild ducks to the train for sale and was even more delighted to find them on her dining table that evening.

Adela noticed poor immigrants boarding the train as well who had passage in the immigrant sleepers. These were simple cars with benches where the families sat, ate and slept on their journey westward. Adela knew she should have been staying in these if she really wanted adventure; yet, she had to admit to herself that she much preferred her first-class coach, sleeper and dining car.

Onboard the train they met other new immigrants with means such as themselves. Most were from England, but a few were from America. The language of discourse was certainly English. When the train stopped at stations along the way and the passengers stepped out to stretch and walk. Adela was fascinated by the different languages she heard along the station sidewalk. She wondered how all these people with their different tongues were going to survive in the new land.

Two little girls often caught her eye. They had long, flaxen braids and spoke a language she had never heard. After discussions with her fellow English speakers, the consensus was that the language was likely Swedish. Upon further examination of the family, she saw there were two more daughters. The girls were shy when she spoke to them, but she realized they did not understand her at all. The parents smiled shyly as well.

Another family caught her eye too. They were much darker skinned, had black hair and colorful clothing. The language was strange and harsh sounding, and none of her English-speaking travelling companions had any idea what the language was. Later, she was to find out that the language was

Ukrainian, and the people were from Galicia. She had never even heard of this place.

All watches were put back one hour as they pulled into Winnipeg. Adela had not done much travelling on the Continent, so she was unaccustomed to this practice. She had reset her watch in New York and believed that would be the only time she would do this. Winnipeg turned out to be much more civilized than Port Arthur had been. It was now a flourishing town of 25,000 inhabitants. This is where the Cochranes were to switch routes and board the train that would take them to their new home on the prairies. From her position next to the window, Adela noticed a city set out in orderly blocks, bordering a great river known as the Red River. Many different sizes of steamships paddled up and down the river, giving it a feeling of haste and industry. The original fort sat behind a city park, and church spires reached into the blue sky in the different communities. The city was completely flat, and the horizon where the land met the sky was very defined. Wharves and factories lined the banks giving the city a true feeling of business, and Adela was relieved, but at the same time a little saddened, to see that here again there was a definite imprint of civilization. She was a little flummoxed, as she kept expecting to see a definite lack of it.

While the streets were made of dirt, the main street sported a streetcar and tracks, and many lovely new three-story buildings. Once again, the couples unloaded from the train and sought lodging in the town. The main street of Winnipeg was sophisticated looking, with most buildings being built of stone. Carts and carriages ran up and down on Main Street, and a streetcar rode the tracks down the middle of the road.

Adela enjoyed the look and feel of Winnipeg, which seemed new and exciting, like a young man in his dress clothes, or a young lady in her finery. While Adela and Evelyn walked up and down Main Street, they were surprised to hear many of the inhabitants not speaking English.

"My goodness, Evelyn, these people are speaking French," Adela remarked. As a lady with a classical education, she had been required to learn French from her Parisian tutor. The language spoken by the Winnipeggers was harsh sounding and hard to understand. However, Adela caught that they were speaking of someone named Louis Riel and that they were mourning the loss of such a great hero of the French-Canadian people.

Upon her return to the hotel, Adela inquired of the concierge about the hero Riel. The man was an English speaker and a look of incredulity passed over his face.

"Hero!" he snorted. "The man was no hero. He was a dangerous, half-insane religious fanatic and rebel against the Canadian nation who was hanged for his crimes."

Adela had heard the bitter alienation the Francophone women felt while she listened to their conversation and she began to feel that she was indeed in a very foreign place where perhaps being English was not always going to be welcomed.

They settled in at the Clarendon Hotel, a five-story hotel built in 1883 that they found at the northwest corner of Portage Avenue and Donald Street. It was new and lovely, and the ladies were able to rest once again in comfort and luxury. Thus far the trip had really been a long, but extremely satisfying adventure, punctuated by respite in luxury hotels that were found in all the major cities. Canada was more sophisticated than Adela ever thought it would be. She found the newness intoxicating and was not bothered in the least by the lack of all the subtleties she was accustomed to.

After a week's rest and good food at the Clarendon, the Cochrane's were seated in the hotel lobby, recounting the wonderful time they had had in the busy city. Billie Cochrane had met a young businessman at one of the card games he found each evening, and this charming gentleman had taken them on a tour of the wonderful new business district growing up in Winnipeg. The Winnipeg Grain exchange, and other commodity exchanges, provided homes to a bustling grain industry in Canada. The buildings were so modern looking. The young man explained to Adela that the architectural style was taken from Chicago, a city to the south in America, that rivalled New York. Adela loved the boldness and newness of it, and this bustling, hustling prairie city impressed her mightily. Its brash self-assurance thrilled her and made her days in Winnipeg exciting. This is what she had been hoping for.

Everything here was new, crisp and audacious. For some reason, this made her think about T.B.H.'s name. There were no other Cochranes on this side of the Atlantic, and she saw no reason to keep calling him by his initials.

"T.B.H., I think it is time for you to be Thomas or Tom here in this country. It sounds like the West, unpretentious. What do you think?" she asked.

Tom frowned at her, and it looked like he was gathering a head of steam to reply hotly and tell her off. Then slowly, the concept seemed to dawn upon him, and the frown turned to a smile, and then to a laugh.

"My dear Adela, I fear you are so right. Tom it is."

The Cochranes were ready to take the final train trip of their journey. Winnipeg to Calgary. If the couples had been travelling even five years earlier, they would have had to set out on the Carleton Trail; however, since 1883, the CPR had pushed the train through to Calgary, which was their final destination. Well rested and ready for adventure, they set off. Finally, Tom, who had settled happily into his new name, seemed as anxious as Adela to reach Calgary and The Little Bow River Cattle Company ranche.

> *May 15, 1887. Finally, we are closing in on my new home. I have seen country unlike anything I have ever seen and met people from places that I never knew existed. Strangely, we are all newcomers and the sense of bewilderment and amazement is apparent in the eyes of us all. We will take the final train ride to Calgary, then be on our way to The Little Bow River Cattle Company ranche. Be still my beating heart – I can hardly breathe for the excitement!*

CHAPTER 8

CALGARY AND THE LAST BEST WEST

1887

Adela could hardly stay seated as the train pulled out of the station in Winnipeg. They were finally on the last leg of their long train journey and would soon be seeing the place that would become their new home.

Within minutes the city of Winnipeg faded into the distance, and the vastness of the prairie unfolded before them. Mile after mile of gentle hills and fields of grass flew by the windows in this mid-May season. Cousin Billie had suggested that they not come until May, as he warned that even in May there could be severe snowstorms. This seemed so unusual to Adela, who had experienced snow only during the December – January months in England, and only rarely during that time. Snow, coming into the summer months, seemed so strange.

Hours later the rolling hills flattened out, and Adela found herself in the flattest plain she had ever seen in her life. All one could see in any direction was a veritable sea of grass; brown, but just turning green with the coming of spring. The great blue sky, broader, vaster and all-encompassing above their heads, met the horizon of grass. The emptiness resonated with that place she kept so locked up inside her heart. Finally, she was seeing the Canada of wilderness she had dreamed about so often. Wild animals could be seen from the windows, herds of dark, shaggy beasts about the height of horses could be seen grazing, and dogs about the size of collies, but the exact colors of the brown-silver grass, could be seen trotting through the lone prairie. Sometimes, a red fox popped up, and great birds of prey, hawks, could be seen diving out of the sky and returning with mouths full of small rodents. Black crows, and their even larger cousins, who she was told were called ravens, could be seen with regularity. Small groves of trees were visible in little valleys, which the conductors told them were called coulees. They had been named so by the French earlier in the century. The leaves were the newest shade of green, which Adela reveled in, as they spoke to her of the newness of this land. Her excitement grew with each passing hour. Now and again the train would stop, and the Cochranes would find themselves in a prairie town. These appeared to consist of a hotel, where fiery whiskey could be tasted at the bar. There were several wooden shacks and houses gathered around the hotel, and sometimes stray cattle grazed amongst the buildings. It was made clear to the Cochranes by the conductors that when entering the North-West Territories that the prohibition of spirits was strenuously enforced; however, in spite of this, whiskey seemed to be procurable with a little management.

Further on down the line the train passed through Regina, the capital of Assiniboia, stopping for the passengers to stretch their legs and look around. Billie told them that this place was the headquarters of the North West Mounted Police, a military organization numbering one thousand. It had been explained to him that Canadians were very proud of the N.W.M.P.

The prairie seeped into Adela's consciousness, and she realized that this train truly was the lifeline that connected the civilized East of Canada to the wilds of the West. Right then and there Adela fell in love, head over heels, with a wild, vast, lonely place. She felt that this place, this land, had a soul completely like her own, and she made a vow on that first train ride, travelling through those flat, bright prairies, that she would come to be one with this place, with this Canada, this Last Best West.

Some of her fellow travelers stopped off at stations in the North-West Territories, before the train reached Calgary. Out of nowhere, it seemed, a station would come into view and a strange name would be called out announcing where they were. The train would stop, usually one family would disembark, and the train would continue on. Adela watched in utter amazement as each family stepped off the train and gazed as their baggage was placed on the platform. Then the doors would close, and often as not, the family was left there in what seemed like abandonment, alone with the sky and the prairie.

As the train doors closed once again, Adela would return to her fascination with the scenery outside the window. Small lakes dotted the prairie, and swans, geese, pelicans and ducks could be seen swimming on them. Strange looking birds called prairie chickens could be viewed in the fields, and the conductors mentioned that shy, small antelope could sometimes be seen, as well. Many trails could also be seen from the train windows.

Adela asked the conductor, "What are these trails I see here?"

"These are old buffalo trails, Madam. It is their bones and skulls that you can see scattered about, as well."

She had to admit to herself that there was a small seed of dread growing in the pit of her stomach, that Calgary might turn out to be the same as these places. It had been announced in Winnipeg that it was 659 miles to Calgary. Once again, the vastness of this distance had amazed Lady Adela Cochrane. As she watched out her window with anticipation and more than a little apprehension, the small station points continued to pass by. She scanned the great sky for signs of snow, like she had been warned, and scanned the prairie in the same way, but saw no signs of white in the veritable sea of brown and green grass. She had procured a printed schedule from one of the conductors (for a fee), as even a printed schedule was a rarity in these parts and watched as the unique sounding places passed by. Sometimes they stopped and people disembarked. Adela wondered if they were as anxious as she was.

"Well," she thought, "they will never think I am not ready for this adventure."

When they had reached the Maple Creek station, the land was dry and very barren looking. Adela glanced over at Thomas, who was grinning broadly. The train lurched forward, and Kincarth, Forres, Walsh and Irvine stations passed before the train actually came to a stop in Medicine Hat.

"What an absolutely peculiar name!" Adela remarked to Thomas as the Cochranes disembarked to stretch their legs and stroll along the platform in the cool prairie air. Here they saw many Blackfoot Indians. Apparently, their reserves, the land granted to them by the Canadian government, were not that far away from the rail line. These people really fascinated

Adela. She tried to imagine how they stayed alive just living on the prairie. They looked rather dirty and poor to her eyes.

Drinking in great gulps of the fresh air revived Adela completely, as she gazed in curious amazement at the little frontier town and its curious inhabitants. The women sat on the ground, some of them smoking, and all were huddled in blankets. The men, in brilliant, colored blankets, stood smoking in groups. A station garden was being built here, and it seemed to be a great novelty to the Indians, who crowded around it. A man was busy planting trees and seeds, which seemed to fascinate the inhabitants. Nothing in jolly old England could come close to looking like these tiny, new villages standing alone and defiant in the midst of the great sea of grass.

Adela noticed that Thomas had been particularly silent as they moved along toward their destination of Calgary. He appeared to be lost in thought, and not at all interested in the surroundings. Adela reminded herself that he had been on this trip four times previously, and therefore was likely not as fascinated as she. They travelled through Stair, Bowell, Suffield and Langevine.

"What a curious mix of Scottish, French and English names these places have," mused Adela, as she watched the station names come and go through the train windows. The passing landscape helped to deal with a large lump that was rising in her throat at the thought of building her own beautiful little village in this strange lonely land. Who in the world would want to settle here once they saw the place? How could anything possibly grow? Then she remembered the station garden and a smile sprang to her lips.

Kinninvie, Tilley, Bantry and Cassils passed, without

the land changing at all. Southesk, Lathom, Bassano and Crowfoot were next. The conductor told her that Crowfoot was a trading point for the Blackfoot Indians, and she was thrilled to see another small band of these people, camping in the distance, as the train rolled through. Once again, this thrill overcame her fear. What exotic people! They had a pointed and painted tent camp, where ragged looking ponies grazed. Savages, real savages.

As the train moved through Cluny and Gleichen stations, the land seemed to get even drier and wilder, and Adela was glued to the window. Beside her, Evelyn sat strangely quiet and perhaps frightened as she observed the scenes around her. As they passed out of Namaka, Adela actually saw with great relief a small lake.

Thank goodness. Water actually exists here, she exclaimed to herself. As the train continued west, the land seemed to grow more verdant and less dry, and by the time they had passed Cheadle, and Langdon had come into view, the landscape looked quite a bit less drastic and more conducive to human settlement. Adela could see that the next station was Shepard, and then Calgary was to be next. They had planned to get off in Calgary and stay a few days while Thomas worked out some business with his mill and tramway. Her excitement started mounting again as they pulled through the gently blowing grasses of Shepard, bound west for Calgary. The great beauty of the Calgary area, the town at the confluence of the Bow and Elbow rivers, became apparent.

Adela's ever helpful train conductor approached her again and asked if she wished to know about Calgary.

"Of course, sir, I relish the idea," she replied.

"Well, Colonel James Macleod, of the Canadian North West Mounted Police, named this lovely place after Calgary Castle on the Isle of Mull. Calgary, North West Territories, Canada, takes its name from Calgary on Mull, which was a favourite summer home of the MacLeods. The story goes that in 1876, after he returned from staying in Calgary Castle, he suggested changing the name of Fort Brisebois. In Gaelic, it is pronounced, "Cala Ghearraidh", meaning Beach of the Meadow.

"You seem to pronounce that very well," remarked Adela.

"Aye, lassie, I do," he laughed. "Me, I come from the Isle of Islay, just south of Mull. Many is the time me dad and I travelled in our fishing boat up to Mull. I have seen Calgary Castle meself, and I agree with Colonel McLeod. It's a grand name for this wee town."

Adela tucked all her new information away for later musing. If she had been taught all these things by her tutor, she would have yawned with boredom, yet now that she was experiencing the adventure, she couldn't get enough new information.

As the train rattled along, Adela was to have another great prairie experience. Ahead of them to the west the brilliant blue sky started to fill with gray and black clouds. These formed into the largest clouds she had every witnessed, with the top being pure white and billowy, while those behind and below grew ominously black. The wind picked up and Adela could feel it battering the train.

"Whatever is happening?" she asked anxiously, looking over at Evelyn, who sat ramrod straight, staring at the quickly changing sky. Their husbands, bent on their own conversations, seemed to pay no notice.

"You're in for a treat, now, milady," the conductor warned. Before she knew what was happening, huge drops of rain began to spatter the windows. In no time the drops became larger and larger, yet all along the prairie sun still shone where the storm clouds had not yet reached. This vast openness where one could view the sky, seemingly forever, astounded Adela. The wind continued to pick up, and Adela could feel the temperature dropping against the window. As she watched in pure amazement, a huge jagged bolt of lightning streaked across the sky, followed by the loudest crack of thunder she had ever heard. She practically jumped out of her skin. The raindrops fell harder and faster. The roof of the train resounded with the din of smashing drops. A huge dark curtain seemed to sweep across the green prairie, bringing with it a cracking and pounding sound on the train's roof. Hail pounded the train, and the noise became a tumult. Hail stones the size of pebbles piled up upon the soft new prairie grasses. Immediately, the ground turned from green to white. As she and Evelyn continued to gasp in astonishment at the unfolding grandeur of a prairie thunderstorm, she noticed the hail had become much smaller, and was now mixed with small, frozen flakes. In no time, the rainstorm had turned to a blinding snowstorm.

"So, this is what they meant by snow in May," she marveled.

It was through this fury the Cochrane families travelled into the station at Calgary. It has been five days on the train, and she was more than ready to disembark, yet she looked around wildly at Tom, wondering how they would even manage to step outside into such a furious force of nature.

Most unlike the cities she had experienced up to Winnipeg, Calgary's station seemed to exist only of a few sheds. There were some democrats with their one-horse nags waiting in the storm. The horses had their heads low to the ground while their drivers had run for shelter in the sheds.

"My God," breathed Tom, "A bloody snowstorm would have to hit while we need to disembark."

Very quietly to herself, Adela whispered, "Adventure."

The station was a red box-like building, with the ticket and telegraph office partitioned off. In the center of the general waiting room, a large circular stove radiated a comforting heat to warm the raw edge to the prairie air. For the last time on this train odyssey, Thomas talked with the station master about where to stay and how to get the baggage transported there. They were heartened to hear that the new Royal Hotel was only one block north of the station.

Even the privileged had to wait out the storm though. A democrat was hired, and as the Cochranes boarded it, they could see that there were only two or three little buildings near the hotel. Directly across the corner was the log store of the Hudson's Bay Company. South and west of the tracks there was simply, a log shack, which the driver informed them belonged to a family named Butler. With absolute delight, Adela thought, "I have found the wilderness of the West."

The driver suggested that he might drop them off at The Hudson's Bay Company while he continued on to the Royal with their baggage. He informed them that they might want to purchase more appropriate clothing now that they had arrived in Calgary. Thomas, ever the dandy, and by now an experienced frontiersman, looked especially annoyed, but Adela and Evelyn were fascinated.

"How thrilling," Adela squealed, which caused Tom to

break into a huge grin. The rain and snow had ceased, and the sun now shone brilliantly again around the little buildings. Adela knew that all the long and unknown days that had led up to this point were so worth it. Adventure was happening. And she was part of it.

Her first sight of the interior of the Hudson's Bay Company log building brought into view piles of gaily colored print cloth and Hudson's Bay blankets. These many-colored wool blankets had a green stripe, red stripe, yellow stripe and indigo stripe on a cream background.

"What lovely blankets," Adela exclaimed.

The proprietor approached them very respectfully, inquiring as to whom he had the pleasure of assisting. Tom replied,

"I am Thomas Belhaven Henry Cochrane, and this is my wife, Lady Adela Cochrane." The proprietor assumed Thomas was also a Lord, which he often didn't correct, and was instantly even more solicitous.

"What an honour it is to serve you, milord and milady," he intoned. The proprietor went on to explain that they were called Hudson Bay point blankets.

"Points are the short black lines woven into the selvage of the blanket along the edge just above the bottom set of stripes," he explained.

"They are about four inches in length, except in the case of half points, which are two inches, and they indicate the finished overall size of a blanket. This allows a blanket's size to be easily determined, even when folded," he finished.

The rough log walls were piled with all sorts of goods. Antlers from some huge beasts graced the walls under the ceilings and rough-hewn shelves lined the walls. The assortment of goods for purchase was very foreign to Adela, but convinced her that indeed, she was now in a new and unknown world.

Would you care to hear the story of the blankets?" asked the proprietor.

"Oh yes, please!" exclaimed Adela.

He continued: "We enjoy these blankets today as much as when they were first introduced into the fur trade in 1780. It is believed that Monsieur Germain Maugenest first suggested to the Company's London Committee that 'pointed blankets' become a regular trade item in the New World. It seems the 'point' system had been invented by French weavers in the mid-18th century as a means of indicating the finished overall size of a blanket, since then, as now, blankets were shrunk or felted as part of the manufacturing process. The word point derived from the French empointer meaning 'to make threaded stitches on cloth. Pointed blankets are very popular with the Indians, milady," he finished.

"I shall take twelve," Adela exclaimed.

"Yes, milady," agreed the happy proprietor, "and now we must find some befitting Western clothes for you."

As Adela began to look around, she saw that the rainwater was leaking into the store through the chinking in the walls, and the piles of brightly colored prints were running with color into each other and down onto the packed earth floor. They obviously were becoming damaged, and a clerk was busy trying to save what he could from the mess.

Adela found some simple sets of skirts and blouses, along with a much sturdier pair of boots to wear. Thomas chose rugged pants and shirts and jackets, and a great "boss of the plains" American broad brimmed hat. Evelyn joined in with

Adela, purchasing blankets and clothing, and sizing Billie up for new boots and clothes, as well. The proprietor looked like it was Christmas morning.

They all purchased capotes as well, hooded wool coats made from the Hudson's Bay blankets. The proprietor assured them that these coats were used by fur traders and Indians alike.

Adela and Evelyn's servants scurried about gathering up all the purchases and bringing them to the hired democrat waiting outside the Hudson's Bay post. They looked uncertainly at the frontier town around them and wondered, not for the first time, what they had agreed to in coming to this new world.

"I will find a woman to come to the Royal and tailor your clothing," the proprietor promised, and the Cochranes set off with their new boots and coats for the Royal Hotel.

Compared to the luxury of some of the civilized hotels from previous cities, the Royal was quite sparse, but it mattered not to Adela. She was having the time of her life on her adventure and knew she would have as many stories as Uncle Henry one day. And here she was a girl, having adventure! Life could not be better.

The first few weeks were busy with getting the new clothes fit and arranging transportation to the ranche at Mosquito Creek.

It would take a few weeks to get the transportation organized, so the Cochranes boarded their old companion, the Canadian Pacific Railway, to explore the area. They took a day trip to Morleyville, passing through what Adela decided was the most beautiful country in all of Canada. Unlike the dry south that they had recently traveled through, or the endless sea of prairie after Winnipeg, this part of Canada was possessed of rolling hills and a beautiful river valley. Very little sign of civilized habitation was evident, and Morleyville, like many of the little stations they had passed through on their trip West, was little more than a station. It didn't matter, Adela was in love with the place. Thomas was amazed by her excitement, and relieved that she really was the adventuress she had claimed to be. Adela could hardly wait to return to Calgary to hire horses and ride out and explore the place by horseback.

Hiring horses was harder than she imagined; but purchasing them seemed to be possible, for quite a pretty penny. The lack of everything in this new land meant that a premium price must always be paid. She often heard Thomas grumbling about the outrageous prices. Luckily, the money transfers did not take too long, yet Adela had to learn a whole new set of rules about paying for items before you got them.

Traveling about the open range of Calgary-area filled Adela with bliss. She simply could not get enough of the new place.

The transportation finally arrived, and in democrats and wagons, the Cochranes headed out to the ranche at Mosquito Creek.

The two young couples started out side by side, but as time progressed, their stories would diverge greatly and end very differently.

May 22, 1887. Oh, my dear heart, how I have longed for this amazing place. It is quite unlike anything even my wildest dreams could have imagined, and I am truly in love.

CHAPTER 9

COMING HOME

1887

It looked like a sight from the distant past, perhaps ancient Egypt. Travel over land by bull team was the common way to get goods from place to place in the North-West Territories, and the Cochranes saw strange long chains of wagons, often ten or more, bound together and pulled by equally long teams of bulls. These were the bull teams of I.G. Baker & Co. The teams averaged about ten miles per day, and everyone relied on their slow but sturdy progress.

The Cochranes slept out of doors, under the wagons. Once again, the bewildered servants didn't know what to think of their lords and ladies traveling in such a style. They had to admit though, that there was absolutely no other way for them to travel. While Adela had impulsively purchased the Hudson's Bay blankets, she was exceedingly glad now to have done so. As well, the warmth of her capote was welcome in the cool spring weather, and she wore it to bed every night. Her lovely lace night clothes never left the trunk; instead, she wore her warm petticoats and capote to attempt to stay warm at night. The kind seamstress had helped her to purchase all the proper clothing she needed and had then tailored it to fit her, so she was now prepared for Western travel. Their own wagons were full of trunks carrying many clothes which would likely be completely unsuitable for her new home. Sadly, the servants began to look a little worse for the wear, as they did not have the luxury of the same warmth as the Cochrane families. Noticing this, Adela offered them some Hudson's Bay blankets to keep some of the chill away at night.

"My, Tom, I must say, this travel is hard on our servants. I have given them some extra blankets to help them stay warm at night."

"Their comfort is little of my concern," was all that Tom replied.

Luckily for all, the weather held for most of the trip, which made the long journey and camping out even more of a wonderful adventure.

They had hired a cookie, a man to cook for them off the back of the chuck wagon. Chuck seemed to be the word used for food out here in the West. Tom complained bitterly about the amount of money this was all taking.

Riding into The Little Bow River Cattle Company was yet another new thrill. Apparently, the staff heard them coming, as they ran out of the doors of the staff bunk houses, where they lived.

"What beauties," the ranche hands laughed.

They looked shyly at the new young wives.

"Welcome back home" they heard from one and all, while the staff vigorously pumped the hands and slapped the backs of the gentlemen.

"Everyone, this beautiful girl is my new wife, Evelyn," Billie started, "and Tom's new wife, Lady Adela Cochrane."

The girls smiled while the cowboys blushed even brighter than before and murmured their welcomes.

Adela sighed a little inward sigh of disappointment when she noticed that the home wasn't made of logs.

THE LOCATION NEAR MOSQUITO CREEK was constructed out of lumber rather than logs which was the first indication that Manager Billie Cochrane was a most unconventional fellow by the standards of the North-West Territories. Cousin Billie was showing that he was bringing civilization to the Prairie, something Adela found less than adventurous. He had hired I.G. Baker and his bull trains to bring all the building supplies and furniture to the site. She knew Tom would be happy with the lumber buildings as she was starting to understand that he needed to show off his wealth.

They all tramped into the comfortable front room of the ranche house, while the cowboys brought in the contents of the wagons.

"So, this is a ranche house," breathed Adela, mostly to herself. It had been in her imagination so long she was now quite excited to see it. The home was a lovely two story, with a formal entrance, dining room, living room, kitchen and back porch. The upper floor contained four bedrooms and a bathroom. Of course, it was hardly anything like the large estates the Cochranes called home back in England, yet Adela could see that one could live very comfortably in a prairie ranche home. She was trying to think like a Canadian already, using the word prairie, the French word used to describe the grasslands of the North-West Territories.

And so began the reality of Adela's great Western Canadian adventure in Mosquito Creek. Now she felt at home on the Cochranes' ranche, The Little Bow River Cattle Company. She wondered if living in a small, unpretentious home was exciting rather than dismaying. Perhaps women needed to act much more like men in this new land, and that suited Adela just fine.

BILLIE, EVELYN AND ADELA WERE gathered in front of the great stone fireplace, relaxing on comfortable chesterfields, with the ladies drinking tea and Billie ready to pour a whiskey for Tom.

Billie and Tom began reminiscing how they found the long, extremely cold winters too much to handle, and how returning to the "old country", as they called it, made for a more hospitable winter. Billie sat back on the chesterfield and began the tale of life in the New World.

"Well, old chap", he started, "Do you remember starting this ranche operation? Times were not easy. We purchased fifteen hundred head of mixed cattle in Montana and had to trail them up here to Mosquito Creek. We were living in a tent then and I didn't have the heart to bring Evelyn out yet, as it was pretty rough. I was lucky to employ Ed London as my trail boss."

"Trail boss, what is a trail boss?" Adela inquired excitedly.

Billie leaned back even further on the chesterfield, ready to answer any questions the greenhorns had. "Well, that will take a little explaining. You see," he began, "a trail boss, about five cowboys, a cookie, and a horse wrangler are needed to trail 1,500 cattle. This is your outfit, and these men hold your fortune in their very hands. The trail boss, why he is just the boss of the whole outfit. He makes sure everyone is doing their job and doing our work, getting my cattle to the ranche. There are a number of trail bosses who work the Montana-Canada trail. Tom Robertson is another great chap. He just trailed about 2500 head to this area as well."

"He sounds like an important person to have!" Adela commented, then continued, "What do the cowboys do?"

"Well now, cowboys, they are a special breed." Billie laughed. They are paid next to nothing, and what little of that they get, they often lose to gambling or drinking. But when they are doing their work, there is nothing like them. They begin to think like both horses and cows. They watch the cows and keep them moving in the direction the trail boss has decided. They are one with their horse. That horse and their saddle, that's about all they have in the world".

"I think I would love to be a cowboy," Adela exclaimed, much to the amusement of the rest.

"Oh, Lady Adela Cochrane, being around cowboys is no place for a lady," roared Billie.

Adela responded, "Maybe being around Lady Adela Cochrane would prove to be quite a match, even for a cowboy," she jousted back.

"But seriously," she said quickly, "how do they get the cattle from one place to another?"

Billie replied, "You see my dear, cattle do not follow a clearly defined trail except at river crossings. When dozens of herds are moving north it is necessary to spread them out to find grass. The animals are allowed to graze along for ten or twelve miles a day and never pushed except to reach water. Cattle that eat and drink their fill are unlikely to stampede. The cowboy's job is to push them just enough to keep them going, without hurrying them. Every once in a while, an ornery cow will just cut out of the herd and skedaddle off. Then the cowboy has to quickly chase that cow and push it back to the herd."

"I want to move cattle," exclaimed Adela, which again made everyone laugh.

"It's not as romantic as it sounds," Tom complained.

"Well, sweet girl, you can definitely do that, if you want. We move the herd many times during the summer to different pastures. You can join the cowboys to move them along," offered Billie, to which Adela clapped her hands, thrilled at the thought.

Thomas was far more interested in the business of the ranche, as he was, after all, a partner. But it was not the talk to be had in the presence of the ladies, so he kept his thoughts to himself.

Evelyn announced she would need to go to the kitchen to discuss the preparations for their dinner with the cook, who had been completely out of sorts the whole trip. Now that she had a kitchen and meals to prepare, she got busy with work she knew how to do. The sparseness of the kitchen surprised her greatly, and she could see now why they had stocked up on whatever food could be purchased in Calgary.

Evelyn and Adela spent the next few weeks adjusting to the lives of prairie ranche wives. Thomas and Billie had managed to get furniture sent out from the east, and after a bit of rearranging by the wives, the house felt quite comfortable. The parlour had lounges and chairs, a carpet and small tables. The bedrooms all had beds and linens. And the dining room contained a beautiful walnut dining table and chairs, as well as a sideboard and china cabinet.

The wives had quite a bit of free time on their hands. Thomas and Billie had been away for the fall/winter season and had a lot of ranche business to catch up on.

Adela and Evelyn spent the lovely May days getting to know the ranche horses. The ranche had riding horses, cow ponies and the large draught horses necessary to do the heavy work of the ranche. As both were accomplished horsewomen, they enjoyed exploring their new surroundings on horseback. Adela loved dogs almost as much as horses, and if the ranche dogs were not being used, they took them along too. Rex and Blackie, imported border collies from Scotland, were constant companions on their explorations.

As young girls are wont to do, they chatted with each other about their old lives, their new husbands and their life here in the Dominion of Canada.

"I shall never miss my life in England," Adela proclaimed.

"I sometimes think that I shall," mused Evelyn.

"This is everything Tom and I have dreamed of," Adela went on.

"I think Billie loves it here, but he is very clear that winter here is not to be endured by Englishmen. I am glad he feels this way as I will be able to return home every year to see friends and family. I quite like that idea," Evelyn said.

"I am sure it cannot be that bad," Adela argued, not wanting anything to intrude upon her dream of adventure.

They had learned that after the hard winters of '86 and '87, the less interested partners sold out to Billie.

"Remember that the partners sold out after the last two

winters Adela," Evelyn reminded her.

Adela decided to change the topic. "What did Billie do before he became interested in the new world?" Adela asked Evelyn.

She replied, "He comes from a long line of naval men, buccaneers he called them, but refused to follow in their tradition. He told me he always preferred horses to the sea."

"Of course, the great Dundonald clan. His grandfather Thomas Cochrane, 10th Earl of Dundonald was nicknamed 'Le Loup de Mers' (The Sea Wolf) by Napoleon," finished Adela. She loved all the stories of Tom's family.

"His father was none too pleased that he did not want to continue with the family tradition of seafaring, but after he left school, he enlisted in the Cape Mounted Rifles of South Africa, where he performed distinguished service in the Zulu Wars. That appeased the family somewhat."

"Thomas spent only a little time in the Navy as well," Adela added, "which I guess is why the two have ended up here on this sea of grassland."

"Billie has some great tales to tell," Evelyn continued. "Apparently, pay was poor and on dark nights he occasionally supplemented his income by strapping a couple of rifles on his back, swimming a river, and selling the smuggled rifles to the enemy."

"Ooh," squealed Adela, "that was devilishly daring."

"Indeed," responded Evelyn. "He is rough and ready, carefree and fearless, and enjoys this range life and the variety of characters that follow cattle for a living."

"Indeed, indeed," Adela said, "what a wonderfully exciting man you have married."

"I believe I will always have to have one blind eye when it comes to my husband," Evelyn said.

"Well, it is the reputation of the Dundonald clan. The Cochranes have quite a wildness about themselves," Adela agreed. "Grandfather Cochrane was dismissed from the Royal Navy following a controversial conviction for fraud on the stock exchange, Tom told me, and wasn't pardoned again for another eighteen years."

"Oh my," Evelyn said. "Billie has not yet told me that. He is always so full of fun and his escapades have enlivened many a staid gathering back home," Evelyn continued. "I am frequently the innocent ally of Billie's pranks, yet, I must admit, I enjoy them as much as he does." She laughed heartily.

Adela was so pleased that this was the woman she would spend her time with, in her new life. Evelyn was not the typical Victorian woman either and this added to Adela's happiness about the life she had chosen as Mrs. Thomas Cochrane. She was happier than she felt she had ever been in her life, and all she could see was great things ahead for the Cochrane cousins.

"I believe our husbands are like two peas in a pod," laughed Adela. "It is certainly what has drawn me to Tom."

At dinner that evening, the Cochrane cousins surprised their wives with an event for the next day. The ladies had both enjoyed the hunt back in England, and a coyote hunt had been arranged, weather permitting. One learned that weather permitting was really the case in the West, as any mild day could turn to a wild day in no time.

Adela was thoroughly enjoying her stay at The Little Bow River Cattle Company, but her long journey with her friend Evelyn would soon be coming to a close. Tom was far more interested in his sawmill and lumber business and needed to get back to them. Now that they were in possession of Lady Adela's inheritance, Tom had been able to connect with a building company in Toronto who had an acceptable house plan and had worked with them during their Toronto stay to decide how to send all the materials to Calgary by rail. The construction of the Cochrane home was to have started once the ground was free of frost, and workers had been sent by train to start this process. It was time for Adela to leave the relative comfort of The Little Bow River Cattle Company, and travel to Tom's new venture. Like many of the situations in her new world, Adela found that she was given little information by her husband, but that was as it had always been in all families, so Adela tried her hardest to just adapt to what Tom told her. It was at the sawmill that Adela would begin the dream of her lifetime, the building of her own village.

> *May 29, 1887. Everything about The Little Bow River Cattle Company is wonderful. Riding each day with my dear Evelyn is sublime. The coyote hunt today was ever so much fun, with Evelyn making the kill herself. I would have been upset that it had not been me, yet I am more thrilled that Evelyn was the victor than I can imagine. Life is so very, very wonderful.*

CHAPTER 10

A SUMMER ON THE BOW

1887

Thomas Cochrane was a man who often changed his ideas like changing his shirt. At times, Adela found this a bit disconcerting, to say the least. While he had been away from Adela each year, he had been busy, setting up his enterprises. What Adela came to understand after staying with Billie and Evelyn was that the ranche was really more Billie's interest than Tom's. In fact, Thomas seemed to have little interest in the ranche at all; he was far more excited about the lumber business.

Adela remained keenly interested in how the ranche worked. The horses and the stables were her favorite part of her home, Henham Hall. She was curious about how it all ran and enjoyed chatting with the grooms and stable hands about the horses, dogs and everything else that was part of the stable world. However, Henham Hall's stables existed for the pleasure of the Rous family, while The Little Bow River Cattle Company ranche was created as a business enterprise.

She and Evelyn regaled each other with stories of the cowboys, their wives (the few that had them), and the adventures of their husbands as they learned how to be ranchers in the Dominion of Canada. Adela laughed heartily with Evelyn as they recalled how Evelyn was chased by a mother sow across the yard until she ran in through the kitchen door to safety. Billie has taken the recommendation of the cookie to raise pigs for the table, but no one was the wiser as to the pigs 'nature.

When he was in Canada, Billie, it seemed, was the lord of the manor. However, when he left during the autumn and winter season, a ranche manager took over the operations. A ranche manager was an imperative for a successful ranche. This reminded Adela about another integral position in ranching and brought to mind the story of the trail boss, the man who was in charge of moving cattle on the long drives from America to the Canadian ranches. Stories about the epic cattle drives were told round the campfires of the cowboys who plied their trade each year and worked for the British gentlemen who owned the ranches.

Traveling with Evelyn and Billie was immensely pleasurable, and she felt sad when it was time to leave the ranche and head back to the site of Toms' other enterprise, the lumber/sawmill business.

Life on the Little Bow sifted to the back of her mind as she and Tom headed north to the site of The Calgary Lumber Company, of which Thomas was president. He had felt that the lumber company and sawmill would be a golden opportunity, because the new settlers would require the much more affordable local lumber that he and his partners, Hugh Graham,

Francis White and Archibald McVittie could provide. This was where he was convinced that he would make his new world fortune.

Tom told Adela that he had planned a nice little house for her, with stables, a barn, sheds and corrals. Of course, the mill wasn't producing income yet, so Lady Adela Cochrane would have to fund it out of her inheritance. As it turned out, they built a two story, ten room house which one day Adela would furnish and finish off with a beautiful piano. For all her love of the out-of-doors, Adela has also grown up being tutored on the piano, and she loved to sit at it on inclement days and play for hours at a time.

Adela's excitement grew with each day on the trail, and as May turned into June, their family group, including servants, horses and wagons, headed to the site of The Calgary Lumber Company.

On a beautiful June morning, with birds singing, sun shining and a south-west wind blowing (as it so often did), Lady Adela Cochrane sat astride her strong chestnut mount and gazed out over the horse's pointed ears to the grasslands ahead.

"No wonder you love this place, Tom. I have fallen completely in love with it too," Adela exclaimed.

"Yes, it is the future, and we will be on top of it," Tom bragged from the back of his horse.

Mrs. Townsend, the cook, sat beside a wagon driver, feeling quite differently than Lady Adela. She almost froze every night out in the open and found that cooking off the back of a wagon or in a pit was not much to her liking. This kind of cooking required a knowledge she had not yet learned, and as a result, the Cochrane group had needed to hire a cookie again. Salt bacon seemed to be the main staple, along with beans and bannock bread. For the thousandth time, she wondered what she had gotten herself into.

Mornings awoke them with birdsong and rustling leaves, with snorting horses and the laughter of the cookie as he coaxed Mrs. Townsend to assist him with the preparation of the morning meal. From her camp-out spot under the wagon, Adela would slowly push herself up on her elbows and open her eyes to the morning camp. She enjoyed just lying in her warm bed, with Thomas still asleep beside her, and watching her camp come alive. Soon the delicious smell of coffee boiling on a campfire, bacon frying in the heavy cast iron pan and fresh bannock baking in the coals, along with the ever-growling of her stomach, convinced her to rise from the warm and dry nest under the wagon and out into the cold June morning. Often the new green grass was covered in white frost, a phenomenon Adela had yet to become used to.

Adela gathered her day clothes and headed to the coulee, where she could relieve herself and change clothes as quickly as possible in the sharp and cold morning air. Around her were new leaves on the wolf willows, aspens and poplars that lined the coulees. Soft green grass pushed up beneath the long, dry and dead prairie grass of the last summer. Beautiful prairie crocuses lifted their purple heads through the grass, and on closer inspection, drops of dew often coated their petals. The air smelled fresh and sweet and full of promise for the coming months. Spring on the prairie came late; June was not yet a month when one thought of summer.

Returning to the camp, she usually had to coax Tom awake.

By this time, the fresh breakfast food was ready, and Adela would tuck in heartily to the fine fare. It tasted every bit as good as many of the fine banquets she attended back home.

Once everyone had eaten, the cookie and servants made short shrift of the packing, and the group was on their way. After some hours in the saddle, they finally approached a new CPR track, and followed it west, past the tiny, scraggly group of tents and shacks that called itself Cochrane.

"Why is this place called Cochrane Tom?" asked Lady Adela.

"I was surprised to hear our name given to it too, Adela, but apparently it is named in the honour of a Senator from Eastern Canada, Matthew Cochrane, who owns the British American Ranche Company up ahead. No relation at all to our family," he responded.

"How very striking. Someone with our name in this very new place. I think it is a good sign Tom," Adela proclaimed.

Where the railway and the Bow River came closer together, Lady Adela was able to get the first look at her new home, the site of The Calgary Lumber Company.

"Oh, Tom, look at this!" she squealed with delight as she saw the saw mill working, the new home and outbuildings being constructed, and the new hotel and store ready and waiting.

Adela pressed her horse into a gallop and streaked ahead to get a better look. As she neared the new house, she pulled the horse up tight, bounced off and jumped up and down, clapping her hands ecstatically.

"Tom, it is stupendous, amazing, wonderful!" she gasped out between giggles of enthusiasm. Tom sat smugly on his horse, a beautiful stallion which he had won at a very high stakes poker game with Cousin Billie.

"It is rather, isn't it," he agreed, looking every bit the returning lord of the manor himself.

"As the house is not ready, we will stay in the hotel until it's completion, which will hopefully happen before we need to leave in the autumn," he explained to Adela. Tom had started the hotel enterprise the previous year, knowing there needed to be a place for the men to live until they could build their own homes, while they worked at the sawmill.

"It is beyond my wildest imaginings," Adela laughed, continuing to bounce up and down with delight.

"Well, my dear, this is who you have married," Tom added pompously, with every bit of pretension imaginable.

Mr. Randolph, a young man hired to work as valet to the Honorable Mr. Cochrane, as well as jack-of–all-trades for anything else that Mrs. Townsend and Miss Brealey, the housekeeper and lady's maid, couldn't do, gathered up the horses and wagons and brought them to the hotel. The servants set about unloading and unpacking, while Tom took Adela on a tour of the site.

He took her to each new building, explaining its place in the new Cochrane world. Adela was thrilled by every single thing Tom showed her.

And where is our manager, Tom dear?" Adela asked, after a few hours of checking out the new venture had transpired.

"I have no need of a manager as I am now here to handle everything myself!" Tom fluffed up his chest, much like a peacock.

"Oh, I see," Adela replied, but rather quizzically, as she had seen the way The Little Bow River Cattle Company ranche had been run and had learned the intrinsic value of the men who managed.

IN THE DAYS TO COME Adela rode with Thomas to inspect the building of the tramway up to the lumber berth in Dog Pound. Adela was interested in the names given to places by savages, and remembering the frieze in her family home, she was therefore so curious to actually meet one. At Dog Pound, she came across a small group of Blackfoot travelling back to their home. Like those she had seen on the train trip, they had dark skin, long straggling hair, and a mish mash of hand-made animal skin clothing and woolen blankets wrapped around their bodies. They neither smiled nor spoke, just looked on at Adela as curiously as she looked at them. Tom ignored them completely.

Uncomfortable, yet fascinated, Adela sat on her horse waiting for a signal from Tom as to what to do next. Afraid of either offending or inciting them, she simply sat on her horse and watched Tom, who went on inspecting the building of the tramway as if the Blackfoot were not even there. Adela found the Indigenous people fascinating, and smiled invitingly at them, but they seemed bored with her, and turned and continued on their way.

"Are they dangerous, Tom?" she asked a little fearfully.

"Adela. Don't interrupt my important thoughts!" he scolded, and she returned to her silent viewing of the back of the savages and their ponies. However, her mind was not silent at all. She was feeling rather vexed with Tom for not answering her questions. Finally, she could stand it no longer, and scolded him.

"Really, Tom. This is my first encounter with the noble

savage. I think you could have given me a minute to help with the greetings."

"There are no greetings. They don't speak, as you can see. They only look at us and move on. Besides, I have important work to complete that cannot be interrupted by these people."

Adela thought this was a rather harsh judgement, but she knew already in her marriage not to disagree too often with Tom, for he was not one to accept it.

They found a lovely spot by a creek to eat the picnic lunch they had brought. While they ate, Adela thought about how hard food was to come by in this strange new land, and yet Mrs. Townsend had somehow procured flour, yeast and all the makings for bread. Young Mr. Randolph had been sent to shoot birds and had returned with some tasty ducks that he had shot along the river. Cold duck sandwiches were quite jolly, washed down with water from the Bow River in their canteens. Not one to dwell on unpleasantness for long, Adela resumed her happy thoughts about the magnificent place she was to call home and her countenance returned to its usual smiling exterior.

ADELA SPENT THE DAYS IDYLLICALLY riding her horse around the area, exploring every nook and cranny she could find. After a few weeks, she was becoming quite accustomed to the area and was really beginning to feel at home. Tom was busy supervising the building of the tramway (or looking like he was busy supervising the building, for in all reality, Tom had never built a thing in his life), so Adela was left to her own devices. Being an excellent sportswoman, she decided she could assist with food procurement by bird hunting. What a difference from her childhood. In those days she had had no idea what happened to the birds she shot. Here, her catch was sometimes the difference between a delicious dinner and a dinner of beans. Fishing was another one of her passions, and she enjoyed nothing more than walking lazily along the banks of the Bow, angling for trout. She would step carefully between the river rocks on the shore, all the while looking out into the river for dark spots indicating pools where the trout were happy to rest and relax. If she dropped a fly into this spot, she often came up with a tasty reward. She was pleased Tom had told her to bring flies from Henham Hall, and had made sure the stable hands, who were also expert fly tiers, had provided her with a generous supply.

Procuring delicious food for dinner, fresh fish caught in the river, or fresh partridge or pheasant, gave Adela great satisfaction. Some days, Tom seemed to be finished with business, and they would meet up with the few other new settlers who owned horses, and they would head off on a deer hunt. Mr. Randolph was responsible for hanging and dividing up the deer and he was lucky to find others in the new site that helped him learn this new skill.

On a wonderfully warm and strangely quiet August evening, quiet as the infernal wind was actually not blowing for once, Adela and Tom were sitting at the confluence of the creek and the Bow River. The creek was known as Horse Creek, a very favourable name, thought Adela.

"Whatever shall we call this place?" Adela wondered out loud. "Saw Mill is just not a pleasant name."

"Well, until we think of a better name, it will do," Tom replied, and that seemed to be the end of the discussion.

Adela looked at him a little sadly. She was having the

adventure of her life in Canada; it was way beyond her wildest imaginings and better than anything she could have hoped for.

Tom, on the other hand, was tasting the other side of The Last Best West and finding there was quite a bitter flavor to it. While the Calgary Herald, the local newspaper from Calgary, had reported at the end of June that, "the Cochrane [sic] Lumber Company have got their railway running and tested their new engine. Everything works in a highly successful manner. The railway is now laid for a mile and a half and the rest of the line will be completed next month," the reality was that there was trouble almost every single day. Tom was often irritated and short with her now and not the wonderfully romantic adventurer she remembered from home in Britain.

As summer drew to its conclusion, it looked like the Cochrane home would not be finished while they visited. And constant problems were popping up every day with the build-ing of the tramway and the licensing of the lumber for the mill. None of Tom's ventures were producing any material nor any money. Undaunted, Tom and Adela forged ahead with their plans for the coming year.

> September 25, 1887. My dear journal – I have little time, it seems, to write down my experiences here in my little village. I have been calling it New Henham all summer, but this name just does not feel right. I shall have to ponder hard all winter back in England to find a more fitting name for this wonderful place my dearest Tom has created.

> Now we will retrace our steps to England. Billie and Evelyn shall meet us in Calgary, and I shall have the delight of returning home with my two favorite relatives.

CHAPTER 11

BACK IN JOLLY OLD ENGLAND

AUTUMN 1887 AND WINTER 1888

It was not often one realized their wildest dreams but accomplishing this brought Adela the greatest satisfaction. She retraced her steps and returned east with Tom, Billie and Evelyn. The ladies' days were passed marveling at the countryside as they passed through it on the train, and talking endlessly about their summers, one on the ranche and one in a tiny little place that Adela hoped would become a village someday.

Spending the summer by the Bow River had given Adela some idea of the enormity of the task the Cochranes had undertaken. Financing this venture was no small task, and though Hugh Graham had been helpful with the ranche and sawmill, Lady Adela decided that she needed to step outside of banking, and into a world with which she was much more familiar, the social circuit of upper-class England. For once she would have an excellent purpose for attending those endless balls. Mama was still trying to marry off Lady Gwendoline and Lady Hilda, so the Rous family would be in full presence at every ball and social event staged during the Season. This would ensure that Adela and Tom could engage with as many of the peers as possible, and secure more investment in their projects.

When Adela got to New York, she remembered once again the difficult time of the seasickness aboard the steamship, but as she always did, she put on her best, British, stoic, stiff-upper-lip and managed the sea days without too much complaining to Evelyn. However, it certainly crossed her mind to wonder if she was "seasick" or "morning sick." She never complained to Thomas as he had no patience nor compassion for "women's" complaints.

After docking in South Hampton, they traveled to the Isle of Wight and Quarr Abbey. Rosetta Cochrane had been notified of their return, and had vacated the family home again so that Adela and Tom could move in.

Adela settled comfortably into life on the Isle of Wight. She was able to visit briefly with Minna Cochrane and Princess Beatrice before the royal family returned to London. She had tea several times with Queen Victoria, who still eyed her rather oddly, and Adela continued to wonder if she had somehow offended the Queen.

After a good rest on the Isle of Wight, the Cochranes headed up to London where Adela had planned to meet with Mama, her sisters and hopefully George. He was much busier now in his role as the 3rd Earl of Stradbroke.

"So, Adela, how have you been feeling in the mornings," laughed Hilda, the youngest.

"Fine…" she replied, with a puzzled look on her face for a moment, and then when it dawned on her what her sister was teasing about, she began chasing her around the sitting room.

Of course, pregnancy was on her mind, now that she was a married woman. She remembered the constant throwing up on the sea voyage, and once again wondered if she might be pregnant. However, once she had planted her feet firmly on the British soil once again, the sickness had vanished, and Adela concluded it was far more to do with the ocean than a baby.

Mama had become pregnant almost immediately after she had married Papa and had produced six children. Adela wondered if that would be her fate as well. She dreaded the thought of so many babies. They got in the way of riding and hunting and building villages.

The autumn days at Henham Hall were filled with that pleasantness that comes from being away and coming back home again. Adela spent much time at the stables, and now she had even more pertinent questions to ask the stable men. She had so many questions about horse husbandry, cattle health, fishing and hunting that the days practically flew by.

While Adela was enjoying time at home, Tom was not particularly happy. He was much more at home on the Isle of Wight, where he enjoyed hobnobbing with the royalty as often as possible or visiting with his mother who had no end of admiration for her son's life in the Dominion of Canada. She would spend countless hours reminding him of his father's exploits as the governor of New Found Land. Thomas loved the comparison and felt quite important in his home on the Isle.

At Henham Hall he was reminded by Adela's brother George about how much the Rous family did not respect him. He put it down to the fact that they were all titled, and he was not. He was not as interested as Adela in the conversation of the stable men and boys, as truth be told, he felt it was quite beneath him. He took to sleeping in late, lounging in the house and teasing Lady Hilda and Lady Gwendolyn, or taking long rides by himself in the Suffolk countryside. Hilda and Gwendolyn found him tiresome, but that was better than George's opinion.

George Rous, 3rd Earl of Stradbroke, found nothing in Tom's behavior to change his opinion of him. Like his father, George felt T.B.H. Cochrane was pompous, pretentious and had little substance to him. Also like his father, he was very unimpressed with T.B.H.'s short navy career. The Cochranes had an amazing naval history and George felt that Thomas owed his family a much better go at service than what he had offered. George did not hide his displeasure from Thomas, who felt very slighted, and as a result, sought to avoid George at all costs.

Invitations to balls had begun to pour in, and Adela put up with shopping for the appropriate new outfits so that she could be nicely attired for the parties. She felt every cent she spent was a waste, especially when she needed to secure funding for the important things in her new life.

Later in the autumn they received an invitation to the Mitford home. Adela was so glad to be able to visit her Aunt Em. Out of all the women in her social circle, it was Emily, Mrs. Percy Mitford, that she most wanted to spend time with. Aunt Emily would understand her excitement about the Last Best West, about building a village and about how grand and amazing it was to be alive and living the life she was living.

Party after party flew by, and Tom as yet had had no luck with securing any new financing. He became petulant and mean, and Adela started to dread these parties again, but this time for an entirely different reason. If only someone would agree to finance the mill and lumber company. She longed for the Tom who had courted her, told her stories about the Dominion of Canada and had thrilled her with thoughts of adventure. He seemed to be entirely different from the sullen, churlish man who increasingly avoided life at Henham Hall, emerging only late in the evenings to leave the house and not return until dawn.

Soon, it was time for the Mitford social, and Adela chose her favorite of the new dresses to wear that night.

"For once, I am looking forward to a party" Adela smiled at Tom, who was fussing with his bow tie.

"Let me help you with that, darling," she offered and moved over to lend assistance.

Thomas pettishly pushed her hand away.

"I can do it myself," he growled.

"Of course, you can, my darling," she soothed. "Is something bothering you?"

"Yes," he blazed at her, eyes on fire. "We have yet to secure any new investment in our businesses. Things are not going well with the mill and we need money!" he seethed.

ADELA COULDN'T WAIT TO GET her dear friend, Aunty Em, aside, at the party. It seemed to take forever for Mrs. Percy Mitford to complete her hostess duties. While she waited, Adela moved around the room, making small talk, silently and desperately willing Emily to hurry. After what seemed like an eternity, Emily Mitford headed over to find Adela.

"My dear, dear Lady Adela, how well you look" beamed Emily. "Obviously, married life in Canada suits you."

"Yes, Aunty Em, it certainly does," agreed Adela heartily.

"Come, let's go and sit on the divan away from the crowds and you can tell me about your adventurous life in the Dominions," and she pulled Adela, who went along very willingly, with her.

Once settled, Emily smiled and said, "Do tell me all about Canada."

"It's better than I ever could have dreamed. The voyage to get to our dear little spot is very long, it takes weeks, but other than the sea crossing, it is fascinating. New York is a wonderful brash city that is full of American fire, Montreal is French, and the food is exquisite. Toronto is completely different again, in fact, it's quite British and feels very homey. The steamers that cross the Great Lakes are magnificent, as are the Lakes, the great inland seas that are larger than you could ever think possible. Then there's the train, the train. It takes you across forests that seem like they will never end, to Winnipeg, a quaint Western town, then westward you go for days across a sea of grass. You arrive in Calgary, which is truly the Wild West. It is simply sheds and tents scattered between a few permanent buildings. It is so very, very new. You always need supplies in Calgary, so you stop to procure them, and then you can ride out the many, many miles to Tom's mill, The Calgary Lumber Company."

"My, my, it does sound quite fantastic" Aunt Emily agreed. "And how is the mill doing?" she inquired innocently.

Adela's countenance darkened a little.

"Well, to be truthful, there is so little help, and everything is so difficult there, it is not yet running. Tom needs to secure a little more financing, but once he does, I am sure it will be running soon. But, Aunty Em, you should see my little town. We have a hotel and store that are nearing completion, and our home is also being built. All of this is on the banks of the lovely Bow River."

"Does your town have a name?" Aunty Em inquired.

"Not yet. Everyone just calls it Saw Mill, but somehow, that name just doesn't fit," Adela replied.

"And what else shall your town have?" her aunt asked.

"Well, now that you ask, I truly want it to have a proper Anglican church," Adela admitted.

"I think that is a splendid idea," Emily agreed.

"I'm so glad you think so," Adela smiled broadly at Emily Mitford. "However, you know that this will take an investment of cash, don't you?"

"Yes, of course, it will Dellie," she smiled again. "Just leave that to me. I have been one of the best fundraisers in the entire Church of England," she laughed. "As well, Percy and I may have some funds to invest in your town, especially for a church."

"Oh, Aunty Em, I can't tell you how wonderful this makes me feel," Adela said.

"How delightful it will be to attend our own little village church each Sunday morning when we are in Canada."

"We shall make it so," Emily replied, then continued, "I am very pleased to help out your ventures in Canada, and I want you to have a wonderful little village to live in."

"You cannot know what this means to me," Adela responded.

"And to think that you, a woman, are building this village alongside your husband. It's positively marvelous," Emily smiled. Their conversation continued on with Adela enthusing about the beauty of the spot at the confluence of Horse Creek and the Bow River, about the endless grassland prairies, the strange and silent Indigenous peoples and the wild winds, rains and snows of the place. They spoke for hours, and when Adela finally got up to look for Tom, Emily Mitford felt quite sure that she was doing the right thing by supporting her dear friend's daughter.

THE CROWDS HAD BECOME QUITE thinned. Adela wandered around looking for Tom. She finally found him talking to a tall young man with a strong Irish accent.

"There you are." She smiled and walked towards him.

Thomas Cochrane tore his glance away from the intense conversation he was having with the young gentleman. For a moment, Adela thought he was angry, perhaps at being interrupted; but the look passed quickly, and Tom smiled and turned and took her hand.

"Ah, my dear! I would very much like you to meet William Graham-Toler, the Earl of Norbury,"

"Hello, Will. Nice to see you again." Adela laughed and took his outstretched hand firmly in hers.

"Good to see you too, Adela. How is George?" he inquired with a grin.

"Taking his duties as Lord Stradbroke very seriously," Adela laughed again.

"Will is very interested in our enterprises in Canada," Tom interrupted. This, of course, brought about a broad smile from

Lady Adela.

"Indeed, it is a country of marvels," Adela responded.

Tom returned to his tales of the wonders of the Canadian West, its beauty, its opportunities, it's excitement.

The three of them talked excitedly until they realized that the house was almost quiet and that they were certainly among the last of the guests at the party. The fires had been allowed to burn down in the fireplaces. Servants at the far end of the room were gathering trays. The Rous ladies had left long ago.

With promises of meeting again soon with the Earl, the Cochranes as well took their leave.

ADELA HAD BEEN KEEPING HER good news to herself until they were safely inside the carriage, but once the horse was stepping out in the direction of home, she could keep it to herself no longer.

"Tom, I have the best news. My dear Aunty Em has promised to raise funds and personally invest in a church for our town," Adela rushed out with her exciting news. She thought he would be ecstatic, take her in his arms and kiss her, but much to her dismay he seemed not even to hear.

"I say, Tom, I have found an investor!" Adela repeated, loudly.

"You needn't shout." He seemed lost in a reverie of his own thoughts.

"Isn't that grand?" Adela pressed, trying to evoke a response.

"What? Oh, yes," he continued. "Money for a church, most kindly of her. Do you think the Mitfords would invest in our other enterprises?" he asked.

Adela was a little taken aback by his nonchalance toward her present news, but she shrugged it off and continued,

"I don't know, my love, but we could certainly inquire."

At this point, Tom broke into an excited babble about the Earl of Norbury and his willingness to come to Canada to see their operation, and all discussion of the Mitford's offer was dropped. Tom talked about the Earl all the way home.

Late as it was when Adela arrived home, she wanted to record her wonderful evening in her journal.

> *January 7, 1888. My, what a delightful evening! I am thoroughly excited by the fact that I have been able to convince my wonderful Aunty Em to raise funds for a church for my town. We really must come up with a name for it soon.*

The season continued on all over London as it always did. Tom and Adela returned to Quarr Abbey. Tom was so much happier there that Adela couldn't let herself to be too unhappy or bored. He was so much more the man she had married when he was at home at Quarr Abbey. They stayed there until he needed to attend a social gathering where he thought he might engage with some investors.

As the Isle of Wight was such a small place, soon Adela became very bored with it. On the pretext of finding more reliable investors for their businesses, Adela went up to London, and also back home to Suffolk and Henham Hall. While there she enjoyed reading letters to her mother from her much older half-sister, Edith Dickensen. Edith had married her first husband, Reverend Belcher, in 1870, and together they had five children. Adela, of course, had never met them. Her half-sister Edith had been fourteen when she was born, and Papa was not keen on Mama seeing her former husband's children, who were raised by Adela's grandparents.

Adela was amazed by Edith and was secretly dying to meet her. Mama explained that in 1886, after the death of her husband, Edith left England and travelled to Tasmania. Adela was thinking about how she had just been preparing to marry at this time. Mama was quite appalled as Edith had left her young family at home in England and had ventured out to the "other" New World to take up nursing. Mama thought it was purely craziness. She had kept loosely in touch with her children from her previous marriage that had ended when her first husband died from a brain hemorrhage.

"Reading Edith's letters reminds me always of you, Adela. How two of my daughters can be so fascinated with the New World befuddles me."

"Oh, Mama, I would dearly love to meet Edith. After all, she is my half-sister," Adela replied.

"I don't believe you are going to have much chance of that, unless you travel to Tasmania," Mama huffed. Still, Adela loved the fact that she had a much older sister who loved adventure as much as she did.

"Mama, may I write to her and introduce myself?" Adela asked. "I would ask her to write me back with her stories of Tasmania. I can share with her my stories of Canada."

"Well, your dear Papa is no longer here to protest, so I suppose that should be fine," agreed Lady Augusta.

Mama had accepted an invitation from Susan St Maur, Duchess of Somerset, to a social gathering at Bradley House, in Wiltshire. Adela wrote to Tom to see if he wanted to attend, and she received a very prompt reply that, yes, he did indeed. His note included, "Adela, dear, Duke Somerset spent many years in the Americas ranching after he left the army. I am sure he will have great interest in our ventures."

Tom and Adela met up in Maiden Bradley, and Adela was delighted to find her old Tom back. When she had left Quarr Abbey to visit Mama, he had been surly and irritable. Not even the excitement of Lord Norbury's interest had brought him out of the melancholy he had settled into on the Isle. Now, though, he was once again the Tom she knew and loved, excitable, dashing and romantic. Adela's heart leapt to see him so once again, he was recovered to the man she adored.

The visit to Bradley House was thoroughly enjoyable, as Algernon St Maur, Duke Somerset and his wife, Susan, were great travelers and great adventure enthusiasts. All social gatherings at Bradley House were predicated on hunting, fishing and riding, so Tom and Adela found themselves very at home.

Adela brought her ball gowns and kept her manners polite during the large social gathering, but she couldn't wait to get to the stables with Susan St. Maur each morning. They mounted horses and rode throughout the day, competing good naturedly in every event. Before the visit was over, they had become great friends.

During the evenings, Tom had been having serious conversations with Algernon, and these had been going very well. Tom was all smiles and grace.

"Adela, I have great news," he spoke excitedly one morning as they rose. "Algernon has committed a substantial sum toward the mill and tramway and is very anxious to come and visit his investment property. They will be joining us at Saw Mill this spring," he finished happily.

"What wonderful news, my dear," Adela smiled fondly at him. A light frown crossed her brow.

"Tom, I have been thinking. I am most unhappy with the name Saw Mill. I have been musing about it very much lately, and I would like to propose that we call our village Mitford, named for my gracious friend and benefactor of our new Anglican Church, Mrs. Percy Mitford.

Tom considered the request for a few minutes.

"Adela, I think it would be far better to save that privilege for a substantial investor," he responded. Adela was crestfallen but was not yet ready to concede.

"Tom, I thought it would be wise for future investors to know that we had named the town after a church benefactor." Tom had paid scant attention to the work Adela had done in getting investment for their town. True, the investment was a church for the town, but at this point, Tom had learned that it was prudent to take any investment offered and to use it for his own means.

"Adela, I think that is a very good idea" he finally agreed. Adela was very pleased, for she was well aware by now that she and Tom did not always agree on decisions. She was glad this one was not going to cause a long and protracted argument between them.

"Mitford it is then" Adela beamed from ear to ear. She couldn't wait to write to Aunty Em with the wonderful news.

Adela had planned to return to Quarr Abbey with Tom, and now that they had completed a successful investment winter in England, Tom was anxious to get back to Canada. They both returned to the Isle of Wight satisfied and happy to continue on with their ambitions in the new village of Mitford.

March 11, 1888. I have so much hope and excitement for the coming year. We will return to Canada and I shall name my new little village, Mitford, after Dear Aunty Em. She has been so generous and kind to undertake fundraising for a little village church. The town will only feel like a town when we have a church and a school for the village children. I am filled with wonder that I, Lady Adela Cochrane, will begin to build a real town in the West. I was disappointed when Tom no longer cared about the ranche, but now I am filled with fervor to create a wonderful village around the sawmill. I am ecstatic when I think of the new home Tom has had built for us, and I am far too excited to sleep these nights before we set sail once again for the Dominion of Canada. That any girl in England should be as lucky as I.

CHAPTER 12

PRIVILEGED GUESTS

SPRING AND SUMMER, 1888

Anxiety nipped at the edges of Adela's brain as the rainy, cold English winter came to an end. The Cochranes were restless to get back to Canada to see how everything was progressing, and to ensure the hotel was ready to receive their investors. As the weather was still quite possibly inclement, with spring snowstorms in April, they planned their arrival for early May. They had invited the Earl of Norbury, William Toler and the St. Maurs, to Mitford, for June. Adela had started to call the village Mitford, and Tom had not complained, so for her the town was now Mitford. She was so excited to think that her dreams of building a new town in Canada were really coming true. She was as thrilled with the naming of her town as she would have been with her first-born child; and was relieved that she had not yet become pregnant. That would make traveling back and forth to Canada almost impossible.

Luckily, Adela had convinced Miss Brealey and Mrs. Townsend to accompany her back to Canada. Without these two Adela would have been able to accomplish much less than she needed to.

Adela had known William Toler much longer than Thomas, for The Duke had been educated at Harrow, like her brother George, and the two young boys had been school friends. William had come to Henham Hall to spend vacations, and Adela always remembered him fondly.

Adela undertook her second voyage to Canada with a much different mindset than her first. Each part of the journey was now familiar, and she knew what was going to be enjoyable and what was going to be tedious. Having the companionship of Billie and Evelyn Cochrane made the voyage once again seem like a holiday, and Adela looked forward to each day until she would again reach her new home. In Calgary, the cousins parted ways, and Billie and Evelyn continued south to the Little Bow.

Once settled in at the Mitford hotel, Adela became busy supervising the arrival of furniture for her new home and also for the hotel. She also began writing letters to the Church of England in Canada to get the church project started. Very importantly, she had also corresponded with William Van Horne, an American, who had succeeded Lord Mount Stephen in 1888 as the new president of the Canadian Pacific Railway. Prime Minister John A. McDonald believed Van Horne had a grand vision of what the railway, and the country it traversed, could become. Adela and Thomas loved grand visions. Her correspondence with Van Horne was over the name of their home. One evening at dinner at the hotel, she shared with Tom,

"Tom, I have written to the new president of the Canadian

Pacific Railway to ask them to start referring to Saw Mill as Mitford."

"I agree, Adela, that Mitford is a much superior name to Saw Mill. Let's hope Mr. Van Horne will agree," he added.

Things moved forward in a flurry of excitement for Adela, who was determined to have her home and the hotel ready for the guests. She and Miss Brealey fit curtains to windows, bedding to new beds, chose carpets for the rooms and placed vases strategically in the front parlour. Adela enjoyed picking the wildflowers that grew profusely in the fields to bring colour and beauty into her home. She waited anxiously to hear about a beautiful piano she had ordered and hoped it would arrive soon. The railway men were none too happy when some of her purchases arrived by train, as the grade of the Mitford tracks was far too steep for the train to stop properly on. Adela was not concerned with such a technical difficulty. She just wanted the train to stop and her purchases to be brought to her. Many unpleasant conversations between herself and the engineer started happening.

For Tom, it was a different story. The timber license, which has caused him so much grief, had finally been granted, and the mill was now fully operational. There were fifty men now employed at the mill, which had produced lumber for a number of small barracks in which they could board. The pay roll tallied up at $30.00/month, including board, for each man working at the sawmill. Thomas was constantly seeking funds to ensure that the men were paid while he waited for the sawmill to turn some profit.

The stresses involved in this financial management were taking a heavy toll on Tom, and he fretted and worried all the time. Such problems had changed Tom from the excited adventurer that Adela had fallen in love with, to a harried businessman, with his mind always on the difficulties he faced every day.

Another constant worry was the railway line needed to bring the lumber from Dog Pound to the sawmill. The grade for the narrow-gauge railway was fairly steep, especially where it ran up to Horse Creek. Almost every day there were constant problems with the railway. Tom was constantly harassed and irritable.

Adela found it most useful just to stay out of his way. If she wasn't busy with her duties settling her home and advising on the hotel, and the weather was fine, she took to roaming the beautiful hills of the Bow Valley on horseback. When she was alone, riding the grasslands, enjoying the beautiful tiny red wildflowers or smelling the heavenly silver bushes, which she discovered were called Wolf Willow, she was completely at peace with the world. Often, as she headed back down-river toward Mitford, she felt her stomach tighten as she wondered what mood she would find Tom in. Usually, the best she could hope for was a sullen, quiet Thomas, who said nothing. If there had been many problems to deal with that day, she sometimes found a nearly hysterical Tom, yelling and seething; impossible to soothe. She hoped that his countenance would improve with the arrival of their investors.

> *May 30, 1888. What an enchanted evening! Tom has had a particularly bad day today as the engine broke down several times. He was in such a state after dinner that I decided to take Napoleon, my trusty mount, for an evening ride up Horse Creek, alone. Napoleon and I*

easily climbed the grade out of the valley. There are still some things that horsepower has over steam power. The ride up the creek was heavenly, heading west into the evening sun. It is so incredible here as the sun does not go down until nigh-on 11:00 o'clock at this time of year. It was with reticence that I turned my horse back east toward home. Riding down the creek, with a soft breeze at my back, rather than the usual gale force wind, was divine. We meandered quietly along the banks, dipping into the much cooler air in the low spots, and climbing back up again to see the sky blazing pink and orange. Is there anywhere on earth quite so beautiful?

June 15, 1888. Today the train slowed as it came through on its morning route. Most recently, the engineer will not stop at Mitford as the grade is too steep. We are plagued by the grade and our railways in this country. The brakeman tossed a package out to me as I waited in my customary spot. We are able to receive telegrams and mail this way without having to go to the Cochrane station. Cochrane is such a bleak collection of shacks; it should never be the train station, and yet it sits upon very level ground and therefore the CPR insists on it being the station stop. Most vexing!

The morning mail brought a telegram from the Duke and Duchess of Somerset, stating that they had arrived in Calgary the day before and were staying at the Royal Hotel. Adela hurried back to the barns and saddled up Napoleon, and they dashed back to the station in Cochrane to send a telegram to the St. Maurs in Calgary. As luck would have it, a freight train from the west stopped in Cochrane as she was finishing up the missive to the St. Maurs. This meant they would receive the telegram in Calgary that very day. Adela invited them to come that evening, if they could manage. Then she dashed back to Napoleon and tore off to Mitford to find Tom. He was at his desk in the house, which was a blessing, and his countenance brightened with the thought of the guests and investors arriving. Adela notified the cook, Mrs. Townsend, and left her to plan a meal for the guests.

"It will be jolly to see Susan and Algernon, here in our own little village. I am so excited for them to see it," Adela grinned.

"Yes, I look forward to their visit and to speaking business with Algernon," Tom replied.

"He is a rare fellow. He has spent much time in the New World. He was here in 1870, in Montreal and Toronto, as well as in America. He was in the army, part of Lord Wolseley's expedition. He explained to me last winter that Wolseley's troops took ninety-five days to traverse from Lake Superior to Fort Garry, as Winnipeg was then called. Most of their travels were by canoe on the network of streams and rivers. Our trip now takes about forty-five hours." Tom laughed. "The pace of change in this country is constant. It moves ever onward."

Much to everyone's pleasure, Susan and Algernon St Maur stepped off a freight train around six p.m. It had taken some persuasion by Algernon to convince the conductor of the train to take them along. When they arrived at Mitford, Algernon offered the man a couple of dollars for his trouble. Much to everyone's surprise, the conductor declined civilly.

The Duchess remarked to Adela as she hopped down from the caboose, where they had travelled, "The gratuitous civility of some of the people here strikes one very pleasantly."

Adela agreed heartily. It was yet another thing about Canada that she loved.

Adela sent Mr. Randolph, who was still in their employ, to fetch the baggage to the hotel. When the Duke and Duchess entered their home, Susan St. Maur exclaimed,

"What a nice little house. Thank you for your kind welcome. The mountains here are spectacular and beyond anything I have seen elsewhere."

After a fine English breakfast, with fresh trout, the next morning, Tom and Algernon left to inspect the mill and tramway. Susan and Adela moved to the porch so that Susan could view the Rocky Mountains once again.

"It is hard to believe they are sixty miles distant," Susan exclaimed. She saw fat, sleek cattle grazing in the distance.

"The cattle make do with the range grass all winter," Adela explained. "They are very hardy. However, the greatest drawback here is the frost at night. Even during summer there is often enough to injure the potatoes." she complained.

"I saw a man planting a garden in Medicine Hat at the station," Susan said as she looked out to the fields beyond the Cochrane home.

"Did you bring the garden seeds I requested?" Adela asked.

"Yes, indeed. I will fetch them from my luggage."

Susan and Adela amused themselves planning the garden. Luckily, Mrs. Townsend was knowledgeable in how to prepare the ground for such an undertaking and had corralled Mr. Randolph with a shovel and a hoe to dig up a garden plot. Beastly hard work, it had taken him days. The soil was hard packed clay, so Mr. Randolph took a wheelbarrow out to the fields and picked up the beautiful fine black loam left above the ground by the pocket gophers. He wheeled this back to his garden, and it had begun to take on a much better look. With some advice on how to plant straight rows from Mrs. Townsend, Adela and Susan started the planting.

"I say, Susan, can you ever imagine doing such a thing back in jolly old England?" Adela laughed.

"I never even knew where cabbages, lettuces, cauliflowers, carrots, beets and beans came from," Susan laughed back.

"Well, I hope to enjoy some fresh vegetables this summer's end." Adela replied. "They are very hard to come by."

Adela took Susan for a walk to show her the wildflowers, which were extremely plentiful. They gathered bouquets for the house and hotel. After lunch, Algernon and Tom set out to building a fence around the garden. Adela had seen what damage the local deer could do to anything planted. Everything they undertook was difficult, yet Adela looked at it with pleasure as part of her new world. Tom, on the other hand, complained loudly all the while until the fence was completed a few days later.

Adela showed Susan the hen house for chickens. Mr. Randolph had constructed it to last through the winter, with a double wall filled in between with sawdust to keep out the cold. Adela told her the poor birds often got frost bitten from the extreme cold in the winters.

The next day, Mr. Kerfoot, their neighbor, showed up to round up all of Adela's ponies. He arrived in a buckboard, a carriage perfectly adapted to rough roads and prairie work. While the Cochrane's were away in the winter, the ponies grazed on the prairies, and quite often required re-breaking before they were taken up again. Napoleon, and Tom's stallion, were ridden all winter by Mr. Randolph to ensure that they would be ready for the Cochranes when they returned. Mr. Kerfoot was known as an excellent horseman, and it was great sport watching him do his work.

That afternoon, the foursome headed to the Cochrane's private railway to see the timber limits, fifteen miles distant to the north. A car was arranged for them to sit in. It was placed in front of the engine, which pushed them along. The St. Maurs were quite thrilled by this mode of transportation. Most unfortunately, the engineer drove too fast, and after only three miles, they felt several great jolts and the car jumped the rails and spilled over sideways. The brakeman stopped the engine, and for a few moments there was great suspense where the couples expected the train to come crashing down on them. Fortunately, this did not happen, or they might have all been killed. Sadly, the only person injured was the brakeman, who had been thrown, and lay under the engine with three bad wounds to his head. His ear, as well, was almost severed from his scalp.

While Algernon and Tom stayed with the brakeman and tried to assist him, Adela and Susan ran back the three miles across the prairie to find the doctor, who lived close by. They arrived breathless and sent him up the tracks, while, after stopping for a short time to catch their breath, the ladies ran on to Mitford where they procured a mattress, pillows, ether and bandages. Mr. Kerfoot and his buckboard were still in the corrals where he continued to work with the horses.

"Mr. Kerfoot," they called as they approached. "there has been a dreadful accident and the brakeman is injured. The doctor is with him, but we need to get these supplies up to him. May we take your buckboard?"

"I can happily take you ladies," he replied.

"We are very capable of driving this buckboard," Susan St Maur replied rather haughtily. Mr. Kerfoot decided discretion would be the better part of valour in this instance, and graciously assisted the ladies into the buckboard.

Susan undertook to drive the team and buckboard, while Adela held the supplies in the madly rocking carriage. It was a wild drive, but the ladies got everything back to the accident site. Soon a wagon showed up to take the poor brakeman, who had fractured his skull in three places, back to Mitford.

The next day, Tom and Algernon went about the business of Mitford, and Adela took Susan to the British American Company's sheep ranche to call on the manager. The sheep ranche was between Mitford and Cochrane. Unfortunately, the manager was away, but his housekeeper gave them luncheon. It was a beautiful June afternoon, so the ladies rode lazily back out to Mitford to pick up their fishing poles for an afternoon of fishing. At first, they were catching fish almost as quickly as they could put the poles in the water, but as is often the case on a June afternoon, a thunderstorm blew up out of the west. Adela told Susan that contrary to the fish in England, the Canadian fish liked to be out in the bright sunshine, and hid away, sensibly, when the storms blew in.

The ladies found shelter under a large spruce while the rain and hail pounded down. Susan was astounded how quickly the hail covered the ground, turning it white in no time. They laughed at each other as they huddled under the branches, grateful for the shelter as the hail was quite painful if they stepped out into it. Within ten minutes the pounding hail had ceased, the white tinged black clouds had moved away to the south, and the beautiful June sun had peeked out again to warm the air.

"What astounding weather this place has," Susan exclaimed. "I have never seen such ferocious hail in my life."

Adela had to agree. The weather was mercurial, it changed so quickly, and often without warning. But Adela thought it was rather charming compared to the incessant days of dull drizzle and rain they were used to back home.

Drenched, they rode back into Cochrane to pick up supplies from the Frenchman, Monsieur Limoge, who ran the small general store. Andre was not a happy man and did not seem to like the prairie life. By the time they reached his store the hot June sun had dried them both completely.

The couples arose the next morning to a great chill. Mr. Randolph and Miss Brealey had filled the wood stove in the dining room with wood and had a roaring fire in the fireplace going. The temperature had fallen to 20 degrees Fahrenheit that night. The St Maurs were incredulous that such cold temperatures could happen in the summer. As it was a very cool morning, the ladies decided to stay inside, but Algernon went for a ride with Mr. Kerfoot, when he came each day to work on Adela's ponies. By the afternoon, everything had warmed up again, and Mr. Kerfoot invited them over to his horse ranche. Enroute, Susan was most impressed with how the horses managed to miss all the gopher holes, if given their heads.

"The gophers abound here" Susan exclaimed, and Adela laughed back, "Indeed they do."

The Kerfoot Ranche was home to more than a hundred

horses, an awesome sight. Mr. Kerfoot explained how he used his corrals to separate and break horses. Algernon always needed sport, so he chose a horse out of the remuda. Mr. Kerfoot lunged the horse on the lariat, saddled him, mounted him and took him for a gallop over the prairie. He returned with a quiet horse. Mr. Kerfoot explained that this was usually all the breaking a horse would get, unless he showed temper. Mrs. Kerfoot invited the guests into their home for tea and cakes, which she had made herself. The ride home across the prairie that evening, with the sun setting behind the mountains and turning them golden and fiery orange, was too beautiful to imagine.

The next morning brought another sight only to be seen on the prairies. A band of Blackfoot Indians rode in, and the chief, Three Plumes, rode up to the house and dismounted, to show the Cochrane's his permit. This was given to him by the Indian Agent to enable the group to leave their reserve for a stated time. This group had been visiting the Stoney Indians to the west. Adela later heard that the guests stole thirty ponies when they were leaving. Had they not shown their permit, it would have been Adela's duty to contact the North West Mounted Police. It was the duty of the NWMP to ensure that the Indians stayed on their reserves.

Later that afternoon, the Earl of Norbury arrived at the Cochrane station, and the engineer once again tossed a packet out to Adela to inform her. Adela had to make it a habit to be in her spot when the train came by if she wanted anything from the train.

Algernon and Tom were busy at the mill, so Susan and Adela procured a wagon and driver, and saddled up three horses to ride into Cochrane to fetch William Toler.

With his friends and investors as guests in his home, Tom became his affable and genial self again. Adela was so happy to have them all in Mitford that some days she thought she would just burst from pride. That evening, it was decided that the men would head into Calgary for business the next morning, and they left at 7 a.m., not to return until the next day.

Adela decided to take Susan to visit more of the neighbours. After breakfast, they hitched up the buckboard to travel to a cattle ranche twelve miles from Mitford. As they finally approached the ranche, they found the spring rains had created a bog in front of it. Adela, and her faithful deer hound, Ginger, jumped down to inspect. Ginger would not go through it. With soaking wet feet Adela jumped back into the buckboard and drove carefully into the bog. They reached the other side with relief.

"Halloo, halloo, Mrs. McKee," Adela shouted, as an old Scottish lady and her two daughters came to the door of a pine log house. The ladies made excellent tea for Susan and Adela. Susan was constantly surprised by the lack of servants, and yet she understood how difficult it was to have staff around too. After all, she had found her lady's maid so annoying on the trip over that she had sent her off to live with an aunt in Chicago. The old lady explained that she could keep no servants there due to the loneliness of the place. Adela secretly was glad that she returned each winter to England as it was the only way she could talk her servants into coming to Canada.

"What induced you to leave Scotland?" Susan asked Mrs. McKee.

She replied, "My eldest son came to Canada and became an engineer for the CPR. He had advised me, a widow, to come to Canada to live with him. While I was preparing to move to Canada, he met a young woman and the two decided Vancouver was a better place to live than the cattle ranche. They stayed until my daughters and youngest son came out here, to take over the ranche."

"How extraordinary!" Susan exclaimed.

Adela, on the other hand, was used to all the extraordinary stories of the hearty folk who made their way to seek their fortune in Canada.

On the way home, Susan commented to Adela, "The hardship those ladies must endure must be unbearable. It may be pleasant enough here in the summer, but in the winter, with deep snow, the bitter cold and the place being shut off from all communication with the civilized world, it must be insufferable."

"Yes, my dear, I do believe it takes more endurance than either Tom or I have to live through a prairie winter. That is why we return home each year."

> *June 7, 1888. My days are filled with such happiness now that Susan and Algernon are here. Thomas is happy again, and Susan and I are enjoying everything about Mitford and Canada that can be enjoyed. Susan is so taken with the mountains. I love to watch the great snow peaks change their aspect with every gleam of sunlight, every cloud that floats by, every storm that passes over and she is as entranced as I. From our arrival to June's end, I will watch them turn from white, to blue, to purple and finally to black, as the last slight rays of sun sink behind them. This morning they were a glory of pink, then orange, then yellow, then white. Nature shares her immense beauty with us daily.*

CHAPTER 13

COAL!

SUMMER 1888

Thomas arrived at breakfast the next morning with a wide grin. He had announced to them all the night before that he was taking them somewhere very exciting. After breakfast, they all saddled up horses and went to see what had made Thomas so excited. As they rode across the green prairie grass, they came across the opening of a coal mine, which had been discovered three years ago. Tom had heard about this potential new business venture and couldn't wait to explore its possibilities. Susan and Adela only went as far as the first gallery, a wide seam of coal, where they met a man and horse bringing up a truckload of coal to the mouth. The men continued on to another gallery, with Mr. Chaffey, of Winnipeg, who was managing the mine for the owner of the Bow River Coal Mine, Mr. Vaughn. Mr. Chaffey explained to them that a new seam of coal had been discovered at the mouth of a badger hole. They set off to inspect the seam, with each of them carrying a Davy lamp to light the way. Upon their return, they visited the now famous badger hole.

At dinner that night there was only talk of mining coal, which Thomas saw as another excellent new venture in which he wanted William and Algernon to be partners. Thomas was at his best when he was soliciting investment for new ideas, and both Susan and Adela were caught up the excitement of this newest venture.

The next days were spent with the men riding out to the mine, and letters were written to Mr. Vaughn with a proposal to enter into a partnership.

While the men were busy with business, Susan and Adela kept busy with the running of Mitford. Susan had become quite attached to the hens in the hen house and enjoyed fetching the eggs in the morning. She felt very sorry for the hens who had lost some of their little toes to the winter cold. Besides Ginger, the deer hound, Adela's hunting dog, there was also Jack, the kitchen dog. Adela had found the spaniel emaciated and almost dead, in a ditch, and had had brought him home and nursed him back to health. Jack would tolerate Adela, but he really only loved Mrs. Townsend, the cook, who constantly fed him scraps. He and Ginger were on the worst of terms and often caused quite a ruckus as they chased each other through the house. Adela purchased a black retriever puppy, Polly, to train to retrieve ducks and pheasants. She was not fond of her lessons, but Adela was patient with her training, and she felt Polly would become a helpful part of food procurement.

"Susan, have you seen Polly?" Adela asked after breakfast the next day. They went out to the porch and discovered Polly chasing butterflies in the back yard. Polly needed to sleep in the back hall at night, as the coyotes would have loved to have her for breakfast, lunch or supper any day. As soon as she could get outside, Polly would run around to her heart's content.

Susan responded, "I don't think she is going to be much of a bird dog," and walked down off the porch to grab Polly, who when she saw her coming, dashed under the house. The houses in Mitford were raised off the ground to try and keep them warmer in the winter, when the frost seeps feet down into the ground. Giving up on Polly for the time being, the two ladies wandered over to check out two pigs named Jack and Jill (not to be mixed up with Jack the Dog) and two dairy cows; one with a wild calf. These animals made up the sum total of the Cochrane's "ranche", a far cry from how Adela had first thought they would live in Canada. She often thought about Cousin Billie's big cattle ranche at Mosquito Creek with nostalgia.

It was a warm and lazy day, and Mr. Randolph brought out an easel that he had made. Susan loved to sketch and had brought charcoal and paper with her. Adela took her to the stunning confluence of the Bow and Horse Creek and helped her get set up. She brought along her fishing pole, as she was not an artist.

The men were still busy the next day, so Adela suggested they ride out to the railway bridge over the Bow River. Adela was light and quick on her feet, and thoroughly enjoyed running across the bridge when they got there. Susan, on the other hand, was rather frightened of walking on the sleepers with the river running beneath her feet. Once safely over the bridge, the ladies walked through the tall grass, noticing the plethora of wildflowers growing so profusely there. It was an idyllic afternoon.

The next day brought lunch guests. Luckily, the men were not out at the mine site today, so a lovely social lunch was enjoyed by all the guests. The cook had to be ever on guard for extra mouths to feed, and today it was two local ranchers. Susan was fascinated by these local men.

"Are these true "western men?" she asked Adela.

"Oh, indeed. Their father is a wealthy man back in England, but he doesn't want these boys returning home. He does send them a remittance to help with their expenses. However, they must work hard; they wash their own clothes and cook for themselves. That is why they look so rough."

The "rough" look included a blue flannel shirt, with no collar, but with a colored handkerchief tied loosely around the neck, a buckskin jacket, a pair of leather chaps with a fringe down the leg, which were worn over trousers, boots and a broad-brimmed felt hat, with a leather band, ornamented with stamped patterns.

Later that day Thomas received a telegram from Mr. Van Horne, President of the C.P.R., saying he was stopping off on his way to Vancouver to discuss business with Thomas. He would be arriving by special train. For the first time since the guests had arrived, Thomas' countenance changed, and he was very upset and angry.

"The mighty William Van Horne is just another of my great annoyances in Canada," Thomas seethed to his guests.

"He steadfastly refuses to build a station in Mitford, claiming our grade is too steep. What utter nonsense. The railway is the lifeblood of the town on the prairies, and it is essential that Mitford have a station. The confounded man will not listen to reason," he raged.

When Mr. Van Horne's special train stopped at Mitford the next morning, Adela and Susan rode out to meet him and saw it was more like a house than a railway carriage. It had a bedroom, bathroom, dining room, kitchen and an excellent cook. Mr. Van Horne had just succeeded Lord Mount Stephen as the president of the Canadian Pacific Railway in 1888. He was a blustery American business tycoon, solidly built with receding brown hair and piercing Dutch blue eyes. He would go on to complete the transcontinental railway in Canada, add ocean liners to the railway system, and build luxury hotels which all would become part of the Canadian Pacific Railway.

Not wanting to be part of the conversation with Mr. Van Horne, the ladies left for an excellent gallop over the prairie while he concluded his business with Thomas. Upon their return, they found Mr. Van Horne's train had left for Vancouver, and Thomas nowhere to be found. He was still seething when they rode into the yard.

"Oh, my dear, whatever did he say?" Adela inquired tentatively. Algernon and William seemed to be elsewhere, and Thomas was pacing along the porch in fury.

"The man still will not see to reason! He claims it is far too difficult for the C.P.R. to stop on this grade. As well, when I suggested that the C.P.R. finance a rail spur, he suggested that he would like to leave all mining to private enterprise. He believes that if the mine is successful, we will recoup our money, and if the mine is unsuccessful, then the C.P.R. will not have lost any money. The man is impossible."

Adela knew it was best to just leave Thomas alone when this happened, and as it was a lovely day, and Susan loved to fish so much, she suggested they grab their rods and go down to the river. That evening, after a wonderful dinner of fresh trout, Thomas had regained better spirits, and suggested a ride up to the timber limits in Dog Pound, as the train engine was typically dysfunctional. Thomas had also been pressuring Van Horne to send out a new engine so that they could get started again.

The St. Maurs had decided to continue on with their journey in a few days' time, and Thomas wanted them to see the timber lease, so a long ride was planned to Dog Pound. They decided instead on an early start, and headed out at dawn, galloping up and down the limitless prairie. With its gentle hills and lovely valleys, the ride was immensely pleasurable to the St Maurs, who loved the outdoors. The Duke of Norbury enjoyed the ride as well. With the five of them cantering along on strong horses, the gentle clouds scudding by and with the wind abated, for once; a feeling of exhilaration and freedom descended upon them all and smiles were to be found, all around, even on Thomas' face.

Mile after mile slipped beneath the saddle, and after traversing over some marshy ground and descending a rather precipitous path, they found themselves in the Dog Pound plain. Adela told them all the story of the name, which amused them as they picketed out the horses. The fishing rods were pulled off the saddle ties, the saddles were thrown off the horses, and the happy group set off to fish for lunch. It was not to be a lucky day though, even though Susan tried three different flies.

"Bollocks! I remember Mrs. McKee telling us that the fish in Canada only eat in the sunshine. They will follow these flies, but they will not bite!" she complained. While they continued to try their luck with the fish, two nice Frenchwomen from the neighbouring ranche came over to visit. Thomas hooked a minnow to his line. Still no luck.

Madame D'Artique and her sister laughed, "You will only catch zeze feesh on a bright sunny day." The group gave in, and started to bundle up their rods, sad that fresh trout would not accompany their picnic. Madame D'Artique invited them to come and see the ranche, of which she and her husband and sister were the managers. The owner lived in Calgary. To their surprise, it was a poultry farm. There were hundreds of chickens, all set up in the French manner with rows of boxes for the sitting hens. An excellent market for poultry existed in the North-West, with a chicken selling for $1.75.

They insisted that the group take skim-milk cheese, which they made from the produce of their dairy cattle, a bucket of milk and a dishful of eggs to add to their picnic. The produce made a wonderful omelette, cooked by Algernon over the fire. His years in the army had provided him with many skills not dreamed of by the rest of the group. It was an excellent repast.

As they were watering the horses in preparation for a tour of the timber lease, four got loose and ran off. Thomas quickly saddled up his cow pony. He chased them for a half mile before he was able to turn them around and head back. He continued to chase them back towards the group and eventually the three rogues were caught. They saddled up quickly and rode around, checking out the timber. The trees were rather small, but tall.

Tom explained, "These trees will still make excellent lumber for settlers' cabins." Adela looked at the diameter of the trees and wondered about that but said nothing.

With a long ride ahead, the group turned back south and

rode for many miles, stopping for tea at another ranche. It was important to know everyone in the area because so few people lived there. Everyone needed to count on each other for survival in this often savage land. Thomas and Adela were always well received by their neighbours. After tea, the group was all rather tired, and the mosquitoes had turned out in full force as well, which was very troublesome. The long, beautiful summer evening was upon them when they finally rode tired into Mitford.

The next day was Sunday, and to everyone's delight, a traveling minister had come to Mitford to give a service in the evening. As there was not a church, the hotel saloon was closed down and all the Mitford residents were invited to the service. Adela thought how alike, in some ways, it was to attending Sunday morning services in Wangford, the town near her home of Henham Hall. However, instead of the beautiful old church, they were going to the saloon bar. It gave Adela a small feeling of home to have all her villagers at Mitford join them for the service. The only piano in Mitford, was unfortunately, in her drawing room, so the congregation had to sing a capella. As they left the saloon to walk home, Susan St Maur asked how many of the men would have come to the service.

"About half, I would say," Tom replied.

"I didn't think much of your minister," she added. "the hymns were not at all cheery, and his sermon was not at all suitable to the requirements of the listeners. One regrets that even such a small luxury as a good service is denied these men."

Adela felt this was a great opening to explain about her church campaign, championed by Mrs. Percy Mitford, and as they sat around on the porch in the lovely evening sunshine, all three of her guests promised to invest in her church project as well. Adela was thrilled.

The next day was to be the final day for the visitors at Mitford. The St Maurs and the Duke of Norbury were all planning to visit Banff next, and the train to take them there would stop in Mitford at 3:00 a.m.

Susan started her morning checking in on the chickens. Since she had arrived, twenty-six chicks had hatched. They were kept in the coop. They would never have survived the weather and the predators (including the Cochrane's dogs) outside of it.

"Look Adela, we have had success with our poultry farming!" Susan exclaimed, as they gathered the morning eggs for Mrs. Townsend.

"Soon you shall have a great poultry operation here like they do in Dog Pound!" she laughed.

Adela had enjoyed the twenty-six days Susan had spent with her so much and knew it would feel so very lonely again once the St. Maurs were on their way.

In the afternoon, they all rode over to the Kerfoot ranche to return the wonderful mount lent to Algernon for his stay. Although he protested, Algernon insisted that Mr. Kerfoot take payment for the time he had used the horse.

Mrs. Townsend had prepared a wonderful farewell dinner, with kidney soup, trout and potatoes; stuffed duck breast, roast beef and roast lamb (procured from the British American Ranche, their closest neighbor), as well as rice pudding, apple pie and cheese. There were also excellent clarets, spirits and beer, and the guests were enjoying themselves immensely, when a tragic event cut the festivities short.

The mill whistle began to blow violently. Another accident had happened on the railway! The Cochranes and their guests rushed to the hotel to find out what was happening.

The engine, returning with four cars of logs, had been thrown off the rails. The engineer had been jammed in between the engine and the logs and had broken his leg in two places. Once again, the doctor was sent for as the men carried him to the hotel, where they laid him out upon a table, awaiting the doctor.

The ladies were surprised to hear him joking with the men as they carried him,

"One cannot believe the strength of these men" the Duchess of Somerset remarked.

After the doctor arrived, they returned to the house to complete the packing. Mrs. Townsend and Miss Brealey had reworked the dinner food into a wonderful midnight buffet, with duck and roast beef sandwiches made up to be taken along for the train ride to Banff. Much more claret was consumed, and the staff packed all the luggage into a wagon. Around 2 a.m. the party climbed into the democrats, and all were driven out to where the train would stop to pick them up, which was before the uphill grade began. This was the only spot William Van Horne would allow the trains to stop.

As all the farewells were being said, Thomas spoke. "Next year, there shall be a station in Mitford, and a reasonable schedule to take people to and fro."

With much regret, the Duke and Duchess of Somerset and the Duke of Norbury climbed aboard the train. They had decided a sleeping car was not necessary as it was only a four hours' journey to Banff, which they would reach at 7 a.m. They would be passing into the Rockies at dawn, and it was a clear and beautiful night. They hoped to be rewarded with watching the light from the sunrise as it poured over the mountains, as they ate their sandwiches and drank a final bottle of claret.

June 25, 1888. It is with such regret that I watch the train chug west through Mitford and onward to the Rockies with my dear friends on board. I hope the success of their visit will keep Thomas in a more amenable mood during the rest of the summer and autumn as we go about our work. Parting is such great sorrow.

CHAPTER 14

GETTING COAL TO RAIL

SUMMER 1888 – AUTUMN 1889

Adela was filled with a surprising melancholy after the departure of the Dukes, and the Duchess. She felt quite alone each morning as she rose to gather up the chicken eggs. She remembered Susan St Maur's fondness for her poultry and was ever so glad that she had been able to spend most of June with her.

Thomas was very busy negotiating with Mr. Van Horne for a way to get his coal to the railway line. He continued to write to him daily about the need for the C.P. R. to build a spur line up to his mine. He tried badgering him, reminding him that the C.P.R. had built a line to the Bow River Mine. Van Horne became quite formal when reminding Cochrane that the former superintendent who had allowed this was no longer employed by the railway.

My Dear Sir,
I do not know under what circumstances or upon what terms the track to the Bow River Mine was

provided by Mr. Egan. If upon other terms than
those fixed by the Board of Directors, he would
have been held responsible for the expense had he
remained in the services of the company.

However, he did concede to let Thomas re-use the no
longer used mine siding rails. The Cochranes would have to
bear the expense of their removal and relaying.

"More expense!" Thomas seethed to Adela after reading
Van Horne's last letter. Adela assured him she would get the
funds for this next leg of the business venture. What did
mollify him somewhat was that Van Horne had replied quite
favourably to Thomas' inquiries about the C.P.R. buying his
coal. As soon as Thomas could get it to the rail line, Van Horne
assured him he would take a large quantity of it. Having a
defined market for the coal was a relief, and Thomas turned
to the ever-vexing issue of trying to build a spur line up to
his mine.

Things did not go easily with this venture though, and
Thomas continued to badger Van Horne to build the spur line.
Basically, he was running out of money, and he had pushed
his investors to the limit. The mill was just not profitable, and
constantly needed funds to deal with the operational problems and related costs. Thomas' dreams of making his fortune
were taking a turn that he had never expected. He returned to
the surly and unhappy Thomas Adela remembered before the
investors had come to visit.

Van Horne suggested building a bridge across the river, but
as this was far beyond Thomas' means, he eventually decided
to bring the coal down Horse Creek on the sawmill railway.
Once in Mitford, it would be transferred to a coal shed.

The rest of the summer and autumn were busy with getting the new venture up and running. It was so time consuming that Tom had little time for the mill, where trouble seemed to constantly lurk.

He had hired a millwright who had come from England with his wife, Mr. William Sargent. He was kept very busy keeping the machinery of the mill running. He was also called on to keep the train in running order as well. Mrs. Sargent was a cook, and her skills were needed to help prepare the food for all the Mitford workers. All the moving parts of Thomas' enterprises needed a close eye and sure hand, and there was often far too much happening for Thomas to be personally involved. Adela stepped in wherever she could, but as July and August passed by, the Cochranes found themselves very overwhelmed and exhausted. Running the Mitford enterprises was far more than a full-time job.

The early autumn of 1888 was beautiful at Mitford. The nights had started to become cold as the days shortened, but the days were warm and beautiful. Thomas' days were taken up with constant problem solving, between the sawmill, tramway and mine. He was becoming so obsessed and troubled that Adela started to worry about his health. She wrote to Billie and Evelyn, asking when they planned to return to England. She received some none- too-welcome news from The Little Bow River Cattle ranche. Thomas had been so caught up with the challenges at his enterprises that he had not kept up with their ranche enterprise. The ranche, like most in this place, struggled to have enough water for the cattle. As well, the herd had contracted blackleg, a bacterial infection that caused necrosis in one or more legs before the cow died. Due to these circumstances, the ranche was not turning a profit. Adela was loathe to share more of the bad news with Thomas, and held on to the letter for a few days before she worked up the nerve to tell him. As she expected, he received the news about the ranche with yelling and ranting.

By now it was getting near the end of September, and Adela knew Thomas badly needed respite. The problem was, they didn't have a trail boss. Adela had learned how integral this person was to a cow/calf operation. Very often the trail boss stayed on as the resident ranche manager, a necessary position if the ranche was to be a success. The mill needed a foreman that was completely reliable, and in whom the Cochranes could place their trust when they left for England. No such man had shown up in the Mitford vicinity, and Adela was unsure who they could place in charge while they were gone. She brought up the subject with Thomas at dinner that night. They discussed the current men who worked for them. They had relied on Joseph Limoges, who had started a trading post, last year, but as so often happened in the land of opportunity, Joseph had sold the trading post to James Johnstone and had moved to High River where he had opened a store. Adela was also finding out that fine breeding did not always make one a good businessman. The Count de Journal had decided to follow Johnstone to High River, so they were in need of a hotel manager as well. Adela and Thomas spent days at the mill, assessing the men, so that they could find someone to be in charge of it, and someone also to manage the hotel. Frazzled and frustrated, they received a letter from Billie saying the other Cochranes were heading home to England in the first week of October. Thomas booked them passage to travel together. Overwhelmed and not sure what to do, Thomas and Lady Adela returned to England.

Once home on the Isle of Wight, Thomas took very ill, and Adela nursed him day and night until he regained his health. She had begun to notice how the stress of the ventures was taking a toll on him, and his month-long illness back on the Isle of Wight reassured her that some her suspicions were proving to be correct. As enamored as Thomas had been of his travels to the Dominion of Canada, the reality of the harshness of the climate and the difficulties of trying to run a sawmill and coal mine, while keeping an interest in a ranche, were becoming apparent. For the first time, Adela began to wonder if Thomas could manage this great dream of theirs. After she had made him comfortable each day, she saddled up a riding horse and rode for hours, pondering on how to assist him. She kept coming back to the fact that a competent manager was essential while they were away, but also while they were in residence. Thomas needed someone to help him with operations; it seemed it was simply too much for him to handle on his own.

This made her examine her life of privilege from a very different perspective. Previously, neither she nor Thomas worried about how life operated. Their homes were managed fully by butler and housekeeper, and the grounds were managed fully by the groundskeeper. Somehow, all this seemed to happen without any effort at all from the family. She had never given it a thought. Life in the Dominion of Canada certainly was teaching her to see the world differently.

Once recovered, Thomas was very happy and settled once he reached the Isle of Wight. Her Mama always planned a beautiful social time at Christmas, and the Cochrane family was always invited to celebrate along with Lady Augusta and her family. All the family were to be there. Her older sisters, Lady Augusta-Fanny and her family, Lady Sophia and her recently married husband, Cecil Fane, would be there. George, ever the dashing bachelor, would also be there, and her younger sisters, as yet unmarried, would be too. Adela lost herself and her woes in the fun of being back at Henham Hall.

"Mama, it is so wonderful to be back home with all of you for Christmas," Adela told her Mama over and over again. Her worries now were over the decorations to be placed on the beautiful Christmas tree her Mama had decided to have this year. Prince Albert had brought the German tradition of the Tannenbaum to England, and as Victoria and Albert were so popular with the people, anything they did was quickly copied by the upper classes. All the Rous family enjoyed the decorated evergreen gracing the library for the holidays.

So simple, and yet, after a while, so boring, Adela thought to herself. While she loved to return to England, she knew after Christmas was over, she would need to busy herself with encouraging investors again.

By the time February 1889 had rolled in, and they had returned to the Isle of Wight, Thomas was facing a financial crisis. Thomas and Adela took the train up to Scotland to have discussions with Billie. In order to cut his losses and focus on his Mitford ventures, Thomas easily turned his grazing lease rights over to Billie. The Little Bow River Cattle Company was all Billie had to worry about, and Thomas was happy to leave it to him. Billie loved the ranche life and was interested in ranching for the rest of his life, while Thomas had never really been interested in ranching, which always saddened Adela.

"This will work out better for both of us," Billie assured Thomas. After the conclusion of their business decisions, Adela and Tom stayed on to hunt and ride with Billie and Evelyn. The ever-present challenges going on in the mine and mill were never far away though, and after a pleasant time in Scotland, the Cochranes returned to the Isle of Wight and the reality of his failing businesses.

Not long after their return to Quarr Abbey, Thomas brought up another visit one morning at breakfast.

"I want to invite Will Toler out to Quarr Abbey for discussions. I believe I can convince him to invest some more in our enterprises to keep them running until they are profitable."

"Oh, I enjoy Will so much, that will be lovely!" Adela agreed. Adela wrote up the invitation that morning and sent it out to Will Toler, and it was arranged he would head over to the Isle in a few weeks.

After Will arrived, Adela, who took her hostess' duties seriously, was in a flurry of activity. She arranged riding, fox hunting and neighbourly visits to all the upper class on the Island. She managed to get Minna, her sister-in-law, to arrange tea with Princess Beatrice, which was always a coup for any socialite. The visit went exceptionally well, and at its conclusion, Thomas had persuaded The Duke of Norbury to form a partnership to help finance both the mill and mine. This turned Thomas from a surly, anxious and angry husband, once again to the charming romancer Adela had married. So, after Will returned home to Ireland, Thomas decided they needed some relaxation in London. Adela arranged for the Rous family London townhouse, and while there they attended the theatre, opera and symphony. Adela also placed an advertisement for a manager for her Mitford store. While she knew a manager for the mill and mines were far more important, Thomas no longer seemed to think this was necessary, so she focused on her ventures at Mitford. She and Thomas read through and replied to many inquiries and set up interviews in the London townhouse.

"Lady Adela Cochrane, and Mr. Thomas Cochrane require a shopkeeper for their General Store in Mitford, Dominion of Canada. The applicant must have previous shop keeping skills and be of sound constitution," the advertisement read.

Both Lady Adela and Thomas were becoming much more adept at understanding who they would need as staff in Mitford.

"I say, Adela, this Horace Hickling seems to be just the right fellow for the job!" Thomas beamed as he read Horace's reply to the advertisement.

"I will write him back today and set up an appointment," Thomas said.

Mr. Hickling showed up the next day and met with Thomas in the study.

"I believe he is the right man for the store operation," Thomas told Adela after Hickling left.

"After all, he has managed Martin's here in London for ten years," Adela concurred, as she had read Mr. Hickling's reply. She was happy to let Thomas make these decisions as she felt he needed to feel in charge of how they could improve things at Mitford.

All plans were set for a return to Canada in April 1889, as there was much that needed to be caught up with over the long winter. Adela also had to hire new staff for the Cochrane home. Given that Mrs. Townsend had lost her adventuring spirit, Adela hired a new cook, and promoted Miss Brealey to the lady's maid position. That meant she needed a new housekeeper as well. Dickie and Amy Smith, who were married in Kent County, England in 1889, were hired by Lady Adela as butler and housekeeper for the Mitford household. Later, from 1892-95, they would become managers of the hotel.

APRIL BROUGHT LADY ADELA AND Thomas home to Mitford. Adela and Thomas greeted their neighbors and employees at a welcome home dinner at the Mitford Arms Hotel, as it was now known. A Dr. Hayden had set up a medical practice while they were gone and had also opened up a drugstore. Logs from the sawmill had actually been used to build the small cabin that Dr. Hayden set up as the drugstore. As well as a medical practitioner, he was also a botanist, and in his spare time was categorizing the abundant wildflowers, of Mitford. However, the constant accidents on the Betsy Line, as the mill railway was called, kept Dr. Hayden busy. Close to Adela's heart, the church would be starting that spring.

Adela was thrilled to be back to her true home. While this home was modest; it was also unique, and so gloriously beautiful, that Adela loved it with all her heart. She spent her days tramping purposefully around the village, talking to the workers and listening to their concerns. A serious complaint from the villagers of Mitford was the mud, as there were yet no sidewalks. Adela arranged for lumber from the mill to be planed and wooden sidewalks to be built by the millwright carpenter, Will Sargent.

Still, the greatest problem continually hampering Mitford and the Cochranes was the lack of a permanent station at Mitford. The train brought mail and supplies, and transported people and animals, the lifeblood of any town. Even though Mitford had a post office, often, someone had to ride to the Cochrane station to pick up the mail. Both Thomas and Lady Adela constantly wrote to William Van Horne, imploring him to move the station to Mitford. At times, Van Horne seemed amenable to the idea, and other times not.

"That confounded Van Horne!" Thomas seethed one night at dinner. "I simply cannot get it through to him how important this station is to us."

Adela, too, was furious. "I have written him as one of his shareholders, thinking that should help "persuade" him, but the bloody American has no sense of British manners and does not realize that it is bad form to treat a Lady in such a manner."

However, the train and train station were only one of the many ongoing problems. The mine was producing inferior coal and the mill had constant issues with supply and mechanical problems with the tramway. Lady Adela had learned that taking off to visit the fascinating neighbors or riding the beautiful valleys on a summer evening was a good way to address the nearly constant stress of the businesses at Mitford. Even still, she loved the place unreservedly.

> June 14, 1889. It is my great escape and pleasure to ride out in the golden evenings, west towards the mountains, or north along Horse Creek. The smell of the evening air is far sweeter than any perfume I have known, and the softness of the evening colors touches my heart in a place that no other has.

CHAPTER 15

IRELAND, MONTREAL, AND THE NEW BEST WEST

1888

"May the road rise up to meet you. May the wind always be at your back. May the sun shine warm upon your face, and rains fall soft upon your fields." This was the Irish blessing that his Ma had said over and over in his childhood until he knew it without thinking. William Percival Bradley, known as Billie to his friends and family, was heading Out West, like many other young Canadian men and women.

in the 1880's, jobs were growing scarcer in the Fitzroy County, Ottawa region, and Ma Lizzie Bradley had too many mouths to feed as it was. Posters for the Last Best West could be seen in store windows, so Billie and his brother Henry decided it was better to strike out for The Last Best West than stay idle and unemployed in Ottawa.

'Course, there was the matter of train tickets and some seed money. But Billie had a way of making that happen. All the years of pugilism while he worked the Ottawa River had left him with a reputation. This had allowed for him to supplement his income as a young man.

And brother Henry Bradley had honed his skills, working the public houses and job sites, building up the bets that would go to the winners, and making sure a good cut went to Henry and Billie. The brothers were also true adventurers at heart. Of course, there was always some unhappy customer complaining and threatening to kill them, and the boys would have to spirit away from the house, as Ma Bradley would have none of the business of the fight around her younger children.

Henry Bradley knew that there was a certain grudge still held by Black Irish Bob, a blacksmith with a bad temper, who had nearly downed Billie once before. He was sure he could stir things up again between Black Irish Bob and Billie, and if he could get enough wagers on the fight, then maybe there would be enough money for train tickets and seed money.

Henry Bradley started hanging around the forge where Black Irish Bob worked. He noted the immense arms which worked the bellows and the tongs, that smashed the hammer into the anvil. He thought, very briefly, about those huge hams pounding his brother's face, but only for a minute.

"Say, Black Irish Bob, I hear you're still mighty sore after Billie Bradley bested you in that bare knuckle brawl behind the forge barn last fall," brother Henry badgered.

Bob looked up slowly, with an angry grimace, but said nothing.

"You think you could beat him in a rematch?" Henry Bradley continued to push.

"I can knock him down so's he'll never get back up" growled Black Irish Bob.

"Name your time, name your place." crowed Henry.

"Next Saturday night, same place." Black Irish Bob growled again.

"Done." Henry Bradley crowed back, then went about the next stage, getting wagers from all over Fitzroy Harbour.

"GENTLEMEN, GENTLEMEN, GATHER 'ROUND AND make your wagers. Black Irish Bob takes on Billie "The Strongman" Bradley in a prizefight." Brother Henry had been making his rounds and had stirred up quite a mob. He had been a great sprinter as a boy, a skill upon which he often relied when a drunk loser decided he wanted his funds back.

He hoped he wouldn't have to rely on those skills, but you never knew when you were going to need them.

Billie had been sparring with an old canvas sea bag filled with rags and hung from the tree in Ma Lizzie Bradley's back yard. And he had been practicing lifting up every heavy thing not nailed down in the area to build up his arm strength. While Henry was swift on his feet, Billie was swift with ducking and coming up with a left hook when his opponent was least expecting it. He had taken a lot of bashes to his head, and had a permanently crooked nose, but typically he had fared quite well and truly was one of the best prizefighters in the county. He was counting on that now, and on the prize money Henry had been coaxing out of the men of the town.

It seemed the Irish whiskey from the backyard stills in the neighboring county farms was flowing freely that Saturday night in 1888. Henry had rarely seen Billie in such fine form. Billie was ready to cut lose for the Last Best West.

They had both found their way to the Land Titles office,

where they signed up for 160 acres of nearly free homestead land in The North West Territories. The train would take them through a little place called Calgary, then onward to Morleyville. From there they would have to make it to their homestead.

In order to make ends meet, Billie and Henry had previously worked on the oat harvests on the surrounding farms in the autumn, so had some small idea of what agricultural life was like.

The lumber trade had certainly provided work and a decent means of making a living for the Irish immigrant Bradley family, who had fled Kilkenny County, Ireland in the mid 1700's looking for a better life in Canada. Like so many others, they had come aboard a lumber ship from Cork. The lumber ships started out in Liverpool and made their way to Cork to pick up poor immigrants looking to improve their lives. The fare for travel to Canada on an empty lumber ship was minimal, which encouraged many Irish to leave the grinding poverty of life in Ireland behind and to seek out a better life in the New World. The ships were not meant for comfortable travel for people, instead they were the worst of the fleet as they were meant to ferry lumber back from Canada. The lumber barons had found out they could make some profit if they kept the fares low enough for immigrants, so they built bunks on the walls of the lumber ships which sailed back full of people, hopeful for a better life in the New World. They also discovered the immigrants provided excellent ballast and the ships made better time when filled with people. The voyages were terrible and hard, and many who sought a new life found theirs ended on the ships.

However, the lumber industry provided work for the new immigrants once they made it to Canada, and Billie and Henry's family had found a decent life in the Ottawa Valley. Now that the lumber business was dying out, many men had nowhere to go to make a living. The New Eldorado of Western Canada offered them hope, especially when it came with nearly free farmland, and the Bradley brothers were ready to strike out again, even further west, to find a better life.

If Billie could just get the money for a ticket to Morleyville, he and Henry would be on their way. All he needed to do was knock down Black Irish Bob the Blacksmith and collect his prize money and they could start their adventure.

Billie had taken just a few snorts of moonshine whiskey to get buoyed up for the fight. He walked behind the blacksmith barn, where a circle of men had gathered around Black Irish Bob. There was heckling and hollering as he walked closer to the behemoth in front of him.

"Are ya ready, ya great Irish loaf?" Billie taunted.

Black Irish Bob replied with a snarl, "Come and find out."

Billie began the fight with a quick jab, and Bob responded in kind.

"A little girl could throw a better punch than that." Henry also taunted from the circle of men surrounding the fighters,

Billie took a smashing to his head, ribs and hands, but like always, he was quick enough to miss a lot of Bob's blows. The Irish Stand Off did not allow a man to back up and recover, and as the fight neared the end Billie's eyes were almost swollen shut. His lips were swollen, his nose was swollen, and his face would likely be black in the morning, but Black Irish Bob was tiring fast, and Billie thought he could outlast him.

"Have ya had enough?" Billie panted.

"AARRGGHH" was all that Black Irish Bob could muster.

Finally, with a mighty swing fueled from God-knows-where, Billie knocked the giant from his feet. He felt brother Henry pulling his arm into the air in victory. He could no longer see or hear anything, but he knew he had won.

Henry was a master of the aftermath. He doused Billie with buckets of Ottawa River water to wash away the blood and mucus. The crowd half carried Billie down the street to the pub, where he was unceremoniously dumped into a chair. He sat, grinning, but mostly unconscious, as Henry paid out the wagers.

"I told you all Billie was the best." Henry cried gleefully to the crowd

"Strongman Billie Bradley wins again. All hail!" the crowd roared.

Henry had paid everyone fairly. A huge crowd had made it to the fight, and many had bet on Black Irish Bob, so the winnings were good for those who had backed Bradley.

"Sweet Mother Mary, Billie, we've done it," crowed Henry when all the business had been done.

The drinking went on long into the night until the barman had to throw them all out. Billie managed some whiskey which definitely helped with the pain, but mostly he sat slumped at the table, exhausted.

Two weeks later the fight was forgotten, the winnings had purchased tickets and the Bradley brothers were on their way to The Last Best West.

CHAPTER 16

THE OLD PORT, MONTREAL, TORONTO & WINNIPEG

1889

With their feet firmly planted on the wooden deck of a ship, Henry and Billie felt at home, and excited for the adventure ahead. The first leg of the journey for them was to get to Toronto, where they could board the Canadian Pacific Railway. Being lumberman from Fitzroy Harbour, they were well used to ships, and therefore decided to sail down the Ottawa River back to Montreal, the route their lumber had taken to market for more than a century. From there, they would sail down the mighty St. Lawrence River to Lake Ontario, and onward from there to Toronto, where they could catch the train to Winnipeg. Heading west from Winnipeg would take them into the Last Best West.

Henry mused, "Our people came from Kilkenny County, Ireland, aboard lumber ships back in '27. Now we will find the Last Best West."

Billie just stared ahead, wary of what might be around

every corner.

At one time lumber ships sailed in and out of the harbor with great frequency, but there was little business now back in England, and the ships were much less frequent in the harbor. In earlier times the harbour had been filled with spruce and pine logs, squared for masts to build British war and merchant ships.

Steamboats now provided passenger service, mail service, brought farmers to market, towed lumber barges downstream and transported politicians and dignitaries. Henry and Billie certainly were none of these. They were ready to sign on as crew and work their way down to Toronto. They waited patiently until a lumber barge was ready to be towed to Montreal. Their job was to pack the cargo tightly, then watch the barge to make sure the logs stayed fastened. It was extremely dangerous work, but the Bradley boys had spent their lives on the river, with logs and hooks, and it was second nature to them. This way they could work their way to Toronto and hold on to the small amount of cash they actually had.

Within the week, they had left Fitzroy Harbour. They had endured a week of hard labour on the barge, with hardly a moment to watch the coast slipping by, and finally sailed into Old Port, Montreal. By 1889 the industry had shifted, and Old Port, once alive with the lumber of the interior, was now strangely quiet. While they had worked the river all their young lives, the men had never had a reason to sail all the way to Montreal. Their steamship towed the barge into the port, and they were busy with the rest of the crew getting the logs secured. Once completed, they looked around at the port. It was huge, with wharves, warehouses, numerous steamboats, and Mount

Royal itself overlooking it. The cries of the longshoremen echoed among the buildings with a distinctive French sound.

"Billie, Billie, what a sight." Henry exclaimed, as he watched the beehive of activity happening in the harbor.

They walked the length of the port, marveling at the new train station and the train that would carry goods from this port west and east to the rest of Canada.

With their meagre earnings in their pockets, they searched out work, and luckily signed on again with the Canadian Steamship Lines, traveling to Toronto. The least they could sign on for was six weeks, and they worked the route between Montreal and Toronto as cargo crew. The money was minimal, it barely paid for their meals and lodgings on the ship, but it got them to Toronto without having to dig into their savings.

At the end of six weeks, they were able to take their leave.

"Finally, off the water and onto the rails" Henry, ever the optimist, smiled. Billie, as usual, said very little. He was worried about this crazy adventure that Henry had him on, but Henry was ever effusive about The Last Best West. He had talked incessantly to passengers on the steamboat. He did, after all, have the Irish gift of the gab, and it seemed there were many people emigrating from Ontario and all over Europe out to The North West Territories. The Government of Canada was providing land through the Dominion Lands Act and that was all Billie needed to hear.

in 1889, there was truly a sense of excitement in the air in Toronto. People from all over Europe and Eastern Canada were heading for the North West to claim the one hundred and sixty acres of homestead land offered by the Canadian government. The government was afraid that the Americans would move north and claim the empty Prairie lands, so a scheme had been put forward to offer immigrants one quarter section of practically free land.

The act gave a claimant the land for free, the only cost to the immigrant farmer being a $10.00 administration fee. Any male farmer who was at least twenty-one years of age and agreed to cultivate at least forty acres of the land and build a permanent dwelling on the land within three years, qualified. This condition of "proving up the homestead" was instituted to prevent speculators from gaining control of the land.

Free to begin their westward quest, the brothers made their way to the Parkdale C.P.R. office, where they purchased tickets to Winnipeg. They stood in line with people who had found their way to the train from many parts of Central Canada. All were looking for the "New Eldorado", the golden West! Many vendors had set up stalls outside the office with goods that the settlers might need. Henry and Billie were shocked to think about what they didn't have. They had a little bit of money, but when they looked at all the tools and supplies the vendors had laid out, they wondered what they would do. They each had a satchel with clothes, and that was about it. Each vendor had a story about what they would need and how much it would cost, and for the first time, Billie saw Henry look worried.

They walked around to the vendors time and time again, looking at farming tools and household goods. They had left Fitzroy with nothing but the clothes on their backs, and they were becoming aware that they had no idea what they would need when they claimed their quarter sections. What were they going to live in?

"I think we may be in for a tough time," Henry remarked as

they looked at the tools.

"We need more money," Billie replied gruffly. "How are we going to get ourselves set up out there?"

"Well, God knows we would be back in Fitzroy if there was work to be had" Henry responded heatedly. "We'll figure it out, we always have."

It was now July and the brothers decided to see if there was any work in Toronto. The train trip was postponed until they could find a little more money for setting up. It was cherry season and they found out they could pick fruit, so they signed on with a large cherry farm and picked cherries from before dawn into the midday. It wasn't much money, but it was some money, and by sleeping in the fields at night they were able to save their board.

"Never thought I'd be sleeping in a cherry orchard," Henry complained.

"Saves us money, and we have to be up so early it would be a waste to pay for a bed," Billie reminded him.

With assurance from other new settlers, Billie and Henry decided to wait until Winnipeg to outfit themselves. With a little bit more money in their pockets, the brothers headed out west. The train was loaded with people from all over Europe. For the first time in their lives, the brothers heard Ukrainian, Swedish, Russian and Danish. It was overwhelming for two Irish lads from Fitzroy but fascinating at the same time. They saw people dressed in clothing they had never seen. The Ukrainian families had brightly embroidered shirts and bright woven woolen belts. By comparison, the plain cotton clothes they wore were dull and dreary. The families had big wooden chests containing their belongings, and often large families with them as well. Billie and Henry felt a little lacking with their small duffle bags and just each other.

The boys had planned to stop in Winnipeg and see if there was any work to be had. They thought it might be good to stay in the area for harvest and find out if they could earn some money haying, or whatever other work was to be found. This might put a little more into their pockets for when they landed in Morleyville. Then they could go on to the Dominion Land Titles office and claim their quarter sections.

As they got off the train in Winnipeg, both Henry and Billie were filled with a sense of adventure. Winnipeg was nothing like their home in Fitzroy. It was a small city, surrounded by large farms of wheat. The boys looked for any kind of work in July, and they found out that indeed, men would be needed to help bring in the harvest. Henry managed to get work in a kitchen, and Billie found some spotty work in the blacksmith shops around the city. If it didn't rain, they were willing to sleep outside, only finding a roof over their heads when absolutely necessary.

It occurred to Henry not to waste Billie's prowess in the fighting ring, and he was able to put together a few matches against the locals, as Billie was the new kid in town. As always, Billie came up the winner, and this put some money into their fund. They even put the money into the bank in Winnipeg in case it might come to be stolen.

September found them part of a harvest crew, long days with a sharp sickle in hand. They cut the stalks just above the ground, then tied them into bunches to dry. It was exhausting labour, but it put much needed money into their account at the bank.

After six weeks of harvest, the work was done. The local farmers were able to think of relaxing after such hard labour, but Henry and Billie were happy to purchase their tickets for Morleyville. After much discussion with locals on the threshing crews, they each decided to buy a bridle, saddle and a rifle, as they were advised these would not be available where they were going. They were on to the last leg of their journey, and on to their new homesteads in The Last Best West. September was drawing to a close as they set out on the CPR.

CHAPTER 17

MORLEYVILLE AND BRUSHY RIDGE

1889

Calgary! The new heart of the golden west. Finally, mid-October brought Henry and Billie into the little town on the confluence of the Bow and Elbow rivers, to investigate their land claim. Calgary was mostly a muddy tent town, but some wooden structures had been built. The sturdy presence of Fort Calgary and the NWMP gave the brothers the impression that there was some sense of law and order here in the wild west. They wandered about until they found the Dominion Lands office and the Office of the Interior, which had grand sounding names but were little more than shacks.

"Well, it's hard to believe that's all it took," exclaimed Henry.

Billie looked around at the dismal little tent town, and muttered, "God only knows what we'll find …."

Henry then turned his thoughts to finding their properties. They had the land descriptions, so they set out to search for their new homes.

They discovered the train schedule, and bought tickets for

Morleyville, the closest settlement to their new land. Much like the journey out from Winnipeg, the train trip west of Calgary was punctuated by stops along the prairie, with often little more than a sign and small platform to greet them. As they continued west, they found large hills to the north and west. This was a surprise after thousands of miles of mostly flat prairie land. While they were craning their necks around from side to side to check out the hills, Henry happened to glance west, and he saw, for the first time, the outline of the Rocky Mountains.

"Billie, would you look at that." he exclaimed.

Billie turned his head around and was amazed to see a rugged outline against the prairie blue sky.

"Say, those are an amazing sight!" he replied. In fact, Billie could not take his eyes off the Rocky Mountains and watched with delight as the train moved ever westward and the mountains grew in size.

The hours and the little stops drifted slowly by, and finally Billie and Henry heard the sound of the conductor announcing, "Morleyville, Morleyville."

Billie and Henry looked at each other. By now the Rockies were filling the western sky with absolute majestic beauty, and the view to the north was that of rolling hills covered here and there with stands of poplar. The Bow River had meandered along out of the south windows, but not long before their stop, the train had traveled over a bridge and they had started following the river along the north side. The large hills now filled both sides of the train windows with a comforting closeness.

As the train pulled up to a stop, Billie and Henry had busily been moving their gear toward the doors. They had picked up some necessities in Calgary, but most of it was stowed in the freight cars at the back of the train. As the conductor opened the door, they mentioned they needed to retrieve gear from the freight section. The conductor led the way, and they moved to the rear of the train where they waited for him to pull open the door.

Their gear was stacked, much as they had left it, in a pile in the car. Two saddles and saddle bags, bedrolls and a trunk they had found for cheap in Calgary sat waiting for them to connect and start a new life. The trunk held flour, salt and baking powder for bannock, ammunition for the rifles they carried on their saddles, small pans for eating out of, and a cooking pot. Canteens for water, blankets and a few extra clothes filled up the rest of the trunk. Their winter coats were thrown over their arms, not quite needed yet in October.

Morleyville. There was so little there. They were relieved to find the stop-off house, run by Mrs. Taylor, who had come to Morleyville a few years earlier, in 1886, with her husband, William, and grown children.

"I wonder if so many people would be saying "Go West Young Man" if they knew what they would find when they got here," complained Henry. Billie was just relieved there seemed to be some inhabitants and a few buildings.

The boys unloaded their gear onto the platform, then watched the train chug off down the tracks, headed for Vancouver. They looked at each other, and Henry broke into his inevitable Irish grin.

"Well, here we are boy-o," he laughed. Billie answered with a weak grin of his own. While they were standing there on the platform, Mrs. Taylor bustled out of the stop-off house and hurried over to greet them. They heard her strong Suffolk accent in her speech as she welcomed them.

"Welcome to Morleyville! Do you speak English?"

"That we do, ma'am," Henry replied, while Billie looked on silently.

"To whom do we have the pleasure of addressing?" he began smoothly, pouring on his considerable Irish charm.

"I'm Mrs. Taylor, and I run the stop-off house here in Morleyville. You must be new homesteaders. Where are your wives? Left them back home while you came out to claim your land?" she finished with a dismissive wave of her hand, and not waiting for a reply, continued on,

"Well, don't stand about on the platform. Bring your gear over to the back sheds where you can store it, and I'll get you settled in the stop-off house. There is no place else to eat or sleep for miles. And if you don't have wives back home, good luck finding one out here. You'll be lucky to find a Stoney woman, if that's the case," she laughed, then turned around and headed for the log cabin stop-off house.

Billie and Henry looked at each other, then bent over to start picking up their gear to follow the formidable Mrs. Taylor.

Once the gear was stowed in the sheds which she had shown them, they walked over to the house and walked inside. The room had a dark, cozy feeling as there were only small windows cut into the log walls. Mrs. Taylor explained the arrangements, got them a room and let them know when meals could be purchased. While they were getting all this organized, Mrs. Taylor's son, Sykes, walked into the stop-off house.

"Come for supplies, Sykes?" his mother queried, as she filled in her register.

"Indeed, I have. Ridden overnight from my place in Springbank," he informed the brothers.

"Is it far from here?" asked Henry.

"A long two day's ride back down the river," Sykes replied.

"Do you know where this is?" Henry showed the land description papers to Sykes, who studied them carefully. After a minute or so, he replied,

"Oh yes, I think I could find that, and for a small consideration, I will do so" he replied.

It appeared part of the fee would include covering Syke's dinner costs, which the brothers divvied up between the two of them. They sat in a small parlour, listening to Sykes' tales of The Last Best West, while they waited for supper to be served.

Mrs. Taylor brought in venison stew and biscuits, then followed this up with more biscuits for dessert, only these were topped with sugar and served with Saskatoon-berry jam. Strong hot tea and sugar finished off the meal.

"Meat and flour are about all you'll get to eat out here," she informed them as she picked up the dinner plates, which were simple tin pans. "The saskatoons are what keep the Indians from getting sick, so you better eat them whenever you can find them," she instructed.

Billie and Henry knew they were going to need to learn a whole new survival game if they were going to make it in the truly wild west.

"The grass here is good for cattle and horses. That is what will make you a livelihood on your new land," Sykes informed them.

Henry had many questions for Sykes, and they sat long into the prairie evening, drinking tea and talking. Morleyville itself had been settled by the McDougall family, as a mission, by the Reverend George MacDougall in 1873. The area had once been the home of a Hudson's Bay Post, and the original mission had been built beside it. George, and his son, Reverend John McDougall, had moved it down the hill to its present home on the flats just north of the Bow. George's other son, David, had followed them out from Cobourg, Ontario, and he had set up a trading post and a ranche.

Morning brought a completely new experience to Henry and Billie, who had shared a bed at the stop-off house. October mornings were already very chilly, and they shaved with very cold water in a bowl in their room. The dash to the outhouse brought with it a view of the Rockies, dark, yet outlined in cold brilliance as the sun rose in the east and cast its first rays upon the sleeping stones.

Breakfast consisted of a large bowl of oatmeal and syrup, which David brought into the trading post and sold to the settlers. They found out that David also sold horses, which was going to be pretty important if they were going to be able to get to their land. David had originally brought horses to Morleyville from Fort Edmonton and had trailed cattle up from Montana. Geography lessons came hand-in-hand with survival lessons.

Sykes was present at breakfast as well and offered to introduce them to the Morleyville inhabitants.

After breakfast they made their way to the Trading Post to meet David McDougall. They were warmly welcomed, and the men began to inform the young greenhorns about what life in the North West Territories was all about.

The men borrowed horses from Mrs. Taylor and rode over

to the David McDougall ranche to look at his horses. David was interested to see that Henry was a sharp trader when it came to bargaining over the ponies. Now that they had horses, they would have the meagre beginnings of their new existence.

"Well, we've almost cleared out our savings, Billie" Henry complained after they left David McDougall.

At their lunch of venison stew and bannock, Sykes told them that he would introduce them to Andrew Sibbald, the teacher and builder at Morleyville. He ran a simple lumber business as well, as all local lumber required for building purposes had to be sawed by hand with a whipsaw. In order to saw lumber, he had erected a scaffold about seven feet high. The logs were first flattened on both sides, lined up with a chalk line to the thickness required, then placed on the scaffold and sawed by two men with a whipsaw. It was brutally hard work, but it was lumber work, and the young Bradley brothers knew all about lumbering. Andrew was happy to hire the two brothers to work at his lumber business. They both needed more money, and time to learn about how to become ranchers. They stayed on at the stop-off house, and went to work for Andrew Sibbald, cutting trees and making lumber from them.

When Sykes was ready to head back home, he agreed to take the brothers out to their new homesteads in Brushy Ridge. They saddled up their new horses, which had stayed on at David's ranche for a rental fee and followed Sykes across the river and south and west to the place where their land descriptions were to be found. All that was there was prairie grass and some insignificant stands of poplar. There were no trees for cutting lumber or cutting firewood. All the larger trees were closer to Morleyville, and the brothers could see it was going to be backbreaking work to haul wood to the homesteads. However, they were thrilled that they had found work and lodgings in Morleyville, and spent the winter bringing in trees and cutting lumber for Andrew Sibbald.

As the long and cold winter was drawing to a close, Henry wrote home to the Bradley family in Ontario.

March 17, 1889.

Dear Mother:

Our adventure to the North West Territories has been something you could never imagine in your wildest dreams. We live in a very small settlement called Morleyville, which is a mission for the Indians who live here. It is also the only trading post to buy supplies. We work at lumbering here for a man called Andrew Sibbald, who brought a whipsaw out from Ontario, and produces lumber for the new settlers in the area to build with. We hunt with our neighbors every week, bringing back ducks and geese in the autumn, then venison and elk for our winter food. There are no gardens, and meat and flour are our only staples. We have been taught to make bannock as well, a Scottish bread that is simple and filling. Mrs. Taylor, who runs the stop-off house, makes jam from the Saskatoon berries which are the only thing that grows wild and can be eaten here. It is a rare, but welcome addition to our diet when she brings some out.

Billie and I have been to our homesteads many times, which are a long day's ride from here. We will need to build some sort of living arrangement for ourselves in the spring, but alas, there are no trees to turn into lumber on our land. It is good grazing land, and we will need to one day buy horses and cattle to begin our lives here.

We miss our family and hope this letter finds you all in good health.

Your sons,

Henry and Billie Bradley

CHAPTER 18

MITFORD GROWS

1890 – 1891

Spring. I will be returning home, Adela thought with the greatest of pleasure. Once again, they had traveled pleasantly with Evelyn and Billie, each couple going their separate way in Calgary. Evelyn and Billie still had to travel overland as there was no train to The Little Bow River Cattle Company.

Once settled in, Thomas began to write Van Horne continually about getting a train station in Mitford. They felt they had really moved forward with a flag station, but knew they needed a proper station for people, mail and supplies for their town. Thomas felt that Cochrane was far too insignificant, and that the simplest thing to do was just to move the Cochrane Station to Mitford. He even offered to cover the expense of the land, a water tank, laying the pipe from the Bow River to the tank, as well as filling in Horse Creek, building a culvert and laying sidetrack. Thomas thought this was a very generous offer on his part, but Van Horne's attitude was now not as amenable as it first had been. He wrote Thomas a letter with the excuse that quite a little town had grown up at Cochrane, and that it would be wrong to simply ignore the rights of the people who were living there. He just couldn't ignore these people for the sole benefit of Mr. Cochrane. Thomas and Adela were flabbergasted that Van Horne would speak to them in such a manner.

"The cheek of the man," Thomas fumed.

Adela thought about it and remembered her meeting with Van Horne the previous year.

"These Americans are so different, Thomas. They have no understanding of the British system, and therefore, simply, no manners. It is always the loudest, rudest people that I meet here that turn out to be Americans. Mr. Van Horne is no different."

The sawmill and the mines continued to be plagued with problems. By the end of June, Thomas announced one night that they must return to England to meet with the Duke of Norbury right away. They had been in Mitford for so little time, Adela was crushed. For once, Thomas was sympathetic to her feelings.

"I know how you love it here, Adela, as do I. However, I must meet with Norbury in person. If things go well, we shall invite him back, as he will need to see what my proposal entails, here in Mitford. We shall return together as soon as possible." Adela could see that she had no choice and spent the next short while organizing the staff to stay on during the summer, without her.

The trip to England was shadowed over by the dire situation that Thomas' businesses were in. His mill was not producing enough lumber to make a profit, and his mines were producing inferior coal.

Thomas left immediately for Ireland to meet with Will Toler, Earl of Norbury, as soon as they returned, and Adela went straight to Henham Hall in Suffolk, to visit Mama and her younger sisters. Gwendoline was now the only unmarried sister. George had not yet married either. Not wanting to alarm them, she would only tell the family that important business needs had brought them back to England early, but that hopefully they would be leaving soon again for Canada.

Thomas spent most of July at William's estate in Ireland. At the end of their time together, Thomas had convinced William to invest in the companies again and had made travel arrangements for them to return in October. Adela remembered the coolness of the nights in late September and was wondering what it would be like in Mitford in October, but as this was something she hadn't done before, she decided it would be interesting to find out. Thomas came up to Suffolk for August, and they returned to Quarr Abbey for September. It was such a boring, sleepy little place which Adela did not enjoy much, but she always put her best foot forward when she was there. The Royal family was in residence, so Minna was there, and the Cochranes spent as much time with them as Minna could manage to arrange. Adela was always afraid that she would offend the Queen and found her time with the royal family very exasperating. Thomas, on the other hand, seemed to enjoy it immensely.

"I say, this had been a good change of scenery for me, Adela," he told her as they prepared to head back to Mitford.

"I am feeling much more positive about how things will go now that I have Norbury on board again."

"William is a dear man, I am very fond of him," Adela replied, but in the back of her mind she was thinking about their current situation. Thomas' previous business partners, even the St Maurs, had demanded to be bought out, and without William Toler, everything at Mitford would be a disaster. William was young and adventurous, like herself, and she hoped everything would finally turn around at Mitford and start going better, for all their sakes.

The first thing to be done upon their return to Mitford was to purchase the land containing the coal mines from the Dominion of Canada government. Secondly, William became a partner-investor in the Calgary Lumber Company, which Thomas had become sole proprietor of the year before. Adela was far too worried to mention it to Thomas, but she wondered what William thought when he could see that the mill was struggling so badly.

Adela busied herself with life in Mitford in October. She was amazed how cold the nights were. As the light shortened each day toward the end of the month, she found that riding was no longer the extreme pleasure that it was in warmer weather. If she wanted to visit her neighbours, she had to wait until the frost melted off the grass, as it was extremely slippery. By the third week of October, a snowstorm had set in. Now, snowstorms can happen on the prairie in almost any month of the year, but autumn snows had a very different feel to them than the spring snowstorms did. They could set in, and Adela could see why the buildings needed so much wood for their stoves for the winter. The floor of her house was freezing cold, and she hated to get out of bed in the morning, as night was the only time when her feet weren't freezing cold.

True to form, a warm Chinook wind blew in after about ten days. The Chinook was the Kutenai name for the warm snow-eater wind which changed the face of Mitford in two days, from white to drab prairie brown. The Chinook never ceased to amaze Adela, and she was grateful for it, like most of the prairie settlers.

Thomas and William busied themselves every day, putting the businesses in working order to the best of their ability, and by early November, before it got cold again, the Duke of Norbury and the Cochranes set off, back to England for the winter.

THE WINTER OF 1890 WAS not a happy time for Adela. Rosetta, Thomas' mother, had insisted that they spend Christmas with the royal family, as Minna had received an invitation from The Family to have Christmas with them. The Christmas season began with an invitation to the palace, to be part of a photograph of the Queen's daughters, that would become the Queen's Christmas card for the year. Christmas cards had become very popular due to Queen Victoria's interest in them. Lady Augusta was flabbergasted at her daughter Adela's good fortune and demanded to come along for the photo day. Much to her chagrin, Adela found herself dressed up like an angel, and bedecked in ropes of roses. Somehow, she managed to stand where the photographer placed her, and in the end, a lovely photo of all the young ladies and little girls was taken.

Adela, as always, felt like she had two left feet when she had to spend time around the royal family. They made her so anxious that she became clumsy, and usually tipped over a wine glass or dropped the salt-shaker, or something, every meal they shared. Rosetta always looked at her like she wished Adela would vanish off the face of the earth, when Adela showed her anxious clumsiness, and Thomas always sided with his mother on these occasions, which made Adela feel all the worse.

"If only I could run away and jump on my horse and ride out of here" she would fervently wish to herself dozens of times over the holiday.

MAMA WALKED AROUND THE GUEST parlor, where they were staying until the Christmas Eve and Christmas Day events at the palace, looking like the cat who had eaten the canary. There wasn't one social event in London that could top an inclusion at the royal Christmas, and Mama reminded her daily that they had made it to the ultimate in social status. The Countess of Stradbroke had spent her life climbing the social ladder, and here, her daughter, Adela, had provided her with that which she had sought her whole life to achieve. Mama was ecstatic.

"Never in all my life dared I hope I would have this honour, Adela," she would say each morning, after they had finished their breakfasts in bed.

"All of London is aware that Lady Adela Cochrane, and her mama, the Countess of Stradbroke, will be at the Queen's family Christmas this year. I now can die a happy woman. I have achieved all my life goals, and this final and most splendid goal is all because of you," she beamed.

"I am so pleased that this makes you so happy, Mama," Adela began. "Please be sure to stay close to me, as you know I will likely fall, or break a glass, or embarrass all of you in some way."

The Queen's Christmas card was sent out, and of course, Countess Stradbroke received hers, and she had placed it with reverence on her mantle, which was decorated beautifully for Christmas.

"Aren't photographs amazing, Adela?" she mused, glancing adoringly again and again at the photo of the rose-bedecked Adela standing amongst the clouds with all of the other Queen's little angels.

Adela thought she had never seen herself look so ridiculous. She was never really sure why Queen Victoria requested her presence, but she felt it had something to do with the stories of Mitford that she was able to share with the Queen. Victoria had never been to Canada, but she was keenly interested in hearing all about it from anyone who had been there.

Luckily, the only time she was really required to be in the royals' presence was during the Christmas Eve service, and for Christmas dinner the next day. Queen Victoria and Prince Albert had had such a large family that the dining hall was filled, and Adela and Lady Augusta were seated far away from the Queen, so Adela relaxed and actually enjoyed herself at the Christmas meal. Rosetta Cochrane watched her like a hawk, waiting for Adela to do something clumsy, and Adela could not even rely on her own Mama for support, as Countess Stradbroke was enraptured watching everything that was going on and paid Adela absolutely no attention whatsoever.

Thomas, and his mother Rosetta, sat at the table looking as puffed up as peacocks. They were immensely impressed with their royal connections, and managed a hauteur that Adela found ridiculous. Adela would have liked to tell Thomas to stop acting like such a fool, but it was wonderful to see him enjoying himself and smiling, instead of wearing the eternal grim face he usually had on because things were not getting any better at Mitford.

Thomas had a lumber company that was producing no lumber, and coal pits producing small quantities of inferior coal. Transportation difficulties thwarted his operations continually. Today, however, he looked like the great adventurer who had built a business empire and a town in the New World. Dozens of gentlemen stopped by the table to hear about the fantastic life he had built in Canada. Some of their wives stopped by as well, asking Adela what life was like in the wild lands of Canada. Adela was only too happy to talk about her dear Mitford, and soon quite a crowd had gathered around them to hear their tales. Mama Rous and Mama Cochrane sat watching on, completely amazed by the social success their children had brought upon them. Of course, it really was Minna Cochrane, as Lady-in-Waiting to Princess Beatrice, who had started all of this.

"I must say," Rosetta started, and turned to Mama Rous, "I really must say that I am completely amazed by what my children have done with their lives. My darling Minna has managed to become Princess Beatrice's confidante, and my son Thomas has braved the difficulties of the New World and is building a business empire and his own town. Could a mother possibly be any prouder of her children's achievements?" She practically purred.

"Adela has been exceptionally lucky to marry into your most incredible family," Mama Rous agreed.

"She doesn't know a thing!" Adela thought angrily to herself, thinking about all the difficulty they were having with the businesses. Or Thomas was having with the businesses. He only allowed Adela to be slightly connected with what was happening, and obviously, he had not kept his mama informed on the true reality of events in Canada.

With agonizing slowness, the party dragged on, and the conversation dragged on, with people continually stopping by to hear their tales. Adela was beginning to think they would have to sleep at the castle soon. However, with a great suddenness, Queen Victoria stood up and wished them all Happy Christmas and retired for the night. This was the cue to leave the room, and all the lords and ladies started to make their way to the coat room to get their winter apparel.

Rosetta and Thomas continued their walk of arrogance to retrieve their coats, completely ignoring Adela and Countess Stradbroke.

"My, my, aren't they very important tonight?" the Countess remarked snidely to Adela.

Adela chose to say nothing, as she could think of nothing to say. Finding her way home and into bed was the only thing on her mind.

The Cochranes returned to the Isle of Wight and Quarr Abbey, and soon after Christmas a letter arrived from Canada for Thomas. It was from the Board of Officers of the RCMP at Regina. In their opinion, Thomas' coal was about half waste and produced very little heat. They also stated it was downright dangerous due to its explosive properties.

Thomas was furious when he received the letter and ranted and raved at Adela over the bad luck he had. There was very little she could say. All she could think of was the cow boss she had met when she came to the Little Bow River Cattle

Company the first time, and how he had been so knowledge-able about the cattle. She wanted to say to Thomas that they should have found a "coal boss" before they went ahead with the mines, someone who might have been able to discern if the coal was good or not. By now she knew that making comments like this would only bring on a barrage of insults and invective from Thomas, so she stayed mute upon the matter.

Each week that winter brought another letter from unhappy customers in Canada. The CPR wrote almost weekly to complain about the inferior quality of the coal, and finally, a letter arrived from Van Horne stating that they would no longer buy any more of the inferior quality coal that Thomas was producing.

Thomas was continually in a state of rage or remorse, and preferred to turn to his mother for solace, rather than Adela.

At first, she burned with resentment and shame that her husband was not turning to her, but eventually she became resigned to the fact that this was who Thomas was. At least, she thought to herself, she was spared from having to deal with his constant complaining.

Yet, with the coming of spring, Thomas was anxious to get back to Canada and to see what was happening at Mitford, so they left Quarr Abbey and traveled back to their home. That was completely how Adela felt about it. Mitford was her home. She wished she could stay there year-round and avoid the tiresome and boring Isle of Wight. The only time she enjoyed herself at all in England was when she could travel up to London to stay at the Rous townhouse, where hopefully George or her sisters or even her Mama would be visiting. Sometimes she travelled to Henham Hall to visit Mama as well, as this gave her respite from what was becoming an intolerable home at Quarr Abbey.

> *February 4, 1890. How very different my life has become. In fact, I feel really like I have two completely separate lives. Mitford and the Isle of Wight could not be more different. Canada and England, while one being child and the other mother, are most dissimilar. My life at Mitford fills me with bliss, while my life in England fills me with dread. When I am in Mitford, I never look back to England for one minute, and when I am in England, I can only look forward to the time that I will once again be in my happy home abroad.*

CHAPTER 19

MITFORD, 1892

IMPROVEMENTS

Adela had a creeping sense of anxiety. After their exceptional success at the Queen's Christmas, Thomas and Rosetta Cochrane spent a few weeks behind closed doors at Quarr Abbey, apparently having serious discussions about something. Thomas did not offer one word of explanation to Adela, and she had learned not to ask. As usual, she escaped to the stables and daily riding, come rain or come shine, to fill the monotonous hours at Quarr Abbey. Quite often, Minna would arrive for these meetings, or the three of them would go out while Adela was riding and would say nothing about their affairs upon their return.

One evening at dinner, Rosetta rose, wine glass in hand.

"I would like to raise a toast to my dear son, Thomas. His businesses are experiencing some growing pains right now, and at my suggestion, he has agreed to take on the work of Lieutenant-Governor of the Isle of Wight alongside Princess Beatrice, the Governor. Congratulations on another great victory, my son." Minna had been there for dinner as well, and all the Cochrane ladies lifted their glass to Thomas.

"To Thomas!" they toasted.

Adela's mind was in a whir. So, this is what they had been up to. Her heart sank and stomach tightened. Adela felt Minna's influence with the Royals must have been used to procure this position for Thomas. This simply did not feel good at all. Her immediate fear was that Thomas was going to pull out of Mitford.

Thomas rose and beamed at his mother and sister, and completely ignored Adela.

"Dear Mama and Minna. How wonderful it is to know that I will have something to help ease the ennui of the winters. I shall have to spend a little more time here in England; however, I look forward to yet another challenge in my life. This island has always been my home, and when I return, I want to make a contribution to it. To the Isle of Wight" he gushed and raised his own glass in a toast.

Adela felt slightly better after hearing that Thomas wanted something to do in the winter. She could understand that, as it was exceedingly boring here compared to their life at Mitford. She breathed a little sigh of relief, but that too was to be short lived.

As they retired to their room for the evening, Adela noticed a flush creeping up Thomas' neck, from his collar to the roots of his hair. He slammed the door to their room and began pacing, a behavior she had witnessed so often when things weren't going well with the businesses, which was almost always.

He turned to face Adela, and with a look of disgust,

started yelling.

"And you, why have you not produced a son?"

Adela was so flabbergasted that she didn't know what to say. He continued to rant at her.

"What have I done in my life to deserve all this ill-luck? My timber leases have no trees, my coal is inferior, and my wife is barren. If I could at least have a son, I would be able to find some comfort in my situation. But the great Lady Adela is barren, and I have no child. My poor Mama! Minna cannot marry, or she would lose her position. It is up to me to carry on the Cochrane legacy, and my bloody wife cannot become pregnant."

Adela simply sat on the edge of the bed staring at him, not having any idea what to say. To her credit, she did not break down in tears, although she would have loved to, but she was not going to give Thomas the satisfaction of that. When she managed to get her emotions under control, and said, levelly,

"I know it has been four years Tom, but babies come in their own time. I have far from given up hope that I will yet fall pregnant and produce an heir for you. I am still young and have many productive years ahead of me."

"Well, I certainly hope that you don't turn out to be yet another one of my great disappointments," he continued viciously.

"I have every hope for that as well," Adela replied.

Thomas' countenance softened, as it so often did after an outburst, and he approached her at the bed and placed his hands on her shoulders.

"Well, we can't fix the pregnancy problem without doing something to encourage it" he smiled and began to undo the buttons at her neck.

Adela smiled, relieved that the rant had been short lived. However, she knew that seeds of discontent had been sown in Thomas' heart. She wondered if they had been started by Rosetta, who really did not seem to like her, or if it was Thomas' own discontent that she had heard.

After, she lay awake for hours, crying silently, and praying that perhaps this time she had conceived and that she would be able to produce an heir.

AS ALWAYS, ADELA PREPARED TO return to Mitford with anticipation and excitement. She was always so happy to leave the Isle of Wight and Quarr Abbey, and happy to be heading to Mitford.

In 1890, Thomas had decided to expand his businesses again, this time with a brick yard. Thomas had been busy starting up the brickyard and hiring a brick master, thank goodness, a Mr. John Cooper. After they were settled in that spring, Thomas took stock of the three primitive kilns and the drying sheds and pondered on how to improve his business. His ongoing difficulty with Van Horne and the CPR had not changed, and he was still having difficulty getting them to agree to give him a decent rate to carry the bricks to market in Vancouver. He continued to attempt to negotiate a cheap rate, but the CPR could not understand why they should carry inferior quality bricks to market in Vancouver, which was already well supplied.

It appeared 1891 was not going to show an improvement in the positive side of the ledgers. None of the businesses were profiting, but Thomas and Adela were far from giving up. Their town now had one hundred and fifty people and was the largest settlement in the area. This made them extremely proud. Thomas was very busy with the businesses and had high hopes now that a brickyard was being constructed. His bitterness over the mill and coal mine had abated and, for a while, he was the hopeful Thomas of their earlier years.

One morning as they returned from their morning ride, they sat on the hill above the town and surveyed its expansion.

"Oh, how I do love the sight of our Mitford," Adela declared happily from the back of her horse.

"It is a beautiful sight," Thomas agreed. "When the businesses are running at full tilt it will continue to expand and bring more and more people to live here.

Adela continued to pour most of her efforts into improving the town of Mitford. She visited with the shop keepers and the hotel manager, always seeking to find out if there was anything she could do to improve their situations. If they were struggling, she helped. If they were running short on cash, she set up loans. If she was fishing and having a great catch day, she would drop trout off at the hotel kitchen. She invited the doctor for tea and worked tirelessly to set up all the needs of her church. She wrote letters constantly, to Aunty Em Mitford describing Mitford and the Anglican church and asking for donations. She wrote to her half-sister Edith, nursing in Tasmania, to Susan St, Maur, keeping her up to date on Mitford's progress, and always back to Henham Hall, to both Mama and George. Mitford was her love and her joy, and unlike the business ventures, Mitford continued to prosper and grow. In 1889 it had boasted a population of one hundred. In 1890, this had grown to one hundred and fifty people.

Adela was so proud of her town and delighted to be its patroness.

Since 1888, the Mitford Arms hotel had served as a community center, and was home to the rifle association, the Bachelors' Ball and the Cochrane Races. Adela attended the rifle association meetings happily when she was in Mitford, and usually Thomas attended too, although, depending on the climate of his business and the resulting mood of the men, sometimes it was better if he did not attend.

The men of Mitford were always very courteous to Lady Adela and were happy to have her at their meetings. They were comfortable having discussions with her around the needs for the growing town, and knew she always had their best interests at heart and would go to great lengths to try and mitigate whatever needed to be done. This was not the feeling they got from Thomas.

The Bachelor's Ball was greatly enjoyed by all the residents of Mitford and area, including the Cochrane residents. Adela, of course, would have stayed away from balls if at all possible, but seeing how much the residents of her town enjoyed it, she could hardly deprive them of this entertainment. It took a great deal of time to find musicians who would be able to play, and quite often Adela herself would play piano. During the long, boring winters on the Isle of Wight, she would practice music that she purchased in London that was suitable for dancing. The people of Mitford loved it when she would play a few reels or waltzes, and the dance floor would be packed. Everyone would dance, and as there were always more men than women, quite often the men would partner up and dance together.

Adela tried to imagine something like that happening back in England. She could see in her mind's eye the horrified looks on faces of the Victorian aristocracy should anything like have occurred. It made her laugh and laugh.

The highlight of the summer was the Mitford-Cochrane Races, which Adela and Thomas created in 1893. On May 20, a general meeting was held, and Thomas was elected the president of the races. The Earl of Norbury was, of course, elected the Secretary Treasurer, and many of the local ranchers signed on to be committee members. One hundred dollars was donated in Mitford alone. This sporting event was held at Mitford on the high ground above the town. It was flat and made a great spot for racing the various ranche ponies and other horses in the area. It was definitely the highlight of Adela's summer life every year, and far more fun for her to plan than the Bachelors' Ball.

Adela loved to race herself. Various races were set up, such as the Quarter Mile Dash, the Green Horse Race, the Local Horse Race, the Indian Race and, of course, the Ladies Race. The horses raced around a rough track that was really just a prairie field but marked out properly with a rail around the entire track. She had the local carpenters build stands, and every man, woman and child from miles around turned out to watch the various riders compete. Adela wrote numerous letters to her old foe, William Van Horne, and he reluctantly agreed to set up a Special Train from Calgary to bring people to the races. Many brought tents and slept overnight just to be ready for the start. Adela purchased a silver trophy, and the Mitford Cup was presented to the final winner. At the end of the races, a huge picnic happened, which was often interrupted by the inevitable summer afternoon prairie thunderstorm. Everyone would duck inside any available shelter, and as soon as the pelting rain stopped, everyone emerged to continue with the picnic. Then, in the evening, the Mitford Arms and surrounding outdoor area was home to the Race Ball, which was really just a country hoedown.

The Mitford Arms was also home to the school. Adela was first raising funds to have the church built, and upon its completion, she would start fund raising for a proper school. Miss Isabelle Monilaws from Bruce County, Ontario, was hired by Adela, in 1891, to teach school. The Cochranes had stopped in Toronto long enough to put a posting in the newspaper looking for a teacher, and Miss Monilaws had applied. Overjoyed that an educated woman would agree to come to her town, Adela hired her and set about making sure she was well set up at the Mitford Arms as her living accommodation. Miss Monilaws taught at the Mitford school for four years until she was persuaded by Mr. Cooper to marry him. As young European women were a scarce commodity in Mitford, Adela was surprised Isabelle had lasted that long. However, Adela was very proud that hers was the only school between Morleyville and Calgary and had twenty students attending. The boys could be a real handful, and at noon hour would sneak out to put large rocks on the tracks to derail the train. As they were needed to help get the train back on the tracks, this afforded them an entire afternoon off school. Another task required of all the students was to first clean up all the bottles and glasses from the previous night's activities so that school could commence for the day.

Of course, the greatest of her achievements was happening

this year, enough funds had finally been collected in England, and the All Saints Anglican Church was to be built. Adela had convinced a British church carpenter to come all the way to Mitford, and with the help of the local carpenters, work on the church began.

It was a tiny little church; one hundred people would be hard pressed to fit in, but it would suit the town of Mitford just fine. They chose a bluff on the east bank of Horse Creek as home for the church. Eventually, the people of Mitford were able to celebrate each Sunday, and also commemorate weddings and baptisms. Adela's house staff christened both their daughters, Violet and Nora, who were born in Mitford, in the church.

BY THIS TIME, MITFORD ALSO had a general store, known as the Mitford Emporium, a butcher, livery stable and the post office. The post was often intermittent, depending on the mood of William Van Horn and the various engineers, as the train did not always stop to drop off the mail. Often, the conductor would just throw the mailbag out the window, or when the train refused to stop, the postmaster had to ride the three miles into Cochrane to pick it up at the Cochrane station.

But Mitford, unlike Thomas' businesses, was thriving. Adela would wake each morning, and regardless of the weather, walk around the town and check up on each building and all the inhabitants. This was her town, and she loved every single nook and cranny, every gopher and crow, every horse and every buggy. When she was at Mitford, she did not have a care in the world. She would wake up to the beautiful, bright morning sun, saddle her horse and ride out while the frost was still on the grass, slippery though it might be. She would follow the river west with her fishing rod, and with a little luck, snag a few trout to bring home to cook for breakfast. Her ponies and her dogs were her constant companions, and they kept her days filled with love. Thomas was usually tied up with his own business affairs, so they saw each other only infrequently. Life often had an idyllic quality to it that she savored every day.

May 22, 1892. Great and glorious is this wonderful land that I call home. My little town of Mitford is an industrious village of hard-working people from all over, and, like I, they work toward building a wonderful future in this Dominion of Canada. The glorious Rocky Mountains wake me each morning, calling me to come and observe their vast glory and splendor. The beauty of the Bow twinkles in the bright morning light, happily babbling toward the east, and providing me with my delicious breakfast. The thunderstorms are not far off, and likely a good snowfall will happen before winter has her last hurrah with us. Each day brings forth something new and wonderful, and life could not be more splendid. Mitford, you are my love.

CHAPTER 20

A TENT HOME IN BRUSHY RIDGE

1892

They were pioneers. Henry and Billie Bradley had become accustomed to the vast distances between their homesteads, and the three small settlements in the area. Their first home on the prairie, Morleyville, was a comforting place to return to. David McDougall's trading post carried supplies, Andrew Sibbald had work for them, and as work was none too easy to find, they could come and use the whipsaw to produce lumber and make some sorely needed capital. They worked together with the whipsaw to cut their own logs that they had felled and pulled out of the trees, behind their saddle horses. Andrew was a master carpenter and helped them to build small frames on the prairie to which were attached canvas upper walls that met overhead in a tent formation. These prairie tents were often the first dwellings the homesteaders were able to put up on their land.

By working for Andrew, they both were able to save a little and purchase a wood stove each. Over the long summer evenings, they rode north of Morleyville into the spruce forests in the foothills, as the hills of the area were called due to the fact that they were at the foot of the mountains and hauled out logs for firewood. They dried, split and cut measures, then hired out a local with a wagon to pile the firewood onto and to haul it out to the homesteads. It got very lonely living in their separate tents, so quite often they would ride over to the other's place and stay over for a while to ease the loneliness. The rough-cut logs were also made into beds and tables and chairs. Some rough shelves were also fashioned and nailed to the log base structure to house their meagre belongings. A large tin flour bin kept the rodents out of the flour. Their homes were extremely simple, and not the warmest when the temperatures dropped to twenty below and colder. However, coyote pelts sewn together with gut made warm winter blankets. Almost everything they needed to acquire here was new to them and required some instruction as to how to adapt the meagre supplies. That was the amazing thing about the hardy folk who were settling in the area. Most brought skills from the old country, to the new, and these were shared easily with neighbours, as there were so few people that it was imperative to swap skills, knowledge and labour in order to just stay alive. All neighbours were friends.

It had taken two years for the brothers to get livable dwellings, and during that time, other hardy settlers claimed their quarters and began to build dwellings of their own. The brothers traveled by horseback to both Mitford and Cochrane as well. Mitford was by far the best of the new settlements. The lumber yard and the new brickyard built by Mr. Thomas Cochrane sometimes had work, and if no work was available, there was the wonderful Mitford Arms to settle comfortably into for a night or two of rather unreserved drinking. Mitford had pretty much everything a body could need, and there was the Bachelors' Ball and Mitford Races to attend to enjoy some sorely needed social activity.

After a few days visit to Mitford, Billie was saddling up his horse at the rail fence to ride back home, when Lady Adela came striding out of the Mitford Arms.

"Good day, Pioneer" she called. "Whom do I have the pleasure of addressing?"

"My name is Billie Bradley," he replied very shyly, for after all, he knew exactly who she was and that she was Lady Adela Cochrane.

"Glad to know you, Billie. Where do you come from?"

It was the question asked of everyone by everyone, for no one came from there, except the Indians.

"Fitzroy Harbour, in Ontario," he replied

"Oh ho. You are already a Canadian. Do you live in Mitford?"

No ma'am," he replied, "I live on my homestead in Brushy Ridge, next to my brother's quarter."

"Right you are, my fine fellow. And if you are looking for employment, please check out the brickyard Mr. Cochrane, my husband, is building." Adela said.

"I would be happy to ma'am," Billie replied gratefully.

COCHRANE HAD ITS SMALL RAILROAD station, much to Lady Adela's dismay, but had very little else of interest to Henry and Billie. And Lady Adela was having the church built this year. As good Irish Catholics (well maybe not so good), Billie and

Henry weren't that excited about the Anglican Church, but it did provide another social event each week, which was something the young men enjoyed.

FOR BILLIE AND HENRY, IT was essential that they find a way to begin to get their homesteads to produce some income. The land was prime for raising livestock, so the early years of their lives were set about earning enough money to buy cattle and horses. Like Lady Adela, they purchased laying hens, then had to work very hard to protect them from predators and the killing prairie cold in the winter.

Any money they were able to earn had to be invested in their ranches, so they were not able to improve their living quarters at all. Henry had not forgotten his promoter ways, and occasionally he and Billie would ride into Cochrane or Mitford to see if they could find someone to take on the fearsome Billie, The Strongman, Bradley in a bare-knuckle brawl. They usually made a little cash on these fights, which was added to the meagre sums they could scrape together to build their cattle and horse herds.

Billie was an incredibly strong man, and it became known that he could lift up very heavy objects. Henry, never one to waste an opportunity, would ride into Cochrane or Mitford on a Saturday night with Billie. They would have a few drinks in the Mitford Arms, then Henry would start his promoting

"I hear there is a new blacksmith in town who thinks he is pretty strong. Well, he can't touch Billie Bradley" and on and on Henry would continue until he had the bets in, and a contest would start. Often, Henry would have them enter a lazy stick pull with Billie. "Maide Leisg" which is Gaelic for

'Lazy Stick', involved a test of strength performed by two people sitting on the ground with the soles of their feet pressing against each other. Thus seated, they each would grab the stick and pull against one another until one was raised from the ground. Billie was almost always the winner.

After a few drinks, Henry could always get the men of Mitford or Cochrane going on who could beat Billie Bradley, who became known around the area as Billie, the Strongman.

Well, Billie became so well known that everyone was trying to come up with opponents who could beat him. Billie even had a horse as his opponent. If the horse was too heavy, it would win, but if Billie could lift it up, Billie would be the winner. Billie won almost every time, and his reputation as Billie, the Strongman, and Billie, the Bare-Knuckle Fighter, kept opponents coming to challenge him. This managed to expand the purse of the Bradley brothers and help them buy cattle and horses. It also provided some sorely needed entertainment to the men of Mitford and Cochrane.

Life was nothing but hard in the early days; however, for Billie, he owned his own quarter section and was building a ranche business, literally from nothing. He didn't expect to get rich quick, but he knew that he could slowly build up his own ranche and be his own man. That was enough for him. Except, of course, for having a family. It was doubly difficult for a man to be a bachelor, as the ranche wife put in a great deal of sweat equity into a ranche operation. She was there to assist with everything that needed doing, and also tended to the household and made meals. Billie could certainly see this would be an asset, and he and Henry, like all the single men who had headed out to claim land, were always looking for possible candidates for wives.

Because of their friendships with Reverend McDougall and Andrew Sibbald, Billie and Henry had met some of the Stoney women who lived in the area. The Stoney had been a nomadic people, living in their tribal territory, but after Treaty 7 was signed in 1877, the Stoney lands had been set aside as a reserve, including Morleyville. But try as they might, neither man could quite imagine setting up a ranche with a Stoney girl as his wife, and they instead waited for more immigrant families to come to the area and bring their daughters with them.

By the mid 1890's, Henry was finding that the adventure of the West was not sustaining him quite like he wanted. He was tired of the endless struggle to keep going, of the difficulty of all the natural elements and of not having a wife. He started writing more and more letters back to Ontario to the Bradley family to keep in touch with how things were going in Fitzroy Harbour. His younger sister Sarah always wrote back about the family and community news in Fitzroy Harbour, and these letters were very welcome entertainment for both Billie and Henry.

Neither Billie nor Henry were particularly religious, but they were both very pleased when Lady Adela built her church. Sunday morning services brought all the settlers together, and Billie and Henry loved to head into Mitford for a night at the Mitford Arms, then a groggy and headache-filled trip to either All Saints Anglican, or up to Morleyville to Reverend McDougall's church, for services. These were the only times they had social interaction, and truth be told, life on their ranches was very, very lonely.

Both men had even taken up reading the Bible, as it

was often the only entertainment they had to fill their lonely evenings.

TOWARDS THE END OF THE decade, back in Europe, Britain had entered into yet another war with the Boer states in Southern Africa. The southern part of the African continent was dominated in the 19th century by a set of epic struggles to create within it a single unified state. British expansion into southern Africa was fueled by three prime factors: first, the desire to control the trade routes to India that passed around the Cape; second, the discovery in 1868 of huge mineral deposits of diamonds around Kimberly on the joint borders of the South African Republic (called the Transvaal by the British), and thirdly the race against European colonial powers as part of a general colonial expansion in Africa.

The British wished to maintain influence in South Africa, and so by 1899, were once again at war with the Boer, and this time, they planned to win. After a surprising early offensive by the Boer, who took three cities, the British sent in massive amounts of soldiers. These soldiers needed horses and sent requisitions to all ends of the British empire to buy horses for the war.

The Boer War was a great opportunity for horse producers, and Billie Bradley was delighted that he could sell every last horse he could raise to the British Boer War effort. It made up in a very small way for the fact that Henry had decided to give up and leave Brushy Ridge.

One night, Henry had ridden over, as he often did, to spend the night with Billie. When he came riding into the yard, Billie heard him and went outside his tent home. He helped Henry get his horse settled for the night in his barn. The men had built barns as these were essential to their ranching operations, but the cost of these had been great and the necessary funds to build even small cabins had not been found. Billie could see from the look on Henry's face that something was amiss. While he boiled up water in a kettle for tea on his wood burning stove, he waited patiently for Henry to tell him what was on his mind.

Henry pulled out a letter from Fitzroy Harbour, and Billie's face lightened up for a minute. He always enjoyed news from home. But Henry's countenance didn't change, and Billie just waited for Henry to start talking.

"Billie, me boyo, I have been doing some thinkin'. Sarah writes and tells me that things have improved a fair bit back in Fitzroy Harbour, and that there is even lumber work to be had again. She also tells me that there has been more new immigration from Ireland as the families have been telling their relatives back in Ireland that there is work again. Oh, Billie, I long for a town to live in again, and a fair Irish colleen to be on my arm on the way to Mass on Sunday morning. I have been done in by the loneliness and hardship of this land, and I want to go home."

"Henry, are you really thinking of giving up and going back?" Billie asked quietly.

"Yes, I am Billie. I have been thinking about it for a long while now. I have saved up my train fare, and I plan to sell out every horse in my herd while the British army is buying. Then, I'll sign the ranche over to you, and you can have a half section rather than a quarter.

Billie was very quiet as he really didn't know what to say.

He knew it was a hard life here, but he watched it grow better, even if only in a very small way, each year. He just couldn't believe Henry was going to give up.

"I'm not the Strongman, Billie, that is you. I just want to go home and leave this God forsaken prairie for forever."

"Well, Brother Henry, if that is what you must do, then God bless you on your way," Billie replied. "You know, of course, that it will be terribly hard on me to be here alone, but I will not give up on this dream. This is my home now, and I am going to find a wife someday and have a family here. I'm not giving up," he whispered, as if to reassure himself that this was the right thing to do.

True to his word, Henry sold off his livestock, then took the train to Calgary with Billie reluctantly alongside, and once there, signed over his land to Billie. He returned to put together what he would take back. The saddle, rifle and clothes he brought out were much the same items he prepared to take back to Fitzroy Harbour.

Billie had to ride over with his team and democrat, and collect Henry at his tent house, because Henry didn't have a horse to get to Cochrane to pick up the train. He did have more cash in his wallet than when he and Billie had set out, and this at least would help him get set up back home in Ontario.

As they sat in silence waiting for the train, each was remembering the near decade of life they had shared in the Last Best West, and the good and bad times that these had been. Then the train pulled into the station from the west, the doors opened, and Billie helped Henry put his saddle and pack onto the train. With a quick embrace so that they did not let out the despair each of them was feeling, Billie stepped back off the train onto the platform at Cochrane Station, and the doors closed on Henry's great adventure in the West. Billie watched the train depart to the east until it had pulled out of sight, then walked back to his horse and democrat with his head hung low. He could hear Henry's wonderful Irish laughter in his ears, egging on the men to place bets on one of Billie's feats of strength. He certainly didn't feel like much of a strongman at that moment, when all he really wanted to do was cry at the loss of his brother.

Billie rode home in silence, as the horse was not much of a conversationalist, and went through the motions of putting away the horse and buggy. He wandered over to the chickens, and rustled up a few eggs, which he took into the tent house. He cut a few chunks of salt pork into his fry pan, then finished up with frying the eggs. He sat down with his dinner and his kettle of tea, and finally let the tears spill that he had been fighting all day. The Last Best West without Henry in it was going to be a very lonely place.

CHAPTER 21

THE BEGINNING OF THE END

1892-1898

The ongoing battle with William Van Horne and the C.P.R. to get a station at Mitford was not getting any easier for Thomas and Adela Cochrane. Thomas sent many repeated letters to Van Horne suggesting options. Ironically, in 1892, Van Horne had been considering moving the station in Cochrane a short distance from its original location, so Thomas pounced on this idea and sent off a new offer to Van Horne. On March 15, 1892, he offered Van Horne a compromise -- he would give Van Horne a site some few miles east of Mitford, of land he had filed under the homestead act. He would offer level land both south and north of the tracks for the buildings to be built on. He would then move the Mitford Arms, school, post office and store closer to the new station site and build a ferry across the river. This would allow Cochrane and Mitford to unite and form a new small town.

Adela had to admit that this was the best argument Thomas had ever sent William Van Horne, and she couldn't see how he could possibly disagree. This would cost the C.P.R. very, very little, and the Cochranes would have to bear the cost of moving their town and its operations. While Adela loved Mitford where it was, she knew that the station was the lifeline they would need to keep Mitford alive. In fact, to her it seemed like her beautiful town was actually ill, and that it would soon start to die. A railway station was the help it needed.

She thought back to those glorious days when they had first come to the confluence of the Bow and Horse Creek, where they had purchased their property, and how they had been so excited to build their town. All they had thought about was that they would have ample water at this spot. They had never considered all the difficulties that this spot actually posed to becoming a real town. Their childish over-enthusiasm mocked her now as she waited in dread to hear if Van Horne would concede and accept their more than generous proposal. He had to accept it, he just had too. Like a mother with a sick child, Adela could feel the death rattle starting in her town and it filled her with dread.

Thomas and Adela were going about their preparations to leave the Isle of Wight for Mitford in April. They were quite pleased to receive a reply from Van Horne on March 22, 1892, as this was only a week after Thomas' latest request. In the reply, Van Horne was polite, yet firm. He responded with: "This matter has been under consideration a number of times and after carefully looking into it, we found so many objections to it from an operating standpoint that we were reluctantly compelled to decide against the change."

Adela expected Thomas to fly into a rage, his usual response to Van Horne. Instead, he just threw the letter to the ground in disgust and headed for the library at Quarr Abbey, where he managed to finish off a bottle of fine French Cognac, while he stared out the windows in bitter disappointment.

Adela went to her sitting room and threw herself down on her chaise lounge. She knew that Thomas' offer had been realistic, and that the area would not cause the C.P.R. operating difficulties. The land offered to the C.P.R. was as flat and easy for the train as the land around Cochrane. And combining the two towns would work well for the inhabitants. There were likely still some challenges to be overcome, but it was clear that the C.P.R. did not believe in the business success of Mitford, and that, she had to admit, was for obvious reasons.

Thomas had hoped that a brick yard could improve his business situation, yet sadly, like many of his previous businesses, his lack of knowledge about the brick making business had caused this venture as well, to be far from successful.

Still, she instinctively knew what was wrong. Van Horne did not like the Cochranes and was not going to oblige them in any way. He did not give a care for the town of Mitford nor its inhabitants. They needed him, but he, unfortunately, did not need them, nor their town.

Well, Adela was not going to sit around and let him get away with it. While Thomas was becoming bitter and resigned, she was becoming angry and protective of her town and its people. Thomas wrote a response to Van Horne in which he threatened that without the station his company would likely have to close Mitford and that a lot of money invested by "a great many influential English people" would likely be lost. It was a last-ditch effort to try and scare Van Horne into changing his mind.

What Thomas failed to realize was that, once and for all, Van Horne was American, and Americans cared little for British society and its influence. It didn't affect his decisions at all. Thomas tried to get T. G. Shaughnessy, the Vice President, to plead his cause to Van Horne. He sent letters to William Whyte, General Superintendent of the C.P.R. at Winnipeg, who assured him that there was even less reason to have a station at Mitford now that Thomas had closed the sawmill business in favor of a brickyard, and in fact, the machinery had been sold to a company in Golden. The C.P.R. just wasn't interested in the Cochranes nor their town.

Adela was not to be dissuaded by this, so she wrote to her mama, and had a social visit set up to entertain Lord Mount Stephen at home in Henham Hall. Thomas and Adela put off their departure to Mitford and headed up to Suffolk. After a lovely meal and party, Lord Mount Stephen, the previous President of the C.P.R., was approached by the Cochranes and pressed to send a letter to Van Horne.

Lord Mount Stephen did so, on April 14, and he explained to Van Horne that he had been obliged by Lady Adela to write to him and ask him for consideration of her application to have Mitford changed from a flag station to a proper station.

Thomas and Adela returned home to Quarr Abbey with hopes that this might change Van Horne's mind, and prepared to leave for Canada, where they arrived in May. Once she arrived in Mitford, she lost no time in writing to Van Horne. In her letter, she discussed her meeting with Lord Mount Stephen, and also disclosed to Van Horne that she was not building a ferry, but a bridge at Mitford, that she thought would be very beneficial to the business of the railroad. She tried as well to use her position as a shareholder of the C.P.R. to help convince him that he should change his mind. Adela really hoped her money and connections could save her town from the certain death she feared would happen without the train station. What she failed to realize was that Van Horne remained not in the least sympathetic to her cause.

Rallying together to try and save Mitford and get it a train station brought Adela and Thomas together again. They decided that while Adela would continue to work on Van Horne through her connections, Thomas should visit William Whyte in Winnipeg and try to convince him to change Van Horne's position.

"Darling, I will use every connection I have to save our town," she told Thomas tearfully as he left for Winnipeg.

Thomas' trip to Winnipeg had some small success. He managed to convince Whyte to place an operator at Mitford if sufficient business could warrant this. However, until that was proven, the Cochranes would have to pay the cost of the operator, which they readily agreed to. An agent was hired and began working at the Mitford flag station in early 1894. It was a very small victory, but for Thomas and Adela, at least it was a small concession from the unenthusiastic C.P.R.

Unfortunately for the Cochranes, the business ventures at Mitford were continuing to go downhill, and finally there was nothing to do but shut down. Without employment in town, many of the new settlers began to look for employment elsewhere. As well, much to the Thomas and Adela's disgust, the town of Cochrane was beginning to grow, as it had the help of a train station and transportation to assist it.

Thomas and Adela continued to come to Mitford each

spring, but Thomas was now spending more time with his duties as Lieutenant Governor of the Isle of Wight. Princess Beatrice found the daily administrative work very boring, and she left all these duties for Thomas, as was expected of his role. Due to this expectation, he could no longer leave the Isle of Wight for long periods of time.

Life was becoming more and more desperate for Adela. For all her involvement in trying to get a station and save her town, it was still considered impossible for her to travel to Mitford alone. She was stuck at Quarr Abbey with Rosetta Cochrane for longer periods of time, which she could only alleviate by riding. There was nothing to keep her busy there, and she became desperately unhappy with her situation. Thomas was spending as much time as possible with his duties as Lieutenant Governor, and the only requirements she had were to be available if he needed her for social engagements. However, the Isle was so small that few government officials came to visit, so Adela really had nothing to do at all.

In sheer desperation she wrote a long letter to Van Horne railing against the C.P.R. and complaining about the interference of railway officials. It still didn't make sense to her that all her connections from Britain were seemingly of no use in this battle with the C.P.R. In all her life, being the daughter of the Earl of Stradbroke, she had never experienced opposition. This, too, it seemed, was a part of the new world, and it definitely was not in her favour.

She begged Thomas to return for the Mitford Races every year, and he was compliant in that regard. At least she knew she would be able to get out of England and back to Mitford for something that she enjoyed.

Thomas had taken over the postmaster position at Mitford from David Crowley, who had decided to move from Mitford to Cochrane, in 1892. He hired this position out but was happy to have control of the post office as he felt it might help with his application to get the station for Mitford.

Sadly, by 1895, Thomas had decided to concede defeat in terms of his business ventures. However, the store, hotel, school and church, as well as the Post Office, were still running in Mitford. As he was now a government official in England, he decided he needed to take a new route in Canada and decided to run for elected office.

Adela was thrilled. If Thomas were to win a seat, they would have to live in Canada full time. She could be on hand permanently in Mitford, to watch every little detail and to make sure her town survived, even if it didn't have a station. She was resigned to the fact that it might remain very small, and even be overtaken by Cochrane, with its C.P.R. station, but that was much better than Mitford dying out.

Thomas was enthusiastic about Canada again, and in his much-improved spirits, gave her the postmastership of Mitford. Unlike Thomas, she planned to do this job herself. The ennui and boredom of the Isle of Wight seemed to vanish. Adela was excited about a full-time life in Canada at Mitford.

For her part, Adela had another disappointment to deal with. To her personal anguish there had been no sign of pregnancy in their marriage. They had been married for eight years, and while Adela had not given up hope, she was less convinced that they would have a child. Her true happiness lay in taking care of her wonderful little town of Mitford. Mama had assured her that after a number of years marriages became quite different, with men and women taking to their own interests, and doing less together. She therefore felt quite justified in loving Mitford more than she did Thomas. After all, Mitford did not become hysterical with anger, or ignore her, like Thomas did.

Adela was also keen to help with the campaign for Thomas, who ran as a Liberal-Conservative candidate against Frank Oliver. Thomas wanted to ensure that his British values were supported at the government level and ran on a platform of preservation of British institutions, the development of vacant lands and the securing of desirable settlers.

Adela had been living in Mitford now for nearly a decade, and she had come to understand the sensibilities of the people who lived there. She had come to appreciate the skills they brought with them from wherever they came; skills that actually helped them to build the new life that Canada offered them. She had realized long ago that all her class had was money, and that money without knowledge and skill did not mean success. She had seen over and over again how Thomas' arrogance and belief in the God-given right of the upper class had led to his failure here on the prairie. She found it interesting that his platform for election was trying to enshrine those rights in the Canadian government. Somehow, she didn't feel that the good, simple folk she had come to love here in her town were going to be too receptive to that.

Sure enough, 1896 did not bring Thomas the success he so dreamed of, and which remained so elusive for him. He was soundly defeated, even in Mitford. His string of failed businesses left no one believing that he could be successful in representing them.

Thomas' defeat in the election left him staggering. It was only Adela's job as the post-master at Mitford that convinced him that they ever needed to come back to Canada. He had completely resigned himself to his job as Lieutenant Governor of the Isle of Wight. He had asked his mother to set up a bedroom for him at Quarr Abbey, and no longer shared Adela's. She had to admit defeat in the heir-producing area herself, which did not add to her gloomy days on the Isle. Rosetta Cochrane got no kinder with age, and Adela became a recluse in the house, and escaped whenever she could. She basically took up residence in the Stradbroke townhome in London.

When asked about her life by her family, she could only sadly reply that nothing had really worked out the way she had hoped, and that Thomas had removed himself mostly from her life. London was truly not much happier for her than the Isle of Wight, and she waited impatiently for the spring to arrive so that she could be allowed to return to her town of Mitford, her only true love. There, in 1897, she resumed her duties as post-master, with the reluctant Thomas along, and attended the Mitford Races and other events, which were the only true happiness that was left in her life.

After the races were finished, Thomas decided he needed to return to his duties on the Isle of Wight, and Adela was forced to return to England in the summer. It was the first summer she had spent in England for over a decade, and she cried every morning when she awoke looking out at the streets of London, instead of the glorious Rocky Mountains.

How was she ever going to live her life without Mitford? That August, Thomas received a letter from the C.P.R. stating it would permanently close the flag station at Mitford. When Thomas finally bothered to tell her about it, with an air of disgust and deprecation, she felt as if the nails on a coffin were slowly being pounded in. She wrote a letter full of anger and frustration to the Post Office Inspector of the C.P.R., in which she complained bitterly about their decisions and the flight of so many men to the Klondike gold rush.

"… so many men have departed to the Klondike that wages have risen horribly. There are so few men left that I shall have to pay a man $35.00 - $40.00 per month to stay up at night and receive the mail bag."

Adela did not want the mail thrown off the train again, so she negotiated with the Inspector to have the mail picked up once again at the Cochrane station. Thomas was allowing her to communicate with the C.P.R. as he had all but given up on anything to do with Mitford. Adela never wanted to give up.

IN ENGLAND, THE WINTER OF 1897 was nothing but grim. Adela moved from Quarr Abbey to London to Henham Hall, whenever the place she was living in became unbearable. She lived at Quarr Abbey until she could no longer take the nasty jibes and comments from Rosetta and Thomas. She would flee to London and live in the family townhome until someone else needed the place, then she would travel out to Suffolk. Home at Suffolk was not a reprieve either, as everyone had now decided that Thomas was an unfit husband, and all the talk from her mama and sisters centered on what an unfit husband he was. While Adela agreed whole-heartedly, it just became too much after a while, and she would head out again to Quarr Abbey, until it became too unbearable there again.

She was completely inconsolable over the slow death of Mitford, and she had no one to share this grief with. The dark skies of an English winter matched her dark mood, and she became less and less interested in any pursuits.

Thomas always demanded that she spend Christmas at Quarr Abbey, as the royal family preferred to spend their Christmas there. His entire life was now centered around his political life on the Isle of Wight, and he needed his wife there to attend all the social events of the royal Christmas. Adela performed her duties perfunctorily. It was an expectation of life as an aristocrat. But she did this with nothing but the heaviest of hearts.

After Christmas, Thomas called her to his office. He stood with his back to her, staring out a window, as she walked in.

"I will be straight to the point, Adela," he started. "I wish to never return to Mitford again. As far as I am concerned, Mitford is dead. Canada no longer has any interest for me, and I will spend no more time on any of my endeavors there. I would like you to return by yourself there this spring and take charge of dissolving the businesses and selling the Mitford property."

Adela felt like she had just received a notice of death. She stood motionless and speechless in Thomas' office.

"Well, woman, don't just stand there," he barked at her. "You have your orders, now go about them," he finished in a commanding tone.

Adela said nothing. She turned and left the office. She had walked over to the administrative offices from Quarr Abbey, and was dressed for walking in outdoor weather, so she walked along the roads of the Isle of Wight for hours, trying to come to terms with what she had just heard. Mitford was dead, well, from Thomas' point of view anyway. She would have no choice but to follow his wishes and sell what was left of the great dream. She felt numb and cold in every part of her body.

In the spring of 1898, when she arrived at her home in Mitford, there were only five families still receiving their mail in town. Most of the Mitford townsfolk had moved to Cochrane, which was now growing, as all prairie towns with railroad stations did. Even her old friends Mr. and Mrs. Sargent, the wheelwright and the cook, had relocated to Cochrane, where he had been hired to build the wooden sidewalks for the town.

Adela spent her time riding, fishing and living in her little ghost of a town, while she organized the sale of Mitford Ranche, as it was called, for the disposal. She wrote a letter to Ellis and Grogan, the auctioneers in Calgary, who placed an advertisement in the Calgary Herald on June 9, 1898. The sale of all the equipment and goods that were left was to be held at noon on June 30. The auctioneers invited people to take the train to Mitford, and also to stay at the Mitford Arms, if necessary.

"How very ironic," Adela thought.

The sale was painful on every level. She tried to keep a stoic British stiff upper lip, but throughout the sale day tears often blurred her vision. Alex Martin, her post office assistant, bought her house. She was glad of that.

It was not a happy time, yet when she could rise in the morning to the glory of the Rockies, ride up into the beautiful hills and fish in the sparking Bow, she still felt a happiness and peace she felt nowhere else in her life.

After the sale was finished, she rode west every day,

watching the mountains grow taller as she approached. She rode out to Morleyville and stopped to visit with the Sibbalds and the McDougalls. They were such good, kindly people who would continue to build up Morleyville. The McDougalls were great friends to the Stoney and had built a church and an orphanage for them. Tears streamed down her face when she said goodbye. She ran into Billie Bradley, who had worked for them briefly when the brickyard was still running. He was cutting and hauling logs. Billie was always shy when it came to talking with women, but Lady Adela shook his hand and wished him the best. She knew in her heart that it was his kind, the simple working men, who were going to build this country, and not her, the aristocracy. Billie wished her well, and she wished him well in return. She continued west, thinking,

"What if I just keep going? What if I get lost in these mountains and never come back?" The idea was tempting, but truth be told, she did not want to die in a storm in the bush around the mountains, so with great reluctance, she turned her horse back around. She had sold the horse to Alex Martin, with all the tack, for a fraction of what she had paid for everything. However, she had retained rights to the horse and tack until she rode into Cochrane to board the train.

She decided she would stay at the stopping house in Morleyville that night. She rode back to eat a meal prepared by Mrs. Taylor, the cook there. Mrs. Taylor was from Suffolk, and Adela had a lovely time talking about the favorite places they both had back in England. It was May and the evenings were long, so Adela got back on her horse and continued to ride up the hills of Morleyville, pausing often just to sit atop a hill and drink in the majesty of the Rockies. She knew there was a very good chance this would be the last time she would see them.

As the mountains turned from blue to black, Adela sat on her horse watching them. She gave the horse its head, and it immediately started to graze on the prairie wool, as the settlers called it, at her feet. She thought about her life. She looked around her and decided that this was her ultimate moment, just being able to sit and stare at the Rockies, all alone. For the moment, she was as free as she had ever been in her life, and her heart filled with gratitude as the tears spilled over and rolled down her cheeks. There was resignation in her tears, but also victory. Mitford had not been a success, for many reasons. At the end of the day, Thomas has proven to be a poor businessman. He had not done his due diligence when it came to purchasing land, leases or mines. He had relied on his position as an aristocrat which had not brought about success. As a result, his businesses had not prospered. As beautiful as the spot was where Mitford was located was, it was unsuitable for a railway stop, and that is what made or broke a town on the prairies. They had learned all this far too late.

But while they had lived their dream, it had been spectacular. It was the life she had dreamed of, desired and achieved. She would never look back on this as folly, foolishness or failure. It was and would always be the greatest adventure imaginable, and she had lived it. She thought about the story of Thomas' father leaving New Found Land with the residents throwing filth at him. At least Thomas had been spared that.

Something happened in her heart right then. The gaping hole that had been there started to find a way to heal.

She remembered the happy times traveling with Billie and Evelyn and thought with envy of how the Little Bow River

Cattle Company was hanging on, despite the difficult, cold winters. The difference, she knew, was that Billie truly loved his new home, and his job as a rancher. Thomas had nothing to sustain him in Canada anymore, and only failure everywhere he looked.

She knew he would never step foot in Canada again.

In July, she finished up the details of the sale, and with dread, made her plans to return to England. She had no idea what her life would hold, but it did not seem like it would be anything she wanted. On her last night, which she spent at the Mitford Arms, she sadly wrote in her journal.

July 15, 1889. Life here has ended. The death of Mitford is the saddest moment I have spent so far. Nothing will ever be the same again.

CHAPTER 22

A NEW CENTURY

1900

Life had been unbearable and unimaginable at times for the new pioneers of the North West Territories. For the people, the weather of the 1890's provided very difficult conditions for them to survive under. It was severely cold in the winter, sometimes as cold as -48 degrees Fahrenheit, which made survival itself difficult.

Billie Bradley had learned how to survive in the cold winters of Canada. He traded cut logs to a trapper for pelts and had the Stoney women make him a fur coat. It kept him warm no matter how cold it got. He was a master of stoking his wood stove just right, so that it gave off the necessary warmth, but never became too hot. He lost livestock to the cold, but with a persistence that marked his kind, he hung on and survived, with only the satisfaction that he was surviving on his own land. He was lord of his own manor, no matter how humble that manor was.

He got to know the Taylor family well. Sykes had been

the first man he met in the new land and they had made a fast friendship. Sykes had traveled from England to Minnesota with his father when he was 12 years old, in 1880. There had been no way of earning a living there, so the two had traveled to Jarvis, Ontario. They had been caught up in the excitement of "going west" and had headed out to homestead in the North West Territories. Syke's mother decided to join her husband and son and had brought his seven brothers and sisters with her. Ma Taylor often included Billie as one of the family, which he appreciated to no end. It certainly helped to ease the loneliness after Henry had gone back to Fitzroy County. Sykes was only a few years older than Billie, but he had the luxury of having his whole family to support him. Billie didn't say much, but Sykes knew that life was very hard for a single man out here in the West.

There was great excitement in the whole area with each new settler family that came to claim their homestead. A few years after the Taylors arrived in Morleyville, another new family arrived from England. They loved to tell the story of how they had arrived on May 24th, to three feet of snow. Having just arrived from England, it was truly a sight to behold. The Smiths found employment in the thriving settlement of Morleyville. But what impressed Sykes and Billie the most was that the Smith family brought daughters with them.

Annie Smith, the oldest, was a sweet young girl. She was very tiny, with curly blond hair and laughing blue eyes. Sykes and Billie fell for her instantly. And so began the great contest to win her love. Both boys paid court to her constantly, inviting her to any social event that occurred, to church, to church picnics and certainly to the Bachelors' Ball in Mitford. There was nothing like the looks of admiration one received bringing a young unmarried girl to the Bachelors' Ball. Annie was safe with Billie, as no man would dare to even approach her when she was with Billie the Strongman.

By 1893 both young men had proposed, but in the end, Annie chose Sykes. This was quite a blow to Billie, as for a while he lost the friendship of Sykes and the company of Annie. However, it didn't stop him from attending their wedding at the church in Morleyville, where they were married by the Reverend John McDougall. Shortly after the wedding, Annie and Sykes, along with all the other Taylors, young and old, moved to Springbank and took up land there.

Billie was very lonely again without his surrogate family, the Taylors, living in Morleyville; however, their home in Springbank was actually not as far away, and Billie soon was coming for dinners with the Taylors again. Billie was very fond of children, and always took time to play with the younger Taylors.

Sykes decided he and Annie needed a home of their own away from the family, so he bought a quarter section out in Brushy Ridge near Billie, who couldn't have been happier. Annie's parents often came to visit, bringing the whole family. When Sykes and Annie were married in 1893, Annie's little sister Alice was only six years old. However, she came to visit Annie often, and Billie too was often visiting with Annie and Sykes. As Alice began to grow up, Billie started to fall in love again. He was getting older and still didn't have a wife, but he had now set his heart on teeny little Alice Smith. Like her sister Annie, she was petite, but she was dark haired where Annie was blond. Billie's persistence finally paid off, and Alice's father gave them permission to marry when Alice turned seventeen. Billie was thirty- four.

Although many European men married Stoney and Blackfoot women in the early years, Billie had been determined to find himself a European wife. And Billie had certainly learned patience from living on the prairies, which had finally paid off. He and Alice were married in March at the Morleyville Church in 1904.

"This is the happiest day of my life, Alice. I have waited so long for a chance to have a family here," Billie told Alice on their wedding day.

Billie and Sykes both had horse teams now and raised chickens and cows as well as the horses they had been providing to the British army for the Boer War. Now that the war was over, the families needed other sources of income. Annie and Alice milked the cows, put the milk into pans and skimmed off the cream which they made into butter. This was either sold or traded for groceries. The families were spending more time now in Cochrane, as to Lady Adela's woe, it had prospered and was continuing to grow due to its railway station. They traveled up to Radnor Crossing, west of Cochrane, to get across the river, as there was yet no bridge in town. Often the two sisters would pack up the butter into the democrat and head to Cochrane to trade it.

"I hope the train has been into town with supplies so that we can trade this butter for something delicious," Alice laughed as she and Annie rode together into Cochrane.

Billie and Sykes continued to take the team to the wooded areas and cut logs, which they hauled to Calgary to sell for fuel for $3.00 a load. There was always a spirit of co-operation and assistance for your neighbor in Brushy Ridge.

Housing was always a priority, and Sykes and Billie both needed better housing than the tent structures they had been living in. As Annie and Sykes had a bigger family, Billie agreed that they should build the Taylors a good solid cabin first. Hunger always had a way of setting priorities, so building a house and barn on the Taylor place in Brushy Ridge took time. Getting logs for the cabin took a long journey north, where there were still stands of trees on unclaimed land. Logs needed to provide income for groceries and heat for the winter, so Billie and Sykes spent long days away from home logging in the Dog Pound area. For the thousandth time, Billie was grateful for his upbringing in logging country in Fitzroy County, as he and Sykes worked the long, hard hours to bring down trees and haul them home.

"The cabin is coming along well, Billie." Sykes smiled with satisfaction as the log structure took form.

"We'll soon be able to start on one for you and Alice."

"That will make her happy. She doesn't think much of the tent," Billie replied.

To Billie's greatest joy, a daughter was born in 1905. They named her May and called her Mamie. They were pleased to think their daughter shared a birthday with their new province. Alberta became a province on September 1, 1905. Billie felt good to think of their home as officially being part of Canada. He had been born in Ontario and now lived in Alberta. There was satisfaction for him that The Last Best West was now Alberta.

All the while he and Sykes were trying to bring home enough logs to get homes and barns built. Billie had built his barn first, but Sykes had neither a barn nor a cabin, so it took long, long hours to get enough logs to build both structures. The men were away for long stretches at a time.

Meanwhile, Alice was home alone. When she couldn't take it any longer, she would wrap up Mamie in a blanket sling, and ride over to visit her sister. Together they would do chores for a few days, but Alice would have to return to milk the cows and gather the eggs. She could only stay away a few nights at most as the animals required care.

Alice did not do well after the birth of Mamie. She had been quite sickly during her pregnancy, but her mother and sister assured her she would start to feel fine again once the baby was born. Now Mamie was here, and everything was not better. Every morning when she woke up, her first thought was, "I can't do this and I'm never going to be able to do this. I can't go out there and milk that miserable cow." Then she would start to cry, every morning, and then she would start to worry. What if Mamie didn't think she loved her? She did love her, but it didn't feel like it some days, most days. Mamie was just another level of work to be done. Mamie cried all the time, and Alice, alone with aching breasts and sore, cracked nipples, wished the damn baby would just go away.

Sometimes her mother rode over to give her a hand, but Ma Smith was not a kind, nurturing soul, never had been. If she found Alice collapsed and weeping on the floor, she would grab her arms and yank her up and shake her.

"Get up you stupid girl and to get to work. There is no place for weakness here," she would yell at Alice. As a sensitive child, Alice had often fled from her mother in terror, looking for Annie, who could always calm her down.

One afternoon Ma Smith rode into Annie's yard looking mean and ornery. Annie wasn't afraid to stand up to her anymore, but when she grabbed the reins to take the horse and tie it up, she heard Ma Smith complain,

"That Alice. What does she think she is doing? I found her sitting on her dirt floor, crying, while Mamie was wailing and hungry. She was complaining her breasts hurt. Whose breasts don't hurt when they're nursing?" she exploded as she climbed down off her horse.

"And she had that look," Ma Smith went on, "You know that look, Annie. That strange look where her eyes seem to roll back into her head.:

"I know," Annie replied simply, not wanting to her encourage her mother.

"Well, she has to grow up and act like a woman now that she's married and a mother. The cows must be milked, and the work must be done. There is no place for a woman who can't hold her own here in Alberta," her mother seethed.

Alice silently willed her mother to stop her diatribe. She smiled at her mother and said, "Ah, you must need a cup of tea and a biscuit Mum, after your long ride."

"I do," replied her mother, and Annie brought her into the tent house and made her comfortable while she made tea and gave her a baking powder biscuit with cream and Saskatoon jam. Her mom settled down, and the two talked of the children and farms for an hour. All the while, Annie was silently panicking. She knew that Alice was in a bad place and desperately wanted to ride over to help her, which was no easy decision. If only she could talk her mom into staying and watching the children. She didn't want to leave them alone, yet she knew she had to get over to Alice's to see what was going on.

In pure desperation, she finally said,

"Mum, can you stay with the kids for a bit while I ride over to see Alice? You know I am the only one who can get through to her when she gets like this."

Ma Smith was instantly angry again. "That damn, stupid Alice."

"Yes, but Mamie is so tiny. I have to get Alice back to herself so she can take care of her," pleaded Annie.

Grudgingly, Ma Smith agreed, and Annie was off like a rabbit to grab her horse and ride over to Alice's place. When she got there, she could hear wailing, like she had sometimes heard from Alice when she was a teenager. She tied up her horse and bounded into the tent, to find Alice collapsed on the floor again. She didn't even move when Annie cried out,

"Alice, it's me, it's Annie."

"Annnniiieeee" she wailed, again. Annie picked her up and half dragged her to the bed, where Mamie had fallen asleep. As soon as Mamie heard them, she started wailing as well. Annie got Alice into bed and got her blouse unbuttoned and her breast out for Mamie. It was hard and the nipples were cracked and bleeding. Alice winced and held her breath while Mamie latched on and began sucking noisily. The baby was obviously famished. Alice sat in bed with a vacant look on her face while Mamie suckled. Annie left them alone, and went to check the cow, whose bursting udder must have felt no less painful than Alice's breasts. She grabbed the bucket and milked the cow, skimmed the cream and placed it in the crocks in the cool water. Then she checked the chickens and brought in eggs. By this point Alice had fallen asleep, as had Mamie. Annie cooked up the eggs and pulled out the loaf of bread she had baked that morning from her saddle bag. She had packed some jam as well. She scraped out the eggs onto a tin plate, and cut a thick slice of bread, which she slathered with butter and jam. She woke Alice, helped her out of bed, and sat her at the little table. While Alice hungrily ate the bread and eggs, Annie made a big pot of tea and brought it to the table. She placed teaspoons of sugar in the tea, and skimmed milk. Alice gratefully took the mug from her sister and started sipping her tea. Mamie cooed and smiled, and Annie found a clean diaper and changed her. Alice had calmed down completely but was hanging her head in shame.

"Don't worry Alice, some women get really sad after their babies are born," Annie said kindly. This brought on a new wail from Annie.

"But I am a bad mother."

"No, no, it's just hard right now," Annie gently told her and stroked her hair. "Just get through your morning chores tomorrow, then wrap up Mamie and come to my place. You'll feel much better there," Annie promised.

"I know it's hard and lonely while Billie is away cutting and logging."

Annie waited until Alice had finished her dinner, then tucked her into bed with Mamie. Then she washed the dishes after she had fetched water from the creek and left them to dry while the two slept.

Annie rode home with a worried, furrowed brow, while she tried to decide how she could help her sister through this difficult time.

LIFE CONTINUED ON MUCH THE same on the Billie Bradley homestead in Brushy Ridge. Mamie thrived and became a lively little girl. Billie continued to raise horses, and cattle and Alice kept the dairy cows and chickens, plus was back-up rancher for any chores that required two. There was no doubt to the fact that it was a hard, hard life. Billie went wherever there was work, to supplement the meagre living they were pulling in from their ranche, the Half Diamond V. Billie had chosen that name to represent the beautiful Rocky Mountains that watched over them from the west.

Hard as it was, Alice and Billie found a rhythm in the ranche life, and Alice returned from the dark sad place she had found herself in after Mamie was born. Everyone marveled at Mamie, for though she had not been born a large baby, she was growing incredibly. When the families got together for church on Sundays in Cochrane, Mamie was by far the largest child of any that had been born that year. It was always a topic of conversation, as Alice was so small.

"Look at that Mamie Bradley, she is such a big girl," the ranche women would all exclaim after church on Sunday.

Alice became pregnant again in '07, and her troubles started up again. She was severely sick, and spent most mornings getting sick outside the barn as she tried to milk the cows. It took so long to get through every job when she felt so sick. Billie tried to be patient, but he often got harsh with her. She just felt worse and worse. Time passed and the sickness wore off, but then the reality of trying to do chores as a pregnant woman took over. Every day was doubly hard now. Alice would fall into her bed in the tent home, almost dead with exhaustion. Little Mamie slept in a tiny bed Billie had made beside their bed, but often as not, Billie was away at night, either working, or visiting the hotel in Cochrane. He went there to drink with the other locals who frequented the place. When he was away, Mamie crawled into her Ma's warm bed.

"Where Daddy, Ma?" little Mamie would ask as she snuggled in close to her mom.

"He'll be back soon," Alice always replied.

For Billie, long gone were the days of the Mitford Arms, as it had closed down with the rest of Mitford after Lady Adela had sold off her home and buildings. Not having the C.P.R. station there had been its final death knell, and the town was just slowly ceasing to exist. The beautiful little church Lady Adela had raised funds for and built had been moved into Cochrane, using logs to roll it and horses to pull it. The All Saints Anglican Church still existed, and it gave Alice pleasure to attend there. She had been such a young child when they had come to Canada that she did not remember the Anglican Church from her home in Suffolk. But her mom had been ecstatic when she found there was an Anglican church built by an aristocrat from Suffolk.

The Smith family left home every Sunday at 6 am to be sure they could get to Cochrane for the service. Each family brought their Sunday lunch with them, and brought it out, picnic style, to eat on the pews after the service was over. As ranchers came from miles around to attend the service, there was a need to eat something before they headed home, so eating in the church, picnic style, became a custom.

And, often as not, Billie stumbled over from the Hotel, where he had finished the night too drunk to make the long ride home to Brushy Ridge. The hotel wanted the business, so they simply closed up the bar at night, leaving the too drunk patrons to sleep it off, slumped over and passed out at the tables they had been drinking at all night. Billie would sheepishly slink in late and join Alice and Mamie and the Smiths and Taylors and other families at the service. Ma Smith would give him looks to kill each time he slunk in.

Alice was often so exhausted from the trip there that she slept through the service. Then she ate with the Smiths and Taylors and prepared to make the long trip home to the ranche with Billie. The Smiths, Taylors and Bradley's often met to do things together. In fact, when Fred Taylor, Syke's younger brother, couldn't find a wife, Billie had written home to the family in Fitzroy Harbour and talked his youngest sister, Sarah, into coming out as a "mail order" bride. The three families were all intertwined.

William Henry was born in 1908 in Brushy Ridge, Alberta. Billie had, of course, wanted to name him after brother Henry, who had married and started his own family back in Fitzroy Harbour. Sadly, for Alice and Henry, the darkness descended upon Alice again. She lay listless, with vacant eyes, after Henry's birth. Billie finally had to take her to his sister Sarah's home, as Ma Smith was vicious with Alice when she fell into this state and it did not help her.

"Sarah, darlin', you have to help her out," Billie pleaded with this younger sister whom he hardly knew.

Annie had wanted to take care of her little sister and had had Billie bring her and the kids there, but Ma Smith would hear nothing of it, feeling her harshness would snap Alice out of her misery. It didn't, so in desperation, Billie had resorted to his sister.

Sarah was having difficulties of her own. Fred Taylor had

not proven to be a good husband, and her life was not filled with domestic bliss. The only reason Fred allowed Alice to be there was out of a sense of obligation to Billie for finding him a wife. None of this was a great help to Alice, who continued to live in her own personal black place of despair. Annie would ride over to help out, and these were the only times Alice would actually perk up a little.

"You're coming along girl," Annie would encourage Alice as the days grew into weeks.

Slowly, with the ministrations of Sarah and Annie, Alice came around. Billie was getting frantic as he needed Alice to be at home to take care of the chickens and milk cows while he cut firewood with Sykes. Poor Annie would make her way over to Billie's when he finally had to leave, to milk the cows and make the butter. Alice was brought home, and Annie rode over to help her after she had risen extra early to milk her own cows and collect her own eggs. Somehow, Alice came out of the blackness and started taking part in the life of the ranche again. Luckily, Henry, as he was known, was thriving well despite the difficulties his mother was experiencing. Billie was so relieved to see Alice improve that he swore to her that he would never step into the Hotel bar again.

Life on the ranche with two little ones did not get easier. Syke's cabin home and barn were now complete; the barn with a sod roof, as it was a good material for a barn. Sykes and Billie were logging to get the material to build the cabin for Billie and Alice, so they were gone for long periods of time again, and as always, when they were home, they rode into Cochrane to frequent the Hotel. The promise made to Alice seemed to have been long forgotten.

Every day was still very lonely for Alice, but she did manage to strap Henry to her body, like she'd seen the Indian women do, and plop Mamie behind her saddle, to ride over to the lake, a prairie slough on their quarter, to have a picnic with Mamie. She'd also ride over to Annie's whenever she could manage it. She stayed away from Ma Smith, who always looked at her with suspicion and often outright disgust. She knew her mother did not approve of her, so she kept as much distance from her as possible.

"It's good to see you back to yourself again," Annie would praise. But Alice knew that the dark clouds that came over her were only gone for the present. She knew they would blacken her heart again when the next baby came. An overwhelming fear would rise up in her when she thought about that, and she tried with all her might to push it far into the recesses of her mind once again.

In 1909 she became pregnant for a third time, and the vicious cycle of morning illness, exhaustion and melancholy descended again. She came to realize that there would be no getting away from it. Women bore children, and thankfully not so many died as they had in her childhood, but instead, it meant that families had now become quite large. She knew her life would simply be a cycle of one pregnancy after the other, punctuated by back breaking labor, worries about starvation, and trying to survive the forty below temperatures that winter could bring. There really was no lightening up. Reality was nothing but survival, and there were days when she couldn't see why she should survive. Billie was able to go to the Cochrane Hotel to drink away his difficulties, but there was nothing to ease her pain, except the occasional kind word from her sister.

Baby Johnny was born in 1910, and the darkness pressed down on her with an oppression she could not resist. She was always relieved that the children were born alive, and she knew it was up to her keep them alive once they got here. Once again, she was unable to leave her bed, and Billie had to lead her and the children into the Democrat they had acquired and take them over to Sarah. Little Mamie was now a four-year-old who could help fetch things for her Ma, and she could also hold the baby. That was a great help to Alice, who dug up a smile from someplace to show Mamie how she appreciated her help.

"That's my girl, Mamie, you are such a good help for your Ma," she would smile at her oldest. Such praise made Mamie glow, then run to her mother to hug her.

But each darkness grew longer for Alice, and it took her longer to recover her health. Sarah was not pleased to have the extra burden of Alice and her kids, so being at the Fred Taylor ranche was far from ideal. Fred complained about this intrusion bitterly to his brother Sykes.

"The last thing we need is Alice and her brats causing us more work,"

Sykes answered, "I know it's hard Fred, but Billie's doing the best he can. We're trying to get enough logs cut to build them a proper cabin. Annie is just not as strong as Sarah."

"I want them outta my place," he raged.

The next spring, when baby Johnny was about six months old, Ma Smith received a visitor. It was her sister's son, come out from Suffolk, and on his way to make his own homestead. The British Columbia government was attempting to settle its north. Mr. Pierce had been attracted by the newspaper articles he had read written by Charles Melville Hays, the president of the Grand Trunk Railway, about the rosy future he envisioned for Prince Rupert. He saw it as a terminus for the railway, and a home for large passenger ships which would spawn a tourism industry. Industrious young families could come and build a life around serving this new venture. It was yet another new great dream in the land of new great dreams, and he meant to follow it.

Ma had planned a dinner to welcome Mr. Pierce to Brushy Ridge, where he hoped to stay and work to gain the money needed to carry on to Prince Rupert. Billie and Alice joined the Smith family, although she never went to her mother's place without a great deal of reticence. Ma had spared no expense to entertain her nephew.

"I want you all to meet Harry Piece. I've invited him to dinner and to bring his fiddle to play for us tonight," Ma Smith announced when everyone had arrived. Ma had baked buttery biscuits instead of the usual johnny cake and had roasted a fine piece of venison. She had managed to get potatoes and carrots from Cochrane and had made saskatoon pies which she served with cream. It was a feast of no small proportion and it was heartily enjoyed by all. Once the dinner had been cleared up, Harry brought out his fiddle. The furniture was pushed to one side and a small dance floor was made. Alice loved hearing the music and felt her spirits lift in a way she hadn't felt for a long time.

"You're laughing my girl," Billie exclaimed in wonder as Alice swirled around the tiny dance floor in his arms.

"It feels good to be alive again, Billie," was all Alice replied.

All the families bunked in for the night, sleeping on the floors as there was nowhere else to sleep. It was the first happy night Alice had experienced in as long as she could remember.

CHAPTER 23

ENDINGS

1910-1915

Mrs. William Percival Bradley of Brushy Ridge, Alberta, had a problem. She was twenty-three years old and was falling in love, but not with her husband, Billie Bradley. Billie, she had known all her life, from the time she was a six-year-old and first emigrated from England to Canada.

The arrival of her cousin, Mr. Pierce, had brought a change in her life she had neither wanted nor expected. There had really been an expectation all her life that she would marry Billie Bradley, a man twice her age, but this she had never questioned. There were so few European settlers in Brushy Ridge, or any part of Alberta for that matter, that it was simply expected that a young girl who grew up on the prairie would simply just marry one of the many single bachelors in the area.

Harry Pierce was her own age and was full of the adventure that Billie might have had long ago, when he started out from Fitzroy Harbour. Hard, hard work and an unforgiving prairie had taken all that away from him. He was hardened into the kind of man who survived here. He didn't understand her sadness and melancholy, and her inner hatred of this difficult life, where they still didn't have their own home yet, because all the logs Billie cut had to be sold to feed the family.

Harry Pierce laughed and teased her when Billie wasn't around and made her long for an end to the never ceasing drudgery of the life of a prairie ranche woman.

She knew some woman glanced out west to the mountains and it filled them with something, but for Alice, they were just another cold hard reminder of this unforgiving country. And Mr. Pierce wanted to leave here and live far away in Prince Rupert. True, it was in the North, which was filled with the long cold winters she knew here, but it was also on the coast of the Pacific Ocean and was completely different from the prairie. Harry Pierce reassured her of this.

She dreamed of escape, of a new life, a better life. She would miss Annie terribly, but Ma and Pa Smith were mean and hard on her and she wouldn't miss them at all. She knew she should miss Billie, but he was just part of the life here that she so badly wanted to escape from, so she let herself dream about a totally new and different reality.

Mr. Pierce grew quite comfortable being a guest at the Smith family home, and all the Brushy Ridge community began to wonder if he was really going to move on to Prince Rupert after all. Of course, Harry Pierce had a reason for dragging his feet.

Billie remained busy trying to make sure that he could feed his wife and three children, and as usual, Alice was left alone. Mr. Pierce took to riding over to the Bradley homestead to help Alice out while Billie was away, which Alice thoroughly appreciated. She still struggled every day with the harshness of her life, the tent she still lived in and the difficulty of raising her young family, mostly alone, on the prairie of Brushy Ridge.

As can happen when a husband is absent, and someone is there to take his place, a new relationship can take seed and start to grow. This is how the romance between Alice and Harry Pierce started out, innocently enough at first. Alice was just so grateful for the help around the homestead that she couldn't turn down Mr. Pierce's help. And he talked about a new exciting life that he was going to build in a new exciting place, and Alice loved to hear his stories.

She absolutely did not mean to, but in the summer of 1913, the year that Mr. Pierce came to Brushy Ridge, Alice fell in love. Harry Pierce also fell in love with Alice. He started to push for Alice to come with him to Prince Rupert. Every day she looked around the Half Diamond V, the family brand and name for their ranche, and saw the tent, the small barn and the prairie grasses in between the two. The thought of being able to escape from her hard, grudging life sounded good. She would never miss milking the cows, trying to grow vegetables, or keeping the children fed, cleaned and clothed. They did have a washtub tub now for bathing, but the tent house was small, so it had to be placed outside when they were finished with it.

Mr. Pierce knew they had a long, long journey ahead of them, so by late May he was anxious to get things underway for leaving.

"Alice, we need to go very soon so we don't get stuck in the snow," Mr. Pierce urged.

"Oh, Harry, I'm so frightened. I just don't know what Billie is going to do. He is the toughest man in the whole area, and I am afraid he might kill you."

"Then we will leave when he is at the Murphy Hotel in Cochrane, drinking," Harry Pierce decided.

"I will have to tell him,", Alice murmured, "but I am so afraid."

"And what about the children?" she asked.

"It would be much easier if you left them here," he replied.

A cold chill ran through Alice like she had never felt in her life. As difficult as it was to be a mother, she had never thought of abandoning her children.

Each morning Mr. Pierce would ride over, and if he didn't see Billie's riding horse, he would stop and spend the day helping Alice.

Annie Taylor knew that something was wrong with Alice. That was common enough, as she had spent most of her life wondering what was wrong with Alice, yet recently, she had noticed that Alice had perked up, was smiling, and happier than she could ever remember seeing her. She looked like someone who had fallen in love.

The more Annie thought about it, the more she started to wonder if that was exactly what had happened to her younger sister. Harry Pierce, her cousin, was Alice's age. Billie, her husband, was seventeen years older than her.

"Well," thought Annie, "For the hundredth time I think I had better go over there and talk some sense into that girl. She has three children and her responsibilities as a wife. She can't go around falling in love with some young man just because he shows up on the doorstep."

As soon as she could fit it into her life, she saddled up her mare and rode over to Alice's place. All the way she thought about what Ma Smith would say if she realized what was happening with Alice. Annie was sure that Ma Smith probably loved Alice, but she didn't think Ma liked her very much. The last thing Annie needed to do was cause even more of a problem between Alice and her mother.

As she rode onto the Half Diamond V, she noticed one of the Smith ponies in the pasture with Billie's horses. As she drew nearer, she saw Alice and Harry Pierce over by the barn, standing very close to each other and talking and laughing. The children were playing in the yard, close to the tent, with their kitten, and she imagined baby Johnny was asleep for the afternoon in the tent house. As she watched them, she saw Harry reach out and take both of Alice's hands, and then reach up and kiss her. Annie's heart nearly stopped. What was that darn fool Alice up to now?

Her mare whinnied at Billie's horses, and Alice looked up quickly to see who was there. Annie thought she saw a look of relief at first, which was probably that Alice saw it wasn't Billie, and then a look of pure guilt crossed Alice's face and Annie knew that this wasn't the first time that this had happened.

Mr. Pierce lifted his hat at Annie, and shouted, "I was just about to take my leave Cousin Annie. Good to see you."

Hurriedly, he made off for his bridle and into the pasture to catch up his horse. Annie strode over to Alice, who looked at her defiantly.

"What in the world just happened here?" she demanded.

Alice realized they had been caught red handed, so she decided that she would tell Annie the truth.

"I am going to leave, Annie. I will miss you terribly, but I hate this godforsaken ranche and my godforsaken life here on it. Mr. Pierce is going to take me to Prince Rupert with him," she finished breathlessly. Annie was stunned. Whatever was Alice saying? She was married to Billie Bradley. She finally managed to stutter,

"What about your children and your family?"

"Well, Mr. Pierce is not too keen on me taking the children as he feels it would be much easier if it was just the two of us. We can get married when we get to Prince Rupert and start our own family there. But this place is too hard for me to leave the children here. Billie is always away working just to keep food on the table, so I know he couldn't take care of the children too. You wouldn't take them, would you?" she asked beseechingly.

"What do I need with three more mouths to feed that aren't mine, Alice?" the stunned Annie replied.

"That is true, Annie. And I've told Mr. Pierce that. It's simply the matter of the children that is keeping us here. We can't agree" Alice finished.

She looked at Annie imploringly.

"Don't tell Mum, Annie. I fear she may come over here with a shot gun and shoot me."

"She probably should!" Annie yelled at Alice and saw her cringe and look at the ground.

"Look Alice, let that bugger of a Mr. Pierce go on his way to Prince Rupert and get these stupid ideas out of your head. Wives don't up and leave their husbands. It just isn't done." Annie warned.

"You're probably right, Annie, you're always right," Alice continued.

Annie could hear the catch in her voice and knew that Alice was going to start crying. Usually she felt sorry for Alice, but this latest problem of hers was just too much. Annie couldn't imagine such a thing happening.

"Now Alice. Stop your crying. The next time that Mr. Pierce comes over here, you just tell him to git on his way to Prince Rupert and leave you be."

'You're right Alice. It's the right thing to do. I can't leave the children, and Mr. Pierce doesn't really want them. I'll do as you say."

Alice made up her mind to follow her sister's advice, because things usually turned out better when she did listen to Annie. However, Billie didn't come home, and three days later Harry Pierce showed up after she was finishing her morning chores. She made sure Mamie and Henry were busy playing with the kitten and met him out at the barn. The moment he saw her he pulled her into his arms and kissed her long and hard. She kissed him back and they tumbled into the barn, where they fumbled with their clothing and fell passionately into the hay. Alice had never experienced the passion she was feeling before and was shocked at the groans she heard emanating from somewhere deep within her. Afterwards, they lay in bliss in each other's arms, and Alice decided that she would go anywhere in the world with this man. In that moment, she was willing to give up her kids and just run away with Mr. Pierce. If he could make her feel this way, then she wanted more of it for the rest of her life. He looked at her very tenderly, and said,

"If we are going to be together, then we must go. I love you Alice Bradley, and I want to live with you forever. Let us start out on our new life together."

Without hesitation she replied, "I love you too, and I want to spend my life doing what we just did. I have never felt so wonderful in my whole life." Then her countenance darkened.

"What about my children? They just can't stay here."

"I know it will be harder with them, but if that is the only way I can have you, then I will have to put up with Billie Bradley's brats. Pack their things and we will leave."

Alice has never been so thrilled, excited and terrified in her life.

"All right, Harry. I will do that. But what about Billie Bradley?"

"Well, he might kill me if he catches me running off with his wife, so let's just pack everything up and leave. I'll get everything together and come for you soon, my love," he crooned.

With another long, passionate kiss, they parted, and Harry Pierce went to catch his horse.

Alice moved like she was in a dream. She didn't want to take anything that Billie would need, as she didn't feel it was hers to take. She took a wooden butter box and started to pack into it Mamie, Henry and Johnny's things. Then she found all her clothing, which didn't amount to much, and tied it together with some rope she had found in the barn. It was a pitiful number of possessions, but she knew Mr. Pierce had supplies for their new life.

Then she waited for one of the men in her life to come home. She got up each morning, milked her cows, skimmed her cream and churned her butter. She drove the butter into Cochrane and sold it, but instead of trading for her usual supplies, she was able to buy some dried meat, pemmican, that the Indians had traded the grocer. She knew this would be a good thing to take with her on a long journey.

She arrived back home and wondered for the hundredth time where Mr. Pierce was. Her resolve was growing weaker and she was getting more and more afraid with every minute that he did not show up.

The next day dawned a fine late spring morning, and Billie came back after a night of drinking in Cochrane with the locals, Ernie Andison and Charlie Pediprat. He rode onto the ranche and saw Mamie and Henry playing with a kitten. Mamie was watching over baby Johnny while Alice was skimming the cream after milking the cows.

Billie thought how good life had become. It was simple, but he had him a wife and children and the Half Diamond V. Soon he would get a house, as the neighbours were moving, and he had arranged to buy their log house from them. He couldn't wait to tell Alice that she would finally have a real log home.

Alice walked over to Billie and he knew that something was wrong, and yet, all he could think was, what is wrong now? Alice always had something wrong with her, and it was very wearing.

Alice looked at her tiny feet, in their tiny boots, then looked up at Billie, then looked at her feet again. With her head hung low, she managed to barely whisper, "Billie, I want to leave". The kids and I are going to head out with Mr. Pierce and head to Prince Rupert." Billie looked at her incredulously, and said,

"I don't want to go to Prince Rupert. I have been working this ranche for twenty-five years and I don't plan to leave now."

"I don't expect you to, Billie." She lowered her voice even further, and said, "I am going with Mr. Pierce." Billie looked at her uncomprehendingly. Then as he started to connect her words, a slow realization came over him.

"You're leaving with Pierce?" Alice nodded her head while she continued to look at her feet.

"The kids and I will head out with him real soon," she managed to whisper again.

"You're taking the kids?" he asked unbelievably.

"I have to. You could not take care of them." This seemed to hit Billie at yet again another level.

He looked at Alice with fury and yelled,

"You ain't takin' Henry. You ain't takin my boy!"

Alice was literally shaking by this point.

"OK, Billie. But I don't know how you're going to take care of him," she whimpered.

ALICE LAY NEXT TO BILLIE that night after he had had his way with her. He didn't say anything and just fell asleep. Alice wasn't sure what was going to happen if Mr. Pierce didn't hurry up and show up. She knew if he took too long, she would give in. She wasn't very strong. It was May and nights in Brushy Ridge were very long at this time of year, and Alice couldn't sleep. She got up, grabbed her shawl and threw it around her shoulders, and started walking. She ended up at her favorite place on the Half Diamond V, the Bradley Slough. It was a small prairie lake on their land, where the cattle and horses migrated to slake their thirst. It was surround by low, low hills that made a perfect place to sit and think. Alice sat down on the hill and looked to the west. With their vista of the tall Rocky Mountains, there really was no other place to look when one sat on the banks of the slough. She knew she would soon hear the frogs singing loud and long at this time of the year. Once she had settled in quietly, they began their courting songs, and Alice managed a little giggle as she thought about Mr. Pierce. She couldn't wait to be with him again, and again and again, she thought.

She was truly terrified at the thought of what she was going to do. She would not miss Ma and Pa Smith. All they had ever been to her was mean and nasty. But Annie and Sykes had been like her real parents, and she loved them dearly. She would miss them. And Henry, her little boy. She realized she would never see him again, and that made her cry. She sat crying quietly on the banks of the Bradley Slough, wondering how Henry would make it without her. She sat for hours until the chill of the night finally drove her to move and walk slowly back to the tent house. When she walked through the flap door, she felt the damp cool of the place as the wood stove was burned out. She saw her family, Billie in their bed, baby Johnny in his cradle, and Mamie and Henry together in their little bed. She knew she would never see this family together like this again in her life. She sat and watched them sleep until the sun peeked over the horizon and began to lighten up the day. Then she finally lay down and slept.

After an hour or so of fitful dozing, she rose and splashed water on her face, then headed out to the barn to milk the cows. They had gathered around the door to be milked, like they always did. She had just finished all the milking when she heard the horses whinnying in the field. She looked out the barn door and saw Mr. Pierce's large wagon, all loaded for travel, bumping across the pasture. Her heart skipped a beat, then before she could really think about it or run away from it, she dashed into the tent. Billie was up and lighting the stove, expecting her to make the morning tea.

She hurriedly grabbed some Johnny cake from her cupboard and slapped it on the table. She turned to baby Johnny and changed his diaper, dipping the soiled one in a basin of water she kept for that purpose, then stepping outside to wring it out. She grabbed the butter box with Mamie and Johnny's things, she had removed Henry's previously, and then she grabbed her small bundle of clothes tied together with a rope. She threw this on top of the box and fled out the door, not being able to stand the silent accusing eyes of Billie on her for another second. Mr. Pierce had hopped down from the wagon, and he carefully took her meagre possessions and untied the tarpaulin he had covering the wagon and stowed her things under it. While he was doing this, Alice ran back to the tent and grabbed baby Johnny, and then took Mamie by the hand and pulled her after herself, with baby Johnny in her arms.

Billie watched all of this with incredulity. He really couldn't believe what was happening in front of his eyes. Just in case she tried to take his son, his Henry, he grabbed the boy's hand and held on tight. Mamie was very confused and asked her mama what was happening as Alice dragged her along to the wagon.

"Just don't ask questions," Alice yelled at her, and somehow sensing things were not right, seven year old Mamie began to cry. Henry heard Mamie crying, and this felt bad to him, so while he stood beside his dad, hand in hand, he started crying too. This just added to the sense of things not being right, and baby Johnny started to cry.

The sight of all her children crying was hard enough for Alice, but when she looked back at Henry, she saw something she thought she would never see in her life. Billie the Strongman, the toughest man in all of Alberta, was standing crying as well. He made no sound, he just stood there holding Henry's hand with tears rolling down his face.

Alice's shame began to engulf her. If Mr. Pierce had not slapped the reins on the big horses' back and started the wagon rolling forward, she would have jumped down off the wagon with the children and fled back inside the tent to her life of drudgery. Instead, they headed toward the Morley Trail and the stopping house at Morleyville where they would board the train for Vancouver. She gazed back at her husband and son, and the tent house and barn that made up the Half Diamond V. She never looked forward until the two had shrunk from sight in the distance. Mamie sat in terrified silence in the back seat, holding baby Johnny. Mr. Pierce had seemed to sense that she needed this time, and he sat silently beside her, urging on the draught horse he had rented from a local. The horse would be stabled at the Sibbald Ranche near Morleyville, and its owner would come and fetch it back. The Pierce's, as they would now all be, would catch the Vancouver train, then head north overland to Prince Rupert.

Billie watched the wagon until it vanished from sight. Little Henry stood silently at his side. He took the boy with him to the chicken coop and rustled up a few eggs to feed them. Inside, he took down the fry pan from its hook, and realized he would be cooking for himself, and the boy, again. A heavy moan escaped his lips, and he staggered back, like he was drunk. He almost dropped to the ground, but although dizzy, righted himself and sat down on a chair. Henry had crawled back into his bed, and sat, wide eyed, with the blanket up around his chin, not knowing what to do. Billie didn't know what to do either.

When Alice had been having the babies at her sister's house, Billie and Sykes had been banished outside the birthing room. They had heard Alice's anguished cries and Billie had wondered often throughout the ordeal if Alice would survive. She always had, but he had thought then about what life would be like without his wife. Pregnancy and illness killed women; he knew that. But a strange man coming to town and stealing his wife away from him, that was something he had never thought about.

The great Billie the Strongman was almost taken out with this event. He had survived so many other difficulties; freezing cold, near starvation and the lonely years before he married Alice. These seemed to jump out at him from somewhere in the past and threaten him with a kind of annihilation. He felt a darkness and dread settle over him that felt like the weight of the world.

LIFE ON THE PRAIRIES WAITED for no man nor woman to come to terms with death or destruction. If one was going to make it, one had to choose to do the things that would allow one to survive here. Billie had to continue. Eventually Annie and Sykes came over to talk to him, but he refused to say a word. They came a few more times, but Billie's stoic silence began to convince them that he was not going to change his mind.

Annie felt so ashamed of Alice. She just couldn't believe her fragile, melancholy sister had done such an unspeakable thing. To them all, Alice was dead.

One day, when His Aunt Annie had come to bring him over to her place because Sykes and Billie needed to go logging, Henry asked her where his Mama had gone.

"She ran away, Henry. She left with Mr. Pierce and went to Prince Rupert," was all she said.

"Why'd she do that?" asked little Henry. Aunt Annie replied, "We just don't know, Henry."

By the end of the summer, Billie Bradley's demeanor was changing. He was no longer shocked and silent; he was angry. He would get drunk at the Murphy Hotel and look for a fight with anyone. As all the men knew about his incredible strength and bare-knuckle brawling prowess, no one would take him on. He had decided that any family who could have produced a woman like Alice who would do what she had done would be a bad influence on his son, so he forbade the Smiths to have anything to do with Henry. Poor Henry. Not only was his Mama gone, but he was no longer allowed to see his Aunt and Uncle, his grandparents nor his cousins.

Billie needed to go away often still, and he would look for opportunities to board little Henry with neighbours. When he came back, he would leave Henry alone, by himself, in the tent, with strict orders not to light the kerosene lamp. Poor little Henry would sit by the stove at night, and open the door a little, to allow some light into the tent. If Billie came home and found him crying from loneliness, he would give him a licking. After that though, he would feel sorry for the lonely little boy and tell him that it would be alright. They got along the best that they could.

That winter, Billie was out cutting logs, so he boarded Henry with two old bachelors named Storey and Doogle.

One day, they needed to chop some meat off a frozen block of meat, and they had Henry hold the block while Storey raised the axe to chop it. The meat slipped and so did Henry's hand, and Storey brought the axe down on Henry's index finger and chopped it clean off.

The two old bachelors got the horse and democrat hooked up and managed to get into Cochrane where they could take Henry to the doctor. Henry managed to survive, but when Billie got back and found out what had happened, he realized he needed a more stable situation for Henry.

Billie asked about this at the Murphy and found out there was a couple who had moved to Cochrane after Mitford had closed down. Their name was Sargent, and they had come over from England. William Sargent was a carpenter and was making a small living doing odd carpentry work in Cochrane. Mrs. Sargent had been a cook at Mitford. They had no children of their own, and Billie sought them out to see if he could pay them to board Henry in Cochrane. It was time for him to go to school too. The Sargents, like all the settlers, were always in need of cash, and they agreed to take on young Henry Bradley.

Henry moved to Cochrane the same year Billie moved a log house to the Half Diamond V. When he wasn't away working, Billie would come and fetch Henry and bring him out to the Half Diamond V. Alice's milk cows were long gone now, and the chickens were mostly eaten up by the foxes and coyotes, or hawks and owls. They would break and train horses all day, as there was always a market for horses. These were happy days for Henry. While he was thankful to have a home where he was well taken care of, his dad was the only true family member he had left, and he wanted to spend as much time with him as he could.

The autumn of 1915 saw Henry back with the Sargents in Cochrane School. He was seven years old and a tall skinny boy. Billie had set out to Claresholm to work on a haying crew. While he was there, he contracted double pneumonia. He didn't think he needed a doctor, but he continued to get worse and couldn't get up one morning to go out on the crew. Two days later, he died. There was no one to bring him back to Cochrane, as he had stopped talking to all the Taylors and the Smiths, so he was buried in Claresholm.

Word was sent back to Cochrane, and the Sargents were informed of Billie's death. Henry felt exactly the same way he had when his mom drove away in the wagon with Mr. Pierce. Only now he was completely alone in the world. He was an orphan. Luckily, the Sargents were kind people, and they decided he would become their son. Will Sargent was not able to find enough work in Cochrane, so they had decided to move into Calgary to find more work.

The Half Diamond V was eventually sold to pay for outstanding taxes, and with it, Billie Bradley's "Go West Young Man" dream finally slipped into the black prairie soil, to remain buried there, like he was, for eternity.

CHAPTER 24

LADY ADELA ROUS COCHRANE

1911

The death of her town had been a dreadful burden to bear for Lady Adela Charlotte Cochrane. Life back in England had been difficult, and often purposeless. As hard as this death had been to bear, it now appeared that life had yet another difficulty in store.

Adela had begun to spend less and less time at Quarr Abbey, until finally, she just stopped going there. Much to her relief, Rosetta Cochrane passed away three years after Mitford. Adela knew it was silly to anthropomorphize Mitford so, but it was truly how she felt. Mitford was her only creation, her only child, as she never bore a living one. With Rosetta gone, Quarr Abbey could have been more comfortable, but truly it was not. She and Thomas were really incompatible now, and try though she might, she really blamed him for Mitford's death. After all, it was his arrogance and incompetence that had not allowed Mitford to flourish. If he had sought more advice, turned to people in the know, Mitford could have been built in a different location and flourished. He had not, so Mitford died. That was how she felt.

She tried to find causes and interests in London, deciding that if she could not be a Canadian business woman she instead would be a British philanthropist. One area that touched her always warm and caring heart was providing relief to the poor of London. She became a Poor Law Guardian, where she sat on a board to help with the administration of assistance to those in need. Here was a place where the amazing kindness and grace of Lady Adela could find a home, and she was able to throw herself into this work to ease the constant pain she felt in her heart over the loss of Mitford.

Southampton had been a city Adela frequented, usually because she was boarding a ship for Canada, but it had become a familiar friend as arriving there from the Isle of Wight always meant she was bound for her true love in Canada. When Quarr Abbey became unbearable, she would often take the ferry across to Southampton, and from there she would set out to other parts of England. During her stays there, she noticed the Hartley Institution, and needing something to fill in her days, investigated it. There she found women studying alongside men, and this pleased her mightily. She loved to walk through the library and observe the students studying at their tables. If she thought she would not disturb them too much, she would often ask a young woman, in a quiet whisper of course, what she was studying.

"Hello my dear. You look so earnest in your work. What are you studying?" she would ask. The replies varied.

"Maths," or "The Law," or" Medicine," were often the answers.

"Please keep up your hard work. It is so important for woman to enter these fields in this new century. I have been an entrepreneur in Canada, in the new province of Alberta. I have seen that women can do well in the world of men."

She was introduced to the Headmaster of Hartley, and soon became a Governor on the board. Hartley became Hartley University College in 1902, which pleased Adela greatly, and she enjoyed her time as a governor on this board immensely. They enjoyed her patronage.

PHILANTHROPY FILLED HER DAYS AND gave her life meaning again, and visiting her brother and sisters gave her the love of family. Sadly, her dear mama passed away in 1901, the same year as Rosetta. Thomas attended the funeral, but it was the last time she was to see him for many years. George had finally married Helena Fraser the year Mitford died, in 1898, and they began a family with the birth of little Pleasance. Many nieces and nephews followed her birth, and Adela was a favorite aunt to George's children. Like her own dear Uncle Henry, Adela would visit with the children and tell them all tales of Canada and Mitford, which they loved to hear. Telling her stories helped to soothe the constant pain she felt, and she visited George and Helena's home frequently.

"Tell us about the Betsy jumping the track and the engineer having his skull cracked," they would encourage her. She would start into this as it was one of their favorite stories.

It seemed Thomas was not done with her yet though. Adela felt they would just live separately and go about their own lives, leaving their past in the past. However, Thomas seemed to have other plans. He had taken up with a woman named Beatrice Knight. Adela was aware of their affair, but truly, it mattered not to her as she had long ago ceased to be in love with Thomas. The wonderful, adventurous young man who had courted her and captured her heart with his dream of adventure in a new land was a far cry from the man T.B.H. Cochrane was today. Adela often reflected on how her dear papa had vehemently opposed her marriage to Thomas, and how as a love-struck young woman she had paid no attention to her papa. He had certainly seen through to a core in Thomas that Adela had not been able to see. However, as the years passed and Adela ceased to see Thomas, she came to the conclusion that without him she would never have had Mitford and her life in Canada, and that though it had certainly not turned out the way she would have hoped, that it was and would always be the most wonderful part of her life. And it was a life they had shared. She was at peace with this decision, and it helped her to build her new philanthropic life in England. Beatrice Knight and Thomas Cochrane were no longer her concern, and she thought nothing about them, until news came to her that Beatrice had given birth to a son, John, in 1909.

Adela received this news with a stabbing pain in her own heart. She had thought she had finally buried all her feelings, both good and bad, about Thomas. However, upon receiving this news, the old wounds flared up again, hot and throbbing. Thomas had been so nasty about her inability to produce an heir, and here this hussy of a woman that he had taken up with had gone and done just that, produced him an heir.

Well, she thought to herself, he may have an heir, but that heir is a bastard and will receive nothing from the Rous family.

But Thomas was not through with hurting Adela yet. When the boy was about six months old, Thomas showed up at her home and demanded a divorce.

Divorce. How ludicrous, Adela thought. But as usual, Thomas was bound to have his way, and to ensure that the boy was not a bastard. He demanded that Adela divorce him, as he had committed adultery and had deserted her. While the two things were undeniably true, Adela was loathe to give him any satisfaction. Her satisfaction came from knowing the boy was a bastard.

With all the nastiness and derision he had learned dealing with Van Horne, Thomas turned on Adela. He would have his way in this matter, and in this matter he would not fail. He accosted Adela at home daily, ranting and railing at her, and demanding she sue him for divorce.

Life, which had been rebuilt to at least a level of satisfaction, became a living hell. Adela never knew where Thomas would show up. When she commanded her servants to stop answering the door, he waited until she left the house, and then followed her, causing an awful commotion as they walked along. The neighbors looked out their windows in disgust at the scene unfolding before them, and Adela, although it was no fault of her own, felt the never-ending pressure one felt in Victorian society and knew she had to somehow stop Thomas.

George, her long-standing defender, was out of the country, as he had taken a real interest in Australia, and in the politics of the Victoria area. He had taken Helena and the children on a voyage there and was not home in London or Suffolk to protect her.

Thomas was relentless. He would leave just long enough for

her to think that maybe he had given up, only to show up again with renewed vigour and harassment. Slowly, Adela's defenses started to wear down. She held on through 1909 and 1910, but these attacks were certainly taking their toll on her health.

I will surely go mad if Thomas does not soon desist, she fretted to herself.

George returned from Australia in the spring of 1910, and Adela, looking frail and haunted, met with him soon after his return.

"George," she practically whispered, "I just don't think I can hold out much longer. Thomas is insistent, and I fear he will never cease with this persecution until I give in and give him the divorce."

"Papa would have him horse whipped and deported if he were alive today, Adela, but I fear there is nothing I can really do to stop him," George lamented.

"My advice is just to give him the divorce. Any satisfaction you may have derived from keeping his son John a bastard is long over. I shall contact my solicitor and inform him that you wish to commence with divorce proceedings."

"I fear you are correct, George. Insanity is no reward for my stubbornness," she admitted sadly.

On August 15, 1910, Adela commenced a divorce suit against Thomas Belhaven Henry Cochrane. On November 28th, the suit demanded that Thomas return to her home and render to her conjugal rights. Thomas, of course, had no intention of doing such a thing and did not comply. The decree was served to Thomas, and as he did not comply, the court found him guilty of desertion, of habitually committing adultery with Beatrice Knight with whom he cohabited and with whom he lived together as man and wife.

Adela had to sit in humiliation in court and listen to the court clerk read out the decision. While she officially won the case, she was decimated by being forced to have her humiliation made public by Thomas, who sat smiling broadly as the decree was read aloud.

1911 brought the dissolution of her marriage. Once divorced, Thomas promptly married Beatrice. The only thought that sometimes gave her respite was that she still didn't really know if John was Thomas' son. Beatrice was obviously a woman of such low morals that she could have been impregnated by another man, and then told Thomas that the child was his in order to get him to marry her. Either way, Adela did not feel that she won anything for herself in the divorce except that Thomas stopped harassing her.

Thomas no longer lived at Quarr Abbey on the Isle of Wight. She had found out as the documents were read in court that he now resided in London. Adela wondered if Princess Beatrice took exception to his current behavior, but as she was no longer in the position to find out if this was true, she had to accept that she would only have to wonder if this was the case.

Adela did not fare well after the divorce was granted. She attempted to return to her life of philanthropy, but she found herself ill more often than not, and unable to travel to Southampton or even out and about in London. The gloomy darkness of a London winter seemed to descend upon her viscerally, and she found she felt better remaining at home, often in bed, dreaming of her life in Mitford.

In these dreams she relived her fabulous adventures: traveling to Canada, visiting the great American and Canadian cities, riding the rails across the ocean of prairie, before finally arriving at her own heaven on earth, Mitford. Her dreams made her heart light, while her body became heavy and unresponsive.

The London Times carried her obituary on May 19, 1911. It informed the readers that she had died on May 18 at a hotel in London, where she had gone to address an illness. It stated that George had been with her when she died. It spoke of her marriage, her divorce and the fact that she had had no children. It regaled the readers with her close relationship with Queen Victoria and Princess Beatrice (her Mama would have been so proud). It spoke of how popular she had been with the people of the Isle of Wight and listed her philanthropic interests in London. There was not one word about her life in Canada, about her adventurous nature or her real love, Mitford. The real Lady Adela Cochrane was not mentioned at all in her obituary.

That girl, instead, was riding the rails back across the prairie to her true love.